LAST MILE

First edition, 2023
ISBN Paperback: 979-8-9886384-1-4
Book Design by Nuno Moreira, NMDESIGN

LAST MILE

THE BEEZE SERIES BOOK #01

DAVID LEE LUEDTKE

To my family, especially Joan,
who is my inspiration and strongest supporter.

CHAPTER 1
Meet the neighbor in his cell,

The algorithms forecasted his fate with an icy certainty. As he opened his eyes, a clawing and piercing little head burst through the wall, like a little gopher burrowing its way in, but actually it was the end of a powerful drill bit coming through the pristine white wall. The scraping was loud enough to wake the dead. What would drive somebody to bore through his wall, particularly here in the quiet Chelsea Pod One?

Manny, jolted awake, stumbled from his recliner and dusted off an afternoon nap. He walked cautiously towards the mysterious hollow in the wall, taking every step slowly as he inspected the little tube sticking its head out from the wall. Pieces of concrete and plaster cascaded down the freshly painted wall. Suddenly the little drill bit disappeared and a wiggly little tube with a tiny glass globe appeared through the hole. Manny thought it might be a tiny camera, but it seemed almost alive as it looked around the room, then it quickly turned its lens onto Manny before withdrawing back inside the hole. He tentatively moved closer to the opening and peered into it. He inched his mouth closer to the edge and yelled out. "Hello? Is anybody in there?"

Manny took a moment before he asked his question again. He tapped the little hole in front of him with one finger and quickly withdrew it when something touched him back. Suddenly, the miniature camera emerged from the wall once again. A muffled voice responded to Manny with a placid tone, "Who are you? Tell me your name."

"Who am I?" Manny responded, dumbfounded. "Who are *you*?"

"Sorry, friend. I'm Theo, your neighbor," the voice said quietly. As it spoke, the small camera rotated, now facing Manny intimidatingly.

Manny stared in disbelief at the little camera, and demanded, "What do you want? Why did you drill a hole through the wall? What are you doing with that camera? What the hell is going on?"

On the other side of the wall, Theo Wiggins spoke through the camera, which he called, "EH4," after hearing the voice come through the hole, the voice muffled but still discernible. "I need food—something I can actually eat." Theo shifted from one foot to another, anxiously glancing up at the little hole in the wall. He frowned as he adjusted his face shield, making sure he could see the video feed from his camera. "I had to make sure you weren't with the Contros."

Dr. Manuel Rio, or Manny as his friends called him, was a respected scientist formerly with the White Cube Research company. When the Contros brought the new neighbor to the next-door cabin, Manny noticed how they replaced the neighbor's door with one of the Controller's signature pass-through doors. It had a card reader on its outside surface and several monitoring devices, along with a one-square-foot reinforced steel cabinet door, painted with a swooshing logo – the mark to label that the person inside was in solitary confinement. Theo was given food boxes through this cabinet door, three times per day, containing a well-rounded, and incredibly boring, gelatinous food substance.

"How would you know if I was a Contro?" Manny asked curiously, recognizing the nickname used for the Controllers.

"I was willing to take that chance." Theo confessed. "Not sure how many Contros would let a solitary-confinement person living next to them."

Manny's thoughts drifted to the new world order. Prisons were a distant memory, replaced by isolated cabins fitted with Radio Frequency Identification (RFID) scanners that monitored people's movement through gates in city streets or when they entered their own pod. Artificial intelligence was so intertwined with the software and technology of the world that the term was rarely even used anymore.

Manny lived in Chelsea Pod One, the first of dozens of Chelsea Pods around the world, distinguished from the rest because it had been the highest bidder for that coveted moniker. Decades ago, it had been part of a sprawling metropolis known as a "city."

He walked quickly to his front door and popped his head into the hallway to see the metal badge reader attached to his neighbor's door. It looked similar to his own, but there were a few distinct differences. He knew his neighbor's door had both an inside and an outside reader whereas Manny's only had the inside one. The monitor on both doors showed the same screen; an RFID reader with a digital display and a badge reader that detected the chips implanted in people's wrists when they passed by it. It was a strange monitoring device, intimidating yet strangely comfortable, like a key back into freedom or a lock keeping out intruders.

A special device mounted on his neighbor's door tracked the inhabitant with much more scrutiny than a regular home. The devices also served as the CATACS's time tracking system—the Controllers of Agriculture, Transportation, Authority, Credit, and Substances—logging each pass into their database. Each person's time and credit was tracked constantly and shown clearly in one of the menu items in each person's face shield—which is connected to the surgically implanted chip in their arm (think Borg).

Manny stepped back to the little camera in the wall and replied to the voice, "I'm not a Controller."

"Are you a Vertical?" Theo asked from the other side of the wall, his voice muffled beneath the concrete. The adjective "Vertical" found itself a new home as a noun.

Manny stopped and looked skeptically at his own front door where the monitor remained blank. Then he walked closer to the camera. "I'm sorry, what did you say?" he asked. "How would you know that?"

"Do you have some real food to share? Are you into VSG?" came Theo's reply.

"Are you spying on me?" Manny waved his hand over the camera, which seemed to flinch in response. Manny swore the little thing must be Theo himself somehow as it slowly rotated constantly while looking around inside Manny's cabin. The sensory and motor responses was evidence of an AI chip that provides sensory feedback.

After a pause, Theo responded, "I saw you through EH4. You have deliveries. Do you have any meat? I can't eat this Contro crap another day." Then Theo added, "And what's with the bandage?"

Manny felt his heart race as he heard the neighbor's question. His eyes widened and his hand flew to cover his bandaged scalp before he quickly pushed the tiny camera back through the wall. He glanced around, panicking, searching for something to block the hole. Confused, he yelled out, "What is EH4?"

"Exploratory Hole Number 4," Theo replied. "I wanted to see your deliveries. I kept seeing the drones flying onto your deck with the food."

Manny looked dumbfounded. "You mean you drilled other holes too?" He rummaged through a nearby drawer, picked out a metal writing tool, and jammed it point-first into the hole. Then he took off his shoe and pounded the tool deep into the hole.

Theo replied in a muffled voice, "I only put one more hole in there—it's out on your deck."

Realizing what must have happened, Manny rushed outside onto his patio and scanned the wall until he saw another small hidden hole behind one corner of the screen that separated their decks. He grabbed another pencil and drove it deep into the hole with another shoe pounding, sealing it shut.

Manny retreated back to his recliner, which activated automatically for him as he sat. He glanced about the room and recognized the familiar objects in it: monitor panel on the wall; a picture of his family when they were all so young; a small pile of electronic magazines piled on his desk; and the bookshelf with various gadgets Manny was inventing.

He looked across the room at the metal pencil sticking out of the wall, then touched his finger to one ear. Nestled on each of Manny's ears was a small, black, arched device that he activated, producing a holographic visor that developed and formed over Manny's face. First, the temple arms developed out of thin air and snapped into place, and then two circular hairline rims emerged from their sides, growing larger until they reached uniformly from his eyebrows to his nose. The shape, slightly bigger than aviator glasses, was barely noticeable and nearly invisible to someone observing this, but from Manny's inside view, the shield showed an augmented reality complete with a menu of options.

Manny moved his eyes to the menu item he desired and double-clicked by moving his eyes on and off and back on to the item on the dropdown menu. Some people had difficulty getting the hang of double-clicking, but most people adapted quickly as the machine-learning of the technology provided constant feedback and adjustment the longer the device was in use. The shield was a way to interact with the world without leaving your home. In public places, other people using their shields often looked comical. They looked like they were talking to themselves and interacting with invisible others. He searched the menu for something about "Solitary Confinement" to do some research. Manny wasn't that familiar with the process and wanted to know more. He reviewed a few articles, but quickly grew tired and drifted off to sleep.

Manny got up from his nap with an ache in his bones from the long jog he had taken the day before, then headed towards the kitchen counter. He leaned down to grab the handle of his adjustable refrigerator and once again wished he had adjusted so he didn't have to stoop over each time. His ex-wife had been much shorter than him and always got what she wanted. After opening the door, he pulled out two cylindrical containers filled with fresh food from the sustainable gardens—FOUPs (Front Opening Unified Pods) are what the containers are called. These pods were three inches in diameter by ten inches long and transparent enough for Manny to make out the steak inside. The other FOUP had a mix of vegetables of carrots, celery, and broccoli.

The lightweight and expensive FOUPs featured a printed barcode taped to the side to track its contents and destination. Drone delivery vehicles stacked them end-to-end during transportation so they looked as if they were carrying long straws down the street. Nitrogen or argon filled each container, keeping the contents perpetually fresh without requiring electronic refrigeration. Moreover, the FOUPs had the ability to fit even through the most minuscule passthrough door that measured just three inches in diameter. This made them less intrusive when compared to the delivery versions of large White Cube food boxes. Many people created their own private passageways for the FOUP deliveries to ensure discretion, therefore avoiding taxes and saving time credits.

Manny lifted the lid of the FOUP, letting the fumes escape before emptying its contents onto the counter. The nitrogen quickly dissipated, releasing the scent of the natural food contained within. The delightful smell of the freshly-cooked meal soon filled his kitchen. He served the meal on the counter, not the most romantic table setting for a single man, but now had become a routine. He glanced over at the growing stack of White Cube food boxes delivered and uneaten for days—nutritious, but dull and gel-like in texture. People with low algorithms ate this boxed food three times each day.

Manny heard a metallic object bounce on the floor like a door chime in the other room. Then he heard Theo again. "Hello! Anybody in there?" This time the voice was louder.

Fuming, Manny went over to the hole in the wall and said, "Come on, man—leave me alone!"

"I can smell the food," Theo pleaded. "Can you share?"

Manny grabbed the metal writing utensil again and thought about gluing it into the hole this time. "Mind your own business," he retorted, then grabbed the little camera that popped through the hole again. "I'm not the one stuck in solitary confinement," he said while holding up the camera to his face.

"Hey, be careful with that!"

Manny's eyes widened as he inspected the small device that he held. It was a miniature, intricate camera, barely bigger than his thumbnail. Manny ran his fingers over its smooth surface, feeling the grooves and bumps of its components as it reacted to his touch like a little animal. He looked up at the hole in the wall in wonderment. "This is amazing. How did you build it?"

"Touch it to your shield," replied Theo, which sounded almost like a challenge.

Manny paused and studied the device, rotating it carefully to see all sides of it. He thought about it for a moment, then thought, what the heck? He touched the little camera to his earbud and, snapping open like twin butterfly wings, his shield quickly assembled and there was a smiling Theo in the viewer. He stared at Theo for a bit, thinking the man was perhaps a little older than himself. Manny said, "Mucho Gusto."

"What?" Theo exclaimed, taken aback at the sight and language of his neighbor. Manny had dark, long hair with no facial hair, in stark contrast to Theo's own gray-blond locks and scruffy beard.

"Oh! Sorry, I forgot to switch on my translator," Manny muttered apologetically. "Nice to meet you."

Theo chuckled. "Ditto. Nice to see another face not with the Contros again. Been fifty days." Theo paced back and forth, but his walking pattern was predictable: ten steps to the refrigerator and ten steps back to the privacy screen at the end of the kitchen and then back again to the refrigerator, only stopping at EH4 for a moment.

Manny wondered what crime warranted the punishment of solitary confinement as he asked, "How much longer are you in?"

"Another ten days. But I got a bad case of cabin fever," he replied instantly. "The food is killing me." He fished some crackers out of his outer pocket and punctured them open with a fingernail claw, scooping up crumbs from inside and sprinkling them on the plain, white, pudding on his plate.

"What did you do?" Manny asked the convict.

"Credit swap is what they claim." An aura of pride radiated from him as he described how the Contros crafted systems that seemed to outsmart even the most intelligent humans as if they were herding cats trying to break free from their cages.

Manny furrowed his brow in thought as he listened to Theo debate the ethical dilemma of credit swaps. Having witnessed those scams firsthand at White Cube Research, it seemed like a funny coincidence that one such scam was now knocking at his doorstep.

Manny shook his head and wondered out loud. "Why are you bothering me about all of this?"

Theo sighed, stared down at the tiled floor for a moment, then looked up, directly into Manny's eyes in the shield. "Well, I drilled some holes through the other side," he said. "But I hit a steel column. Took me a week to drill that one. Then I hit the back of a video screen on the next one. I don't want to talk about the third one."

Manny whistled in disbelief. "Jeez, hope you are not a surgeon or something." Curiosity getting the better of him, he asked, "What do you do when not in solitary?"

"I work as a scientist at ARS," Theo answered swiftly, detailing his occupation in the Autonomous Robotic Surgery organization that had become so common within medical facilities.

Manny couldn't suppress a short, soft laugh as he considered the irony of book smarts without common sense. He recalled his grandfather's oft-repeated sayings, "You cannot teach an old dog new tricks," and, "You can lead a horse to water, but you can't make him drink." Manny couldn't help but smile as he recalled his wise grandpa's words.

Theo gawked at the size of Manny's cabin as he peeked through the camera lens. The cabin had numerous doorways and seemed to stretch on forever, with more halls than Theo could count. "Your cabin looks huge!" he exclaimed.

"It was good for the kids," Manny replied, recalling his twins running through the halls.

"How about you? What do you do?" Theo asked.

Manny was about to reply that he previously worked at White Cube Research, but that felt like ancient history now, almost as if he never did it. "I'm between gigs right now," he said instead.

Theo mulled over the answer, unsatisfied with its vagueness. He was on the verge of launching another volley of inquiries when he realized his steps brought him to the edge of his privacy screen. With a heavy sense of uncertainty, Theo turned back to the tiny opening in the wall to continue his pacing until the next limit.

Manny made a decision and said, "Hang on, let me try something. I'll get back to you." With that, he turned off his shield to disconnect from Theo.

The delightful aroma of Manny's dinner clung to the air as he stepped out onto his patio, pulling the sliding door open as he went. He peered over at the privacy screens that separated his patio from his new neighbor's. These walls were an innovation adopted during the Great Pandemic in 2019 and extended out farther than either patio deck—a design created to keep viruses from spreading. The privacy screens not only blocked out potentially dangerous viruses but also provided plenty of privacy in the cramped cabins inside the pods. The popularity of the feature spread far enough to make it an aesthetic staple across all tall cabin structures, rendering them to look like enormous waffles placed on their ends. Manny's cabin was on the top floor of the Redwoods Cabin Structure.

Leaving the patio door open, Manny moved to the refrigerator to grab a FOUP with a steak in it, which he then attached to the magnetic holder on the underside of his green delivery drone. The toaster-shaped drone gleamed in a bright green hue and featured the iconic smiley-face logo on its underside. A pair of eggbeater-like blades whirred inside a protective enclosure that surrounded them, and below the blades rested a magnetic holder for delivering food orders efficiently. He'd built many prototypes for himself during his time at White Cube Research and could afford luxuries like this. "Good to keep your day job," is what his grandfather said to him.

Manny activated his shield and it lit up with a pale green light. The drone also sprang to life and hovered an arm's length away, ready to obey his command. Manny double-clicked on his shield, giving the drone its instruction to fly past his privacy screen, around the corner of his patio, and onto Theo's patio next door. He watched as the video feed from the drone zoomed around the corner, revealing all that lay beyond in vivid detail. As soon as it reached its destination, Manny instructed it to set down the small, cylindrical FOUP. Then, he double-clicked on the link to Theo and spoke through the speaker of the drone, "Bon Appetit!"

Theo gasped as he saw the drone come around the corner, his heart pounding. He couldn't help but think it was the Contros coming for him. But then he heard the voice of Manny calling through the drone, muffled by the patio glass door. He hesitated for a moment before double-clicking in his viewer on the recent caller ID labeled: "Unknown Caller." Theo asked into his shield, "Manny, is that you?"

Manny replied through the shield as he saw Theo's face pop up on his screen, "Thought you might like this."

Theo cautiously opened the patio door, sliding it just enough to fit his arm through. He gingerly picked up the FOUP, turning it around in his hands to inspect its efficient design. His jaw dropped when he saw what appeared to be a piece of steak nestled inside. Glancing quickly over his shoulder, he could see the monitoring station in the main room, and although they respected prisoners' need for privacy, Theo knew he was being watched at all times. He smiled in appreciation as he looked back at the FOUP and its prized contents. "Thanks, Man," he whispered into his shield.

Although he was on display 24/7 in the main area, the Contros realized that each convict deserved a small amount of privacy and thus allowed internal privacy screens for certain areas such as bathrooms, dressing areas, and kitchen areas. However, no funny business was to take place behind these screened areas, which meant that all convicts had to appear for at least eight hours per day in the viewing area.

Manny replied, "Enjoy!"

Theo was about to rush into the kitchen and thought about eating the steak raw until he looked at the drone again, hovering at the edge of the patio, "Can I see the drone?" Theo asked, admiringly. The lime-green shell had a smile painted on it, making it look like a tiny robot wanting to make a new friend.

Manny spun the drone around in front of him, displaying it proudly. "It's a prototype. I call this one, Greenie," he said with an excited grin.

Theo smiled back in response, charmed by the little machine. "Cute drone. I almost want to pet it," he added.

Manny nodded in agreement and chuckled. "I gotta run," he said before steering the little robotic friend back home. "Oh, and do you mind keeping that camera out of the wall?" he asked as an afterthought.

"Oh yeah, sure thing—sorry about that."

After delivering the steak to Theo and disconnecting from his communication, Manny felt a growing sense of anxiety about his new neighbor, and though he wasn't sure why, he couldn't quite shake it. He thought he might find some comfort in seeking out information from someone he knew within the Pod Police.

Manny opened up his augmented reality menu and watched the holograms of contact icons appear in a three-dimensional grid. He scanned the list of names, looking for one specific name. He felt a burst of energy as he double-clicked on it—this connection would be key to getting what he wanted.

Manny had a powerful friend in the Pod Police. This network of authorities kept every Pod in check and communicated with other Pods and their Clusters around the globe. They were a subsidiary of the Contros and the whole CATACS organization, which now was the fourth branch of the United States government. His heart raced as he waited for this "PoPo," as they were called, Michelle, "Mickey" Killian, and watched as her face appeared in his visor.

CHAPTER 2
Neighbor's fate and time must tell,

After weeks of eating bad food, Theo Wiggins finally consumed a proper meal. Now energized, he carried his wiggly little camera to store it in a hidden compartment beneath the desk. He barely managed to not drop it, considering how costly and lengthy the process was to locate the parts and assemble it. His most successful builds came when he was in isolation. But this time, the Contros relocated his cabin, and his supplies became disrupted. He'd wisely used his time credits, so he was able to get back on track eventually.

He went to his desk in the general area and held the camera gently in his palms. As he rounded the corner, he tapped his shield, and the holographic visor returned to its resting place inside his earbuds. It was time to video chat with the Contros—he was two hours behind on today's objectives.

Theo looked to the Contros panel on the far wall and he saw his reflection backlit by an analog clock ticking off each second. The sinister device reminded him of his long sentence—sixty agonizing days, fifty of which were already served. Theo was one of the lucky ones, he was able to live with a round-the-clock watch in a normal cabin. In Chelsea Pod One, there is a special accommodation for those prisoners who cannot behave appropriately in solitary confinement. A few hundred of them are redirected to psychiatric clinics where they can receive round-the-clock care. This keeps them off the streets while simultaneously keeping them away from any negative interaction with society. Theo's crime? A time swap violation, and it seemed the Contros were determined to squeeze every penny out of him in order to make their taxes. He only fudged a little data and got caught this time.

He stopped typing and leaned back in his chair to stretch, inadvertently catching a glimpse of himself on the monitor. He ran his fingers through his disheveled hair, noticing for the first time the streaks of gray that now wove through his beard and mustache. He stroked his chin thoughtfully as he pondered the implications of this development; he would need to tweak the algorithms that controlled the ever-changing time credits, life expectancy projections, and resource correlations between people. He mentally noted down the changes he needed to make to the Algos, referring to the algorithms by their nickname.

Theo heard a low rumbling sound as the little pass-through door at his front door suddenly opened. He squinted in surprise as a perfectly white square box appeared in the opening, about the size of a bowling ball. Appropriate, because the stuff inside tasted like a bowling ball too. He wrinkled his nose at the impending smell of the bland food when he opened the box—nutritional but lacking all flavor. It reminded him of the food used to feed animals at the zoo. His heart yearned for the Vertical Sustenance Growth, or VSG for short, food he used to obtain by swapping time credits. For example, celery tasted like real celery because it was real celery. And now after meeting his new neighbor at his new cabin, Theo thought he might have found a key to obtaining that same type of real food again. Maybe he would like this new neighbor after all.

He must diligently perform repetitive motions in front of the Contros monitor during his eight-hour shift, or else an extra day would be tacked onto his sentence. But beyond the scrutinizing gaze of the Contros monitor, Theo was crafty and resourceful; he'd managed to create a hand drill and a tiny camera out of parts of disassembled items in his cabin, and a few smuggled bits of high technology. If the video feed detected any discrepancies with the RFID chip implanted in Theo's arm, PoPos—short for "Pod Police"—were dispatched within minutes. The Controller's algorithms alerted the authorities to any suspicious activity and recorded it all on video.

Sometimes, a stern face would appear on a screen near the front door, questioning Theo from afar; other times, a real-life PoPo would arrive, unannounced, and search through Theo's cabin and take whatever they pleased. When Theo one-time trusted a PoPo, he quickly realized it was a mistake. As a consequence, the PoPo confiscated a month's worth of his hard work, and Theo suffered greatly.

Theo rose from his desk and took measured steps to the front door. He knew he would find one of the familiar White Cube deliveries in the pass-through. His finger rested on the door's release, and with a soft swoosh, it opened. On the tiny monitor beside the frame, he saw his own face, large and bright. Out of habit he smiled for the camera, knowing that it would register as little more than an algorithm's declaration of happiness. Back at his desk, he reached for the cube, its stark whiteness contrasting against the dull room that seemed to encompass Theo's mood. He questioned whether or not to consume what lay hidden in the box. To eat crap food, or not eat crap food, that was the question.

Theo carefully opened the white box, unzipping the thick plastic bag within. He inhaled deeply, hoping for a delicious aroma to fill his nostrils, but the box was strangely scentless. Several small packages lined the lid of the box, labeled with various scents like salmon, chicken, and spices. Theo plucked out one labeled "barbecue chicken" and tucked it into his pocket. A sense of longing filled him as he thought about what real food must taste like outside of solitary confinement—a meal with real texture and flavor tastefully seasoned to perfection. But for now, this was as good as it got. He was desperate for real food and the only way he could get it was if his new neighbor was willing to help. If not, Theo knew he would have to wait another ten days until he was released from solitary confinement and could re-establish his supply chain.

Theo ran his finger along the row of aroma packets, stopping at "Filet Mignon." His mouth watered as he recalled the succulent steak he had eaten several months ago. The packaged scent didn't quite smell the same. It was close, but he knew what a real filet mignon tasted like. He opened the packet and inhaled deeply, savoring the memory of that tender bite. Turning back to the packages in front of him, Theo vowed to break away from the White Cube's cubic food packs. He started assembling his meal and unwrapping each package before pouring its contents onto his plate—vegetables, proteins, and carbohydrates all meticulously portioned into perfectly bland cubes and rectangles. This was meal number 152—only 28 to go until he could get access to proper nutrition again.

Theo reclined in his chair and kicked his feet out from under the desk while adjusting his black pants. He was certain he needed a new pair of shoes, but the Algos disagreed. They recommended he get his feet checked for any abnormalities that could be wearing down his footwear. Theo knew that to avoid paying hefty fees for transportation, he must walk everywhere and not pass through security gates since those would register him and result in a credit deduction. In order to thrive in the system, Theo learned the hacks of dodging the system—always stay on the move. And do every little activity that rewarded him with points.

He had a gift for tinkering and making useless gadgets of his own. Even as a small child, visiting his Grandparents' cabin was like a playground for him. One day, he noticed the strange contraption his Grandma Elizabeth had affixed to the washing machine. It whirred and buzzed and made an interesting noise. Being the curious boy he was, Theo decided to investigate. He unscrewed the device from the machine and spread its components out on the kitchen table—inspecting each piece carefully. As time quickly ticked away, Theo's desire to figure out how the device worked shifted to panic at the thought of his grandma discovering what he'd done. He hastily reassembled it back into place, praying she wouldn't notice.

As Grandma and Grandpa ambled back to the cabin, Theo patiently waited for his punishment. He knew he was in big trouble after tinkering with the washing machine instead of playing outside. When they arrived, the grandparents set about preparing their typical White Cube meal, as Theo nervously fidgeted and wrung his hands.

Grandma began loading up the washing machine and soon enough the sound of water swishing filled the room. Soon after, a wafting smell of artificial flavoring saturated the air from their boxed dinner that was now prepared. But before they could sit down to eat, Grandma took one last check on the laundry and was baffled when she found the damn thing actually worked again. Grandpa said proudly to his wife, "I knew you would get it fixed."

Theo smiled inwardly at his secret success without showing any trace of emotion on his face. He managed to mistakenly repair the broken washing machine. After a moment of internal celebration, he quickly sunk into the background again, knowing it would be better not to show anyone what he'd done.

CHAPTER 3
Discovers the neighbor's true plight,

Dr. Manuel Rio, or Manny as his friends and family knew him, had a string of contacts in many walks of life. He recalled his grandfather's advice before he'd died: "Be strong like the river; be steady and constant and you will slowly wear down the problems in life." Rio Constante, strong river, is what they called his grandfather.

Manny was able to make an extra number of credits through his research books about self-sustenance in isolated areas, such as space travel, undersea exploration, and living in metropolitan areas during pandemic lockdowns. His research gained recognition in the form of a small but loyal cult-like following in the Vertical Sustenance Growth area. His ex-wife Sarah found it boring, while his children Amy and Alex admired their dad for it. The VSG followers thought it was brilliant.

Manny double-clicked the menu item of his shield and scrolled through the list of names. He knew most people didn't trust the PoPos, but Mickey was different. They had grown up together in the Bronx Pod, a place so much more improved now than it was decades ago. Manny and Mickey were like siblings in their youth, attending the New York University Pod together and eventually both marrying their college sweethearts. Manny met and married a complicated woman named Sarah. That ended poorly. Mickey met and married a woman named Barbara, and that also ended poorly.

Now at 40 years old, Mickey, or Michelle Killian as most knew her, had made captain in the PoPos in the Bronx Pod. As Manny clicked on her name, he couldn't help but smile with admiration for his oldest friend.

"Yo, Mickey," said Manny to his old friend. He added, "How youuu doin'?" in the Bronx-flavored accent that he adopted for those times when he was portraying a character from an entertainment program called *Friends*. They loved this show so much, between the two of them they watched every episode at least three times (though now it felt as if Joey Tribiani and Monica Geller were family friends). Manny and Mickey discovered this series from the 1990s in the archives on a cloud site, called, *Television Archives*. The people in that old show met at a coffee shop every day to talk face-to-face. No shields, no personal communicators, no time restrictions. They even used paper dollars as the currency! Must have been really cool to live in those times.

Manny saw Mickey in his viewer. She sat alone in the corner of her office in the Pod Police headquarters, her dark blue uniform fully pressed and clean, while leaning her tired body against the back of her high-topped chair, her voice was cold and dismissive as she spoke, "Well, Rio, long time no see."

Manny shifted his weight uncomfortably and said softly, "Been a while. How's it going?"

Mickey, feeling uncomfortable, picked a topic to fill the silence, and replied quickly, "Have you been following the pandemic in Russia?"

Manny paused for a moment before taking a sip of his lukewarm tea. Ignoring the news lately kept his mind in a more positive attitude. The Sunnyside Farm, job applications, and a little surgery captured his full attention. But he could not ignore the lockdown in Russia, and the increasing number of COVID cases still spreading in many parts of that country. Manny cleared his throat, feeling anxiously uncertain. "Only bits and pieces," he said, trying not to think too hard about it. "Looks like it's spreading to the east and south regions. I heard Ukraine is still open."

"We better get prepared," Mickey said as her eyes clouded over and she sighed. "This lockdown could spread here again if we aren't careful." She remembered the last lockdown—three months of misery that nearly destroyed their economy. An uncomfortable silence settled between them, both recalling a night months earlier when their judgment was impaired by wine and sorrow. That night, they'd shared an awkward yet tender kiss. But for her, it felt like kissing a dog. Kissing heterosexuals was not her thing. Immediately after the kiss, she slapped him across the face.

Manny had a reason for calling but danced around the subject, "You still have Gary there?"

Mickey adjusted her shield the full length and a faint whirring noise began to fill the room. Gary stood across the squad room, with his face also hidden beneath an opaque visor. "He's on another call with Sarah," Mickey said, her voice dripping with sarcasm. She watched as he shifted uneasily in place, a sure sign that he was uncomfortable, and an unmistakable smirk crept onto her lips. "Not a bad PoPo before she got a hold of him."

Manny felt his chest tighten at the sound of Sarah's name, the ache of all those years together suddenly rising up inside him. He had no desire to revisit that part of his life—eighteen years was enough. But still, he couldn't help but imagine some kind of revenge for the PoPo who arrested him when false charges were filed during his divorce. His mouth quirked up in a wry smile as he knew that at least Mickey severely reprimanded Gary for his actions. He finally responded, his voice low and rough with emotion, "I hope you have him on the night shift at least."

Mickey chuckled and agreed, then asked one more time, "OK, what do you really want?"

Manny hesitated for a moment. "Can you give me some information about my new neighbor? He's in solitary." Manny left out that the man drilled a hole through the wall and set up a camera. Too much information to share even with an old friend.

Mickey paused slightly as if to emphasize how serious an inquiry this was. Was it ethical to look up somebody for a friend? Her face softened as if recalling a distant memory and she responded, "Okay, I'll get back to you. That's the least I can do for an old Bronx buddy. Do you have a name?"

Manny leaned in closer. His voice lowered to barely a whisper as he revealed, "First name, Theo. That's all I got."

"Alright, let me get on it." Mickey replied, looking like she felt the weight of all of their words, unspoken and spoken, that were exchanged since that stupid kiss. She looked at Manny's face, searching for any sign of recognition, but Manny was miles away in thought. Taking a deep breath, she mustered up her courage and broke the silence. "How's the Big C?"

Manny shifted uncomfortably in his seat and let out a heavy sigh before responding that he went through another Mohs surgery last week and all of the margins were negative. He was grateful for the good news but obviously tired from going through so many surgeries.

When Mickey asked about any new tests or treatments, Manny stopped cold and looked away. His typical expression when he didn't want to talk about something cast a heavy shadow in the viewer. Mickey looked like she could tell there was more going on than what he initially said, but she chose not to press him.

"Good to hear," Mickey responded. "Any new biopsies?" She remained pensive with the ensuing silence but looked strained while waiting for Manny to speak up.

He let out a humorless laugh. "Too many." He glanced at her from the corner of his eye, and watched as Mickey's stomach seemed to sink. How long was it since his diagnosis? Four days? Five? Anything over seven days meant bad news.

Mickey added, "Stick with it, Buddy. You can beat this shit."

Manny felt reassured about their friendship now and replied, "I know that now. Last time I saw you...was different."

As Manny spoke on the shield with his friend, he walked from the kitchen towards his living room and brushed past a smooth white countertop, accidentally spilling some liquid from a cup. The red fluid in the cup landed on his leg, making it look like blood was spilled. He kept talking to Mickey while grabbing a tool mounted on the wall and pressing it against his pants leg. It resembled a miniature hair dryer but performed differently. Manny waved it around and triggered it, which started a bright light and high-pressure wind that dried up the liquid stain in seconds. His self-cleaning nanotechnology clothing was made with a tightly woven surface that repelled dirt and stains. He then pointed the tool at the floor and hit another switch that sucked up the dried crumbs. All was back to normal in his orderly cabin. Additionally, he cleaned up all traces of paint chips and concrete pieces on the floor made by the hole in the wall.

Manny stood in front of a mirror and surveyed the bandage taped across his forehead. The edges were still pristine, but a small spot of blood seeped through in the center, a sign that he should be wearing a hat again. He sighed, feeling a heavy wave of disappointment wash over him. His algo and credit ratings were already reduced by the numerous surgeries undergone, reducing his predicted lifespan to just 69 years. The loss of his job only made things worse, leaving him struggling to make ends meet on the income from his VSG and book sales. As he turned away from the mirror, Manny determinedly set himself to the task of reclaiming as much time and as many credits as he could.

CHAPTER 4
Battle is on for the first fight,

Manny heard the pleasant chime in his earbuds that signaled a "friendly" was calling. He tapped his futuristic visor, and Roberta Ceglia's name appeared on the menu. His lips curved into a smile as he double-clicked on her beautiful face. "Hi, Roberta!"

"Manny!" she replied. "James said he's coming with fresh steaks, but he doesn't have any FOUPs to seal them."

An exasperated groan escaped from Manny's lips. "I'm headed out soon. I'll contact Coop again and see what I can do."

"We need it today, or else the meat will go to CATACS," she said gravely.

Manny knew that meant the Contros would mix the fresh meat produced at Sunnyside Farm with thousands of pounds of White Cube food if not consumed fresh. "What a waste of fresh meat," he muttered.

"I can always give it to the cats, you know. Fresh meat mixed with their cat food keeps their fur in great shape." She glanced fondly at the cats wandering through the kitchen. Roberta loved her cats. And her husband loved his Roberta. Otherwise, he would not be much of a cat lover.

Standing nearby, James shouted loud enough for Manny to hear him through Roberta's shield. "Get some goddamn FOUPs here fast!"

Manny sensed the camaraderie with James, having been through tough jobs together many times during their volunteer work at the vertical farm. James stepped closer to Roberta and slid an arm around her waist before letting his hand drift down to rest on her buttocks. Despite her playful wriggle, he kept his grip firm and looked like he enjoyed feeling her curves beneath his hand. His own dark skin was rich in melanin pigments, smooth and silky, contrasting with Roberta's lighter black skin.

Roberta's cheeks flushed as she realized that Manny could see them embracing. Trying to cover up her embarrassment, she mentioned that they needed to get back to work at the farm. James sighed and reluctantly let her go, knowing that they would have no time for love-making later that day—his workload at the office was too high since it was nearly the end of the quarter.

Roberta stepped away from James and said, "I have to get back to the farm." James looked mildly rejected but Roberta nodded to Manny in the viewer. "We have the harvest to do."

"Do you guys ever keep your hands off each other?" Manny teased.

Roberta knew that Manny could see her face in the shield. "Just get the damn FOUPs."

Later, Manny slid his arms into the sleeves of his black "leather" jacket. He was still getting used to wearing clean, strangely soft clothes each day and he tugged at the collar to loosen it as he thought about how much he'd changed in just a few short months. The jacket tingled against his neck, reminding him that this coat wasn't merely fashionable clothing, it was an advanced piece of technology designed to be comfortable and flexible like a second skin. The jacket's special nanotechnology resisted dirt, stains, and wear and tear, making it last far longer than any traditional outfit made from natural materials. The similar nanotech fabric kept his blue pants clean and sharp-looking no matter what he put them through. The pants fit securely over his hips but flared out below his knees then tapered inward toward his feet where they ended with shiny black boots with thick soles. Unusual for farm work, but this was no ordinary farm he was visiting and guiding.

Manny pressed his thumb against the reader on the door, and a satisfying click-whirr resounded as the motorized door latch disengaged. He glanced at the monitor and saw his own face reflected back, illuminated by the surrounding white light. He let out a small smile in acknowledgment—the Algos were always watching people's expressions and giving them extra time credits for leading a happy life. Knowing he just received credits for his good behavior, Manny grabbed a fedora from his growing selection of hats, and stepped through the doorway, allowing the RFID chip embedded in his wrist to register his passing. His eyes scanned the neighbors' door next to him—a nondescript white one with the standard passthrough, but also an additional monitor featuring CATACS's ubiquitous green apple logo with the thin swoosh that always struck Manny as looking more like a penis than anything else.

Manny made his way down the hallway and into the elevator, passing through another chip reading. He stepped out of the lobby and onto the street and was scanned again. The traffic was minimal and there were few people around. It was a typical scene in the middle of an autumn afternoon. As he marched off to the doctor's office to check on his status, he zipped up his jacket all the way up to his neck. He admired the colors of the leaves this time of year. He thought about getting his paint set out again. He also imagined the leaves gently falling from the variety of vertical gardens around Chelsea Pod One, and thought of the sheep needing to be sheared at Sunnyside Farm. The sun was bright that day and he could feel the heat trying to burn its way through his hat.

Manny glanced up from his face shield, his stomach flipping as he took in the sight of van-shaped vehicles passing by a little too closely. The sides were a glossy black and they were nearly identical, boxy like an old Volkswagen van from the 1960s. People called them "Beeze" after the leading manufacturer who supplied them exclusively to the Controllers. They had called the project Beeze after their prototype E, as part of a manufacturing agreement with the Bureau of Environmental Engineering and Zoning (BEEZ). The term Beeze stayed with the vehicles no matter how hard the Contros tried to rename the fleet.

Manny watched as the Beeze vehicle gracefully dovetailed in and out of the lanes, like a school of fish swimming together, responding to one another's movements and signals. Their artificial intelligence systems learned from each road, each vehicle, and each driver. He had heard of rare accidents, like the one last month when one drove straight into a brick wall, but luckily the passengers remained safe within the cocooned interior. Traffic today moved as smoothly as ever.

The etiquette of the streets required people to use the crosswalk at the exact moment that the signal changed. It sensed Manny's presence and switched the traffic lights to give priority to the pedestrian. An approaching Beeze slowed to a crawl in deference to him, as did several other Beezes interconnected to this one. He was about to cross halfway through the intersection when he looked down at the road and noticed one of the electromagnetic charging wires was damaged. He wondered if the vehicles in the area were receiving the proper dose of energy from the damaged wires, or whether the vehicles became weaker because of the loose wires.

Manny carefully stepped between two lanes of vehicles and crossed over to get a closer look at the damage to the power wires. The smell of ionization cut through his senses, but he ignored it and observed how closely together each wire was placed on this section of the street. A quick inspection revealed some places where small chunks were torn out by accident, leaving behind blackened edges that could not conduct power any longer.

He eagerly made his way to the doctor's office, taking in all the sights and sounds of the journey. He heard the familiar chatter of customers coming from a nearby coffee shop, and he could smell the distinct aroma of freshly brewed java wafting through the air. As he continued, he saw intricate pieces of art carefully arranged along the street, showcasing a wide range of vibrant colors that seemed to dance in the dappled sunlight filtering through the trees overhead.

Everywhere he looked there were signs of life, of hope, and yet he felt a sudden pang of sadness, not knowing if hope was enough for himself. He noticed the familiar faces of people he'd seen many times before, but today they seemed to regard him differently with a quiet understanding that the future was uncertain. He kept walking, determined to wait until he reached his destination before he allowed himself to be overwhelmed by his own thoughts.

Manny's ear pods vibrated and he activated his shield to take a call. The pavement below him sped by as he walked faster, adjusting the augmented reality view of his shield so he could stay on course while accepting the call from Mickey. Her voice echoed inside it. Her face appeared on one side of the screen while a map of the city filled the other half. It almost looked like Mickey was standing in front of him but he could see around her to keep from walking into a pole or other impediment on the sidewalk.

"Theo Wiggins is a genius at a robotics company. He has some credit issues," Mickey revealed and then continued reading from the data file. "He's in for some sort of credit problem. Looks like he scammed the algorithms at CATACS, but they don't have any proof."

"Why is he in solitary then?" Manny asked, stopping in his tracks on the sidewalk near a shady tree.

"I don't know," Mickey replied, "but sometimes the Controllers do that to interrupt the cycle. They hope the data reveals itself when the suspect is put on hold for a while."

CHAPTER 5

The doctor is in,

Dr. Rosita McKenna hurried along the corridor of her doctor's office in Chelsea Pod One, checking on her patients amidst the whirring and clicking of robotic medical assistants. She smiled and worried at the sight of a child brought in for treatment, then headed towards the check-in station.

Suddenly, she noticed a dark red spot on her pant leg, a stark contrast to the pale blue of her doctor's smock. She reached for the cleaning wand next to her desk and activated it with a flick of her wrist. The beam of light caused the stain to evaporate and break into pieces that fluttered to the floor. Nanotechnology had revolutionized the cleanliness of medicine, and robotically-assisted surgery had changed the practice of medicine. Before, healing from surgeries previously took weeks or months but now recovery was nearly instantaneous. However, Rosita knew there were still some diseases that resisted technological improvement.

In the gleaming hallways of the hospitals, which had become research centers attached to universities, robots of all shapes and sizes hummed along. Doctors specialized in their respective fields and practiced out of their own offices scattered throughout the pods. They worked with deep-learning algorithms that played a key role in medical diagnostics. Chemists at the university hospitals cooked up new medications for treating diseases, while auto-docs assembled intricate prostheses and replaced organs missing from patients' bodies. Some of the specialized robots traveled as needed to the doctor's offices when required for a specifically delicate operation.

Rosita strode toward the check-in station and reached up to her ear pods, tapping twice to disengage her shield, which hummed as it swirled away, allowing her to hear the soft sounds of the hospital hallway. "Are we all logged in?" she asked without looking at Dr. Cheryl Blanding, her trusted protégé for so many years, standing before her in a white medical smock that hung off her thin frame like a tent. As always, black-rimmed glasses sat perched atop her freckled nose and her light brown hair strained against the ribbon holding her ponytail. Cheryl's fingers danced across the surface of her electronic pad. The pad chirped as if answering questions and then glowed a soft turquoise blue. "Yes, Doctor," she said without looking up.

Just then, Rosita heard a small thump on the countertop. Looking up, she saw a little girl, her face barely visible under the front brim of her shield. She was bouncing on the balls of her feet, and grinning with all her teeth. Most settings on the shields allowed for an opaque view of the real face, but this one was set to full transparency. The little girl's eyes lit up when she caught sight of Rosita, who smiled warmly back at her. "Mommy, are you done yet?" the girl asked.

Rosita stroked her daughter's soft, brown curls, nestling around a large, oval bandage. She knew that beneath the sterile gauze, a robotic surgeon recently wielded a scalpel to cut away the malignant tissue that spread across the little girl's scalp like a spider's web. The surgery peeled back layer upon layer of skin in search of hidden pockets of cancer cells, right down to the bone. Every so often, the robot would pause and send each sliver of flesh to the lab for analysis, then continue on if the lab detected more cancer cells. Sometimes these surgeries would take hours until they were sure they removed the spreading cancer.

Margaret McKenna, or Maggie as she preferred, was just eight years old, too young for a disease as serious as melanoma. She already underwent three surgeries to fight it, and her scalp was stitched up each time afterward. Unfortunately, the internal stitches began to pop prematurely, sending sharp jolts of pain through her head with each one that burst. To make matters worse, she'd been diagnosed only last year. Rosita finished double-checking Margaret's vitals and smiled at her reassuringly. "Okay, kiddo, we can head home now."

"Look," Maggie said as she pointed to the crisp new bandage, her voice joyful with excitement. She leaned closer to Rosita and spoke in a soft, conspiratorial tone. "They gave me a fresh one so there won't be any more blood stains.

Cheryl glanced at Rosita's daughter, recalling another blue-eyed patient they treated just weeks earlier. Rosita had performed a nearly identical Mohs surgery to remove melanoma cells from his scalp, a particularly common site for the disease due to its sensitive skin and frequent sun exposure. Despite attempts to stay inside and out of the dangerous rays, some people were unlucky enough to be genetically predisposed to melanoma, as was evidently the case with Rosita's daughter. With a blend of Irish, Spanish, and Norwegian heritage, her heredity sealed her fate at birth. Cheryl cleared her throat and spoke up, suggesting that Rosita take over the log-in process while she stored the records on the cloud.

Cheryl recently noticed that the patients she treated shared something in common—their heritage and ancestry traced back to Vikings from the old world. Despite this, there were many theories as to why the Vikings had stopped their southward expansion. One of the strongest explanations seemed to be related to their Nordic nature: the low levels of melanin in their skin made them more vulnerable to getting skin cancer. Studies show that people living in northern parts of Europe and Scandinavia are far more likely to develop skin cancer than those in the warmer climates of the south. And as the Vikings traveled further south and had more cases of skin cancer amongst their population, they began to understand and recognize the dangers of the new world, which eventually led them to retreat northward.

Cheryl mulled over the biopsies from both of her patients that would soon be assessed by the Cancer Board. This committee, which rotated three doctors every four months, convened once a week, with an additional six doctors waiting to rotate into the panel. All three members had to unanimously agree on what stage the cancer was in; stage one meant malignant yet highly treatable, while stage four implied immediate death. The consecutive progression through these stages felt like a march toward death.

Stage two cancer patients may receive immunotherapy and if it proves ineffective then the doctors prescribe chemotherapy. The famous phrase, "That which does not kill you makes you stronger," certainly applies to chemotherapy. An unfortunate reality, the Algos not only forecast how a patient will respond to treatments but they also decide who gets access to the lifesaving drugs. Without the best treatment, most people will eventually progress to later stages of melanoma, and succumb to it.

The ground-breaking mRNA treatment (Messenger Ribonucleic Acid) method began development in the early 2000s, used to combat a pandemic that had killed millions around the world, lasting nearly two decades before an mRNA vaccine finally beat the virus. The process works by identifying a protein that can treat a disease and then creating a vaccine to deliver the treatment specifically to the part of the body that needs healing. This involves extracting DNA (Deoxyribonucleic Acid) from the cell's nucleus and transporting it to the outer watery area of the cell, where instructions from the vaccine synthesize with the protein.

Though these vaccines are now available for even common illnesses, cancer treatments remain expensive because each one targets each individual's DNA. Scientists extract blood from each patient, and they develop unique mRNA for injecting each patient multiple times to combat the specific cancers. AI-powered algorithms monitor the process closely to ensure that only those who will benefit from the treatment will receive it.

An experimental new method of treatment for cancers, mRNA is very expensive and only delivered for those with the right algorithm. Clinical trials on the west coast lead the way, picking off one cancer at a time. Unfortunately, this means that only those who can afford such expensive treatments are able to enjoy its life-saving benefits. And those with a cancer still not targeted by the clinical trials, may die long before the scientists discover the cure.

CHAPTER 6
We wanted a win,

Manny entered the doctor's office and immediately observed the sterilized atmosphere. He felt like an intruder, and absent mindedly did not think about activating his face shield as he strode confidently toward the check-in station. Three people seated in the waiting area turned to look at him, their face shields fully extended like protective bubbles that blocked out germs and bacteria. But Manny neglected this precaution until he heard a stern voice calling his name, "Dr. Rio, please engage your shield."

A flush of embarrassment rose to his cheeks as all eyes turned towards him; the patients' opaque face shields made it impossible to make out complete facial expressions, but he could feel their judgment nonetheless. He quickly tapped his earbud and was soon enveloped in a personal bubble of filtered air. "Sorry about that," he mumbled to nobody in particular.

Manny strode to the check-in station, gaze narrowed as he leaned in and spoke in low tones to Dr. Cheryl Blanding. "I want to know my results. It's been eight days already." He noticed a little girl standing off to the side of the counter that he'd seen before, with her face partially concealed by a face shield, but smiling up at him all the same.

Cheryl shook her head. "I'm sorry. We don't have any new information for you yet, Dr. Rio."

Manny was beginning to lose his patience and looked visibly upset. "You can't keep doing this to me."

Just then, a voice from the next room made everyone freeze. "Do what to you, Dr. Rio?" Slowly, Dr. Rosita McKenna stepped into view wearing casual black pants and a crisp white blouse which she was busily buttoning as she entered the room. Her eyebrows raised in suspicion as she stopped short and stared directly at Manny. "Really? Are we going to have this conversation again?"

Manny raised his voice a bit too much for the small waiting room, "Damn right we are. You can't make us sit and wait to hear the results like this. What does it take around this place to get an answer?"

The little girl standing nearby disengaged her shield and replied firmly in a brave little voice, "You have to wait your turn, Mister. That's what my Mommy always says." She stepped toward Rosita and held her hand.

Manny glanced down at the little girl with confusion; she may have been young, but she had a strong presence and stood confidently in her answer. She wore a purple tutu, like a little ballerina, over her jeans. He tried to keep a straight face, but amusement tugged at the corners of his mouth. He turned towards Rosita and tried not to smirk as he said, "She says that, does she?"

"Yes, sir. About twenty times a day," the little girl replied without missing a beat. The room suddenly filled with laughter.

Manny couldn't help but grin; Rosita's mommy-daughter duo was quite the reckoning force. He thought about his last few doctor's appointments and how that must have made an impression here, though not necessarily a good one. He looked back at the little girl and gave her a warm smile, then removed his cap, "Looks like we both have bandages," he said and quickly put it back on.

"Yours is bleeding though," she whispered and pointed at the top of his head.

He glanced over toward the check-in station again and sighed heavily at the two doctors. "Sorry, Dr. McKenna," Manny said. "It's been eight days since my biopsy. I know what that means when you don't get the results right away. I don't want to go through another round of your shield calls again."

"Dr. Rio, the Board is reviewing your results and they have not made a decision yet." She looked Manny square in the eye again, her gaze unwavering. The unspoken weight of the words hung heavy in the air between them, thick and suffocating.

"You will have to wait for them to decide," Rosita continued, her tone flat and clinical.

Manny felt his heart sink into his stomach. He knew that the Board's decision was required to be unanimous, but it still stung to hear that his fate was up in the air.

"Sometimes two Board members will vote the biopsy to be stage 1 cancer for example and the third will vote stage 2," Rosita explained further, her hand absentmindedly fiddling with her pen.

Manny's mind raced as he absorbed the gravity of what she was saying. Depending on the stage of cancer determined in the diagnosis, the doctors must adjust the treatment plan, which would then affect the patient's algorithms, lifespans, and earnings.

"Stage 1 means the patient has cancer," Rosita pressed on, as if sensing Manny's confusion. "Whereas stage 2 means it already reached the deepest layer and may have spread through the lymph nodes. Stage 3 means it went to other organs, and stage 4…" she trailed off delicately, letting the severity of what she didn't say hang heavily in the room

Manny felt a wave of confusion wash over him; he thought of the words "malignant" and "benign," trying to make sense of what it all meant. When someone hears, "My test was positive," does that mean a good result or a bad one? He shook his head and likened malignant to being lazy, but it is just the opposite. He murmured quietly, "If they haven't decided in this much time, that means it's malignant again."

The little girl emerged from around the desk and approached Manny, her eyes wide with worry. Her tiny fingers trembled as she reached out to take his large hand in hers. "That means another surgery" she whispered, her words barely above a hush. She tugged at his hand slightly for emphasis as she added hopefully, "I hope it's not a big one this time."

Manny could feel the weight of her concern in her touch, but he also felt something else: strength and resilience that belied her small stature. He released her hand before turning back to the reception desk and stating, "I'll hang tight for the doctor's call then."

As he moved toward the door, Manny noticed a picture hanging on the wall that showed an intelligent-looking woman of about 70 years-old boasting a doctorate degree in Biomedical Engineering. Manny deduced this may be Rosita's mother due to their similarities and looked back at Rosita, who was watching him. His eyes went to another photo on the wall—that of the same woman alongside a man receiving an honorary doctorate from UC Berkeley for his achievements in autonomous driving vehicles.

Manny looked between the photos and Rosita once more before leaving the office with even more questions than when he had arrived. He decided to take a Beeze home and drove along, marveling at the intricate details of these autonomous vehicles and wondering how they had come into existence.

CHAPTER 7

Travelers go to the coast,

Manny stood at the edge of the street, contemplating the trip ahead to Sunnyside Farm, the vertical farm he volunteered at out on the Long Island Pod. His impatience for his ride began to increase when he noticed a school of Beezes change their pattern. One of them broke away from the formation and glided towards him. Manny waited as it stopped right in front of him, its double doors opening invitingly. He double-clicked on his farm destination to make sure the Beeze had the right address. This would cost him some credits, but it would get him out to the farm and back before his allotment ran out.

He stepped inside, carefully keeping his head down to avoid knocking against the doorframe. Settling himself into the seat, Manny felt the belt automatically moving around his waist to secure him in place just as the doors closed. He became aware of another figure hurrying towards the Beeze, evidently intending to join him in his ride. Seeing an occupant inside this particular Beeze, he waved and turned aside, hurrying off towards another Beeze that arrived for him nearby.

This city was practically crime-free. Cameras tracked everyone's movements and advanced algorithms anticipated any potential problems before they occurred. Those who did break the law were immediately placed in solitary confinement—a small cabin where the Contros monitored their every move. Health officials treated mental health issues with compassion and dignity, leaving homelessness at zero. The one exception to this rule was the penal colony for the unforgiven, an isolated cluster where the Contros sent the criminally insane to live out their sentences. Even urban legends could not quite capture its reality. The exaggerated accounts of violence and breakouts served to entertain more than anything else.

Manny studied the menu in his shield and scrolled through a list of lighting options to set the interior lighting of the Beeze. He selected SAD, or Seasonal Affective Disorder, which cast a low blue light over the interior of his Beeze. Manny knew that this gentle light would help fight off the depression he was experiencing since the triple whammy of his divorce, job loss, and cancer diagnosis all in one year. Not to mention the fact that both of his twins left home for college pods recently, leaving him with an empty nest syndrome that he did not anticipate. Maslow's Hierarchy of Needs was familiar to Manny. He knew well enough to not take on more than one of life's biggest challenges at a time.

Manny's Beeze hummed along the city streets, its electric motor purring quietly and the soft blue interior lighting setting the mood. He welcomed the bright sunlight streaming down through the skylight, feeling invigorated by the warmth despite the air conditioning in the car. With a gentle glide, the Beeze moved onto the connecting bridge that would take him from Chelsea Pod One to the Long Island Pod. As he crossed over to the other side of the bridge, Manny looked out of his window and saw the smaller steel and glass cabins dotted around this area of town. No towering skyscrapers here, buildings were at most ten stories high. Some lucky folks had a view of the ocean from their cabin windows, but most gazed out wistfully at the cityscape below. But whether or not you had a view was determined entirely by algorithms and this new game of life.

Manny's Beeze slowly detangled itself from the "chain" of other vehicles, each linked wirelessly to the next. The Beeze quickly changed speeds, adjusting to the slower pace of traffic on the surface streets as they crawled forward in a wave-like formation. Manny could see buildings in the distance that housed the vertical farming complex and felt a tingle of excitement as he approached a place that he loved.

As Manny's vehicle made its way through all the turns, his mind began to wander. In light of all that had happened over the past two years, he couldn't help but feel mental weariness. Did this change him? Or were any changes minor and insignificant enough so he did not notice? His thoughts trailed off to a book he'd read about rewriting one's own internal wiring. The book explained how each neuron in the brain fired signals in standard patterns, but that changing the patterns produced different results. Some signals fire into a certain dendrite while others branch off into an entirely new axons of a different neuron. When neurons do not fire regularly, or get bombarded by alcohol and drugs, they can start to wither away and will eventually die. Thus, the term arose during a hangover that the person fried their own brain.

Most people think along a single path of neurons, like a Beeze vehicle choosing an exit on a traffic roundabout. Every time the Beeze goes from Point A to Point B, it exits at the same first roundabout, unless there is a roadblock that forces it to take the second exit and reroute. But something was changing. Suddenly, Manny stopped self-medicating with alcohol, which he jokingly referred to as "Forget Me Juice." Refraining from numbing his emotions, he gradually became aware of his thoughts and feelings—an epiphany in which he finally accepted that it was time to move on. He slowly broke away from his old habits. No more sleeping pills to get him through the night, or working and drinking being all that filled up each day, and he began to focus on counting up successes instead of surgeries.

Manny felt the weight of time pressing down on him like a lead blanket. Every night he tried to sleep, but his body ached and refused to relax. He reached for sleeping pills, but they provided only temporary respite. They weren't a real solution. Desperately, Manny tried to make sense of his life by breaking it down into smaller increments. He calculated that he had only 348 full moons left, a timeline so short he shuddered. He looked at all of the animals' lives around him—the cows and chickens whose arrival and departures measured in dozens of full moons, and the gnats who only lived half a moon. By this calculation, Manny's life amounted to the lives of about 700 gnats.

The Beeze pulled up to the vertical farm and veered onto a gravel drive, slowing as they approached an immense granite boulder that marked the entrance. Manny and James Ceglia had purchased that rock at the end of the Long Island Pod and used a transport vehicle to carry it to the farm. They'd dug a deep hole into the peat moss soil for the boulder to stand upright in when they dropped it in; a one-shot opportunity to create a monument instead of leaving a large rock flat on the ground. The driver of the truck, a man named, Coop Cooper, laughed so hard at the concept that he helped Manny and James, "stick the landing."

The Beeze drove past the rock, with a sign on it that proudly greeted, "Welcome to Sunnyside Farm: Vertical Sustained Growth." The Beeze was now in full view of the farm, a five-story steel structure with glass on all its sides. Inside the structure was no ordinary farm like those in the pods of the middle of the United States Cluster. But then, those pods were so far away, their produce used CATACS repositioning money and then delivered solely to White Cube distribution centers. Sunnyside VSG Farm was right here inside the Long Island Pod instead to make deliveries easier and shorter.

As the pods became more separated and transporting food products became difficult, vertical farms became necessary alongside the pods. The standard delivery process from big vehicles to smaller ones, to even smaller ones for "The Last Mile," then to a human's hands was expensive and labor-intensive, while those who filled this delivery position considered themselves unworthy by society's algorithms, so the jobs became difficult to fill. The artificial intelligence built into all systems now used a deep-learning process that shaped self-fulfilling prophecies.

The answer to this dilemma was to grow fruits and vegetables hydroponically on the walls of various buildings inside the pods, while livestock and other proteins grew in vertical farms immediately adjacent to the pods. People from the vertical farms harvested the food and divided it into sealed FOUPs with barcodes for tracking purposes and delivery to every customer inside the pod. The Sunnyside VSG was a pioneer in the development of vertical farms and other similar farms were now popping up in other pod clusters.

Rolling drones, small machines resembling minivans from the early 2000s, delivered the vegetables to the pods. These drones loaded the organics and produce into the FOUP containers, which they then transported to the cabin structures. Once at the cabins, smaller drones resembling cute little robots took over. The motion-sensing devices navigated through the halls with their cargo of vegetables, becoming a source of fascination for some children who would stop them and pet them. Kind people would even occasionally help out if the robots got stuck or tipped over.

Humans gather at the vertical walls to harvest the precious fruits and vegetables, loading and unloading rolling drones as they began their deliveries to other people inside the pods. The owners of the cabin structures tended to the colorful, lush vertical gardens with care and happily shared their produce with the others, who in turn shared what they grew. Their labor of love was too precious to be left in the hands of robots—they preferred picking, packing, and shipping food themselves. Despite this, the White Cube system remained dominant for proteins like beef, poultry, freshwater fish, and saltwater fish due to their higher space requirements. To remedy this issue, some members of the vertical sustenance growth group developed vertical farms in underpopulated areas of the pod, attempting to distribute this higher-quality food to those who wanted to break free from White Cube.

Manny glanced up at the gleaming Sunnyside Farm. The five-story building was an architectural marvel of glass and steel, with a unique feature at the top—a massive fish tank that split off into both saltwater and freshwater tanks for raising regional species of fish. Pumps moved the saltwater from the nearby ocean on Long Island and filtered the water through a reverse osmosis system to feed the freshwater fish. Meanwhile, the bleed-off from the freshwater tanks created nutrient-rich water that cascaded down to the livestock beds on the bottom floor providing nourishment for growing grains to feed cows and other four-legged animals raised for dairy and beef.

The zone between the fish tanks and the lowest level of livestock is where the poultry reside—mainly chickens, with some pheasants and ducks mixed in. A winding spiral walkway herded the poultry toward the middle floors when their numbers start to dwindle due to an out-of-balance system. Then, the farm required exterior sources from traditional farms outside of the city. This hasn't happened in close to a year, because the scientists are constantly working on improving the self-sustaining process.

The fragile ecosystem within the dome required a meticulous balance of biomechanical feedback and adjustments. Dr. Manuel Rio and his team of college interns, volunteers, and a small paid staff of scientists, had worked tirelessly to keep the fragile ecosystem within the dome in balance, allowing for successful harvests and sustainable growth. But when Manny left White Cube Research, the grants dried up and his project needed an influx of new resources. Determined to find a solution, Manny approached NASA, the premier space agency on the west coast, looking for a grant that would allow them to continue their work. Although they were hesitant due to already having plans to colonize the moon on their own, Manny remained steadfast in his desire to convince them of a cooperative agreement.

CHAPTER 8
Only one is diagnosed,

Manny's Beeze pulled into the parking lot and came to a stop near the entrance to the vertical farm. As he stepped out, a cool gust of air blew past him, carrying with it the smell of fresh-cut wheat and damp soil, while the double doors of the Beeze opened and closed with a swooshing sound. Coop Cooper greeted Manny with a friendly smile, a hand ready for shaking. With his broad frame and towering height, Coop looked like a giant compared to Manny. When they shook hands, Manny's normal-sized hand was almost engulfed in Coop's large one. "Are you ready for harvest time?" Coop asked.

Manny noticed that Coop's beard had grown even longer since their last meeting, cascading down his chest in an array of gray hairs. Despite this, he still looked fit, like he could take on a football team if need be. "How many are we doing this time?" Manny asked.

"Thirty-five cows," Coop said, peering over the electronic clipboard in his hand. He ran a finger over the pad and counted off figures in his head. "Seventy of the poultry, and five-hundred from the fish tanks."

"Not bad." Manny stood beside him, surveying the farm. He thought it was a good load of orders—as long as it didn't throw off the biosystem too badly. They ran into trouble with that last year. One wrong move and the whole vertical farm could be thrown off balance. Too much of a harvest and they can't sustain themselves, but too little and they drown in their own excess. Delicate was the choice. "Is Roberta involved in the count?" he asked.

"Of course," Coop replied, pride in his voice.

Manny knew Coop loved the vertical farm, although the income was only a fraction of his trucking dollars but a larger part of his time—a true labor of love.

Manny started walking towards the loading dock, ready to inspect and take part in the activities. He turned to Coop and said, "You know we are out of FOUPs, right? No sense in harvesting if we can't ship."

Coop responded with a proud grin as they rounded the corner and saw Coop's truck, loaded to the maximum with stacks of containers. Coop put his arm around Manny before slapping him good-naturedly on the back. Manny winced from the impact of Coop's burly hand, who must have forgotten that normal people cannot withstand such force. And he also didn't know about the surgeries, specifically the one in the middle of Manny's back only two months ago. Coop's expression shifted to concern. "Oh man, you alright?"

Manny forced a tight smile and ground out, "No problem. Just… a sore back, that's all." He felt the weight of Coop's gaze as he spoke, his friend's sympathetic concern mixing with a hint of suspicion—the subject of Manny's divorce became fodder for gossip at the farm, and Manny knew it.

"Sorry about that," Coop said finally. He gestured to the truck bed and continued, "You okay to do some lifting? Those FOUPs aren't gonna move themselves."

Manny nodded, then squinted up at the stack of containers on the truck. "How did you get so many of them?" He knew the long journey these parts took—the PVDF plastic piping cut to size in Wisconsin, the nitrogen fittings added at Armeden Labs, the magnetics assembled by Magneto Corporation—and finally reaching their destination in Coop's truck.

"Hooper Corporation had a leftover shipment from a canceled project for the Contros," Coop said with a hint of pride. "I know a vice president there pretty well and we arranged a bigger load this time."

"That should get the supply chain problem all sorted out." As more FOUPs were utilized to deliver food, their circulation size increased, but the loss rate was incredible. Misplaced, lost, broken, or forgotten, the quantity of FOUPs was always dwindling. Each individual FOUP had a lifespan of one delivery, and then only occasionally found its way back to the vertical farm with the same drones that brought them to each destination. The farm contained a reprocessing plant and an Automated Storage and Retrieval System, known as ASRS, that cleaned the FOUPs and sent them back to the harvesting area for another delivery. The PVDF material, although expensive, was deemed the most hygienic way to transport the food. The ASRS storage was the most efficient method of storing and moving the FOUPs since they could be connected end-to-end like straws before being bundled together in groups of twenty-five into long packages measuring fifteen inches by fifteen inches by ten feet. Manny and Coop shared the patent for this design along with ten other scientists from various pod clusters, and the whole network of vertical farms and supply chains kept expanding.

Manny turned to Coop and asked, "I want to see the farm first if you don't mind. Have you toured it today?"

Coop shook his head. "No, I just got here too. We can start unloading the FOUPs later."

The two men made their way up the brick paver path that led to the vertical farm. At a security checkpoint, they presented their identification cards to a private security officer sitting at a desk. The guard ran his scanner over the cards, activated his electronic shield, then double-clicked on each shield menu item to confirm access permissions. The officer looked up and recognition sparkled in his eyes, but he seemed momentarily startled before dropping his shield. "Hello, Dr. Rio. Hello, Mr. Cooper," he said, looking sheepish as he added, "Sorry I didn't recognize you. I'm new here."

"Good afternoon, Officer Henry," Manny said while reading the guard's nametag, while Coop just gave a curt nod.

"What can I do for you?" Officer Henry asked as he stood to attention, squinting in the bright sunlight that streamed through the windows.

Manny asked several questions about the status of the farm. He then asked, "Is Roberta Ceglia here?"

A slight shift in the officer's eyes suggested discomfort but he responded with, "Yes, Sir" nonetheless. Manny heard a faint grunt from Coop, no doubt caused by the truck that had to be unloaded today and probably some issue that occurred with this guard before.

Manny began walking to the lab but turned back to the officer, "Oh, one more thing, can you ask Randy Jorgenson to take a look at Coop's truck? We have some unloading to do, so we better get started."

"Will do." The officer must not have understood much of what was going on at the farm but he kept his mouth shut, glad for having found this kind of job—one that offered him better pay than most others and free lunch during work hours. Even better, the guards took one hot meal per day back home to their families. Some guards packed the FOUPs so tight that the lid would not close.

Manny and Coop strode along a monochromic hallway before taking a right turn into the lab. The combination of soils and cleaning odors was impossible to miss as they entered. Manny punched in a code into the wall-mounted console, revealing a metallic door that opened and shut behind them with a hiss. The inside of the laboratory resembled something out of a sci-fi movie. Six women draped in white coats and carrying an electronic clipboard stood at white consoles. All smiled widely at the sight of the two men as they entered. Roberta stood in their center like she was awaiting an embrace. As soon as she saw Manny and Coop's entrance, her face lit up with a smile, and she exclaimed, "There you are!" Both men couldn't help but grin back and moved closer to receive the hug.

Coop smiled and opened his arms to Roberta for a tight hug. He thought it strange that he blushed when greeting her, but couldn't help himself. He waved to the rest of the room as he stepped back from the embrace, feeling the admiration from the group in return.

One of the scientists motioned for him to follow her near a computer screen where she stood. "Kunichiwa Cooper-san," Naoko Nakamura said, but the words in Coop's shield translator made the words sound like affection in any language as the words became translated into "Hello, Mr. Cooper."

He smiled, tapping his shield before meeting her eyes with admiration. She often reverted to her native language for emphasis when speaking of important matters.

Naoko, the leading scientist under Roberta, transferred to NYU from the Kyoto Cluster. She wore her protective face mask partly reduced so she could discuss the intricate terms used in the lab. Many languages adopted the same words when it came to scientific jargon, but the native languages were translated through the shields. Naoko, tall and willowy, quietly moved with elegance. She sported the same white attire that everyone wore in the lab, yet she managed to make it look stylish.

Naoko pointed to the screen and her shield translator continued on as she spoke to Coop, "This is the harvest count, diet selection, and culling stats. We are currently gathering up the herd. Will your truck be ready to accept the filled FOUPs in four hours?"

Herding cattle today was far different than the ways of the old wild west of the last millennium. Now herding used RFID chips attached to the animals that activated doors and gates as they moved toward their designated harvest rooms. Redirection of those cows harvested on the lower floor sent them for a quick walk straight to the end of their milk-producing lives. The selected chickens and other poultry used a spiral walkway path that led them to the final destination of their egg-producing days. And fish simply plopped into tanks in the harvest room with a splash. Everything selected was based on predetermined algorithms not too dissimilar from those methods employed by Controllers to herd people.

"I need robotic assistance to unload the new FOUPs before the loading. I've got ten thousand in the back of my truck," Coop relayed to the group as he looked around the room. His tall, bulky frame towered over the other scientists. With broad shoulders and a thick neck, Coop seemed more like a black bear than an intellectual.

"Yoku yatta Cooper-san," Naoko said while beaming at Coop. "Well done, Mr. Cooper," said the translator. She stood up and gave a slight bow to him. He smiled even wider now.

Roberta started moving towards him, her strides swift and determined. She threw her arms around him, her cheeks flushed with excitement. "Ten thousand FOUPs? How can we ever thank you enough, Coop?"

The embrace caught Coop off guard. He wasn't one for physical affection, not even as a child, but here he was, standing in a room full of geniuses, being praised and hugged by each of them. It felt strange but oddly comforting too. "No thanks needed. I'm only helping where I can."

Manny clapped his shoulder, the customary sign of camaraderie between men. "Let's go harvest some protein," he said.

Roberta proposed they start at the top of the vertical farm. "Manny, we have workers to prepare the harvest and load it into the FOUPs," she told them. "That will take about four hours to finish. But we need your help with the desalination system again."

Manny took a few steps towards the exit, then suddenly spun back around on his heel. "Is Randy looking at it?" he asked.

"Yes, he's in the facilities room right now," she replied.

Manny tapped his shield and double-clicked on Randy Jorgenson's name to initiate a call. He began walking out of the lab, conversing with Randy as he went, and turning right down the long hallway towards the elevators. Coop hurried to catch up with him, casting one more glance back at Naoko. She smiled warmly and nodded her head in encouragement.

The men stepped out of the elevator on the highest floor of the vertical farm and saw two massive tanks, each one twice as tall as them. There was a slightly greenish tint to the freshwater tank while the saltwater tank had a bluish hue running through it. Multiple dividers within each tank created different compartments for various species. Tiny beams of sunlight cascaded throughout the tanks, giving the occupants and their natural surroundings blinking colors as they bounced off the fish and their environment. Above the tanks were several solar panels that shielded them from direct sunlight but still allowed enough into the tanks for kelp and other weeds to flourish.

The tanks were like miniature versions of reefs in nature, complete with kelp beds, rock formations, bottom feeders, moss, and ferns dotting both tanks. No wonder why the fish tasted so amazing!

Manny gazed as he stood before the giant saltwater tank, captivated by its sheer size and complexity. Schools of fish darted beneath the shimmering surface, their iridescent scales flashing in the sun's rays that cascaded down from the skylights above. He examined the network of tubes installed along the walls which pumped filtered seawater into the aquarium at a precise temperature and salinity balance. The largest specimens were almost two feet long and Manny watched them with awe, marveling at how they could go about life so peacefully in this man-made environment.

Building the fish tanks at Sunnyside became necessary in response to heavy-handed regulations imposed by the Controllers on the fishing in the nearby ocean, so the vertical farm set up its own operation to get around those mandates. The majority of the Controller's catch went straight into the White Cube system, where they transformed it into a gelatinous substance far removed from its original form, then distributed to citizens across the region in unappetizing pudding-filled bags.

Manny and Coop stepped through the door near the end of the saltwater tank, the stark contrast of bright white light illuminating the equipment room. A loud hum filled their ears as they moved closer to the desalination plant, where Randy stood waiting. He noticed them approaching and signaled them to activate their shields so they could speak to each other in the loud room. He activated his and Manny and Coop followed suit, extending their shields out to full length, activating their HEPA filters and noise cancellation devices.

Manny smiled and extended his hand in greeting. "What's up, Randy?" Coop nodded in recognition and waited for Randy to respond. They stepped close to the large reverse osmosis system that was the heart of the desalination plant.

Randy pointed at the monitor displaying a dark screen with a blue graph line in the shape of an s-curve and a red curve running slightly to its right. "The high-pressure pump is off the pump curve a bit, but we switched the lead pump and now it's coming back on track," he explained. All three men looked up at the monitor with satisfaction.

Coop bent down to study a low meter and glanced up from his crouched position to ask, "Can you fix the lead pump?"

Randy shook his head. "No, we have to send it to the Chicago Pod for a rebuild. Don't worry," he continued, gesturing to a row of pumps near the membrane filter system on the right side of the room. "We have a third backup that should keep us going until then."

"Nice design," Coop acknowledged, always proud of the physical labor and ingenuity it took to run a vertical farm.

Manny nodded in agreement before squinting up at Randy. "Roberta said you needed help, so why are we here?"

"Oh, not with this," Randy replied, gesturing to the array of pumps and pipes surrounding them. He began bundling up his various tools and measuring instruments before stashing them away in a large red tool chest with about a dozen open black drawers, depositing each tool in the perfect spot, and closing the drawers quickly and efficiently. "It's the concentrate discharge that's got the problems."

With that information, Randy began moving around the large platform that held the reverse osmosis system, containing pumps, a dozen thin cylinders about twenty feet long that held the membranes for filtering, and a half-dozen sand filters and ion exchange beds that brought the clarified water to perfectly balanced pH levels. He pointed to a flowmeter on the system displaying a flashing red number on a black screen. "The reject water flow is way too low."

Coop nodded in agreement. "Let's start with the discharge tank," he said.

Manny nodded in agreement, "We need the discharge water for the harvest." He then motioned them to follow him down the hall and into a massive room stuffed with tanks and pumps. In the old days on ocean-faring vessels, knowing how to operate pumps and replace O-rings was essential.

Manny and Coop got to work. They opened panels, followed piping, and checked wires that ran along the tight confines between the walls. Manny occasionally stopped to check his time credit allotments on his shield with a sense of relief that his labor wasn't being charged from the three-hour balance he had left.

Manny stood pondering his work and life after he checked his time allotments. Those thoughts of dread popped into his mind and he could not shake them. Trying to brush off the impending biopsy results, Manny remembered the "Three D's" from psychology books—Delay, Distract, Deal. He figured distracting himself was reasonable in this situation, so that is why he went to the farm. But the third D, to deal with the situation before allowing it to bottle up, was the most difficult because he had no choice but to face it eventually. Taking note of his own advice, Manny made plans to make an appointment soon when he returned home.

Manny and the team soon spotted the problem—a flat cable was tangled in the metal frame and prevented a flowmeter from regulating properly. As he and Coop set to work unraveling it, bits of insulation stuck to their hands and arms. They cut away the bad section and spliced a new length into place. Upstairs, the fish tank showed no signs of trouble—the red light on the flowmeter glowed green again.

Coop shook Manny's hand and clapped him on the back. An unexpected jolt of pain shot through Manny, and he winced visibly. Coop noticed his reaction immediately and frowned. "Okay," he asked. "Are you going to tell me what happened to your back?"

Manny forced a casual shrug, though worry painted his face. "Nothing serious," he said, trying to sound more confident than he felt. "Just a recent surgery—should be all healed up in a few weeks."

Coop squinted at Manny in disbelief. "You didn't tell me you had another surgery."

"Todo esta bien," Manny replied automatically, this time switching to English. "I mean, everything is fine."

Coop turned from Manny as they left the maintenance area, then paused to walk side by side. After several seconds, he put his arm around his friend's shoulder. He cast about for something comforting to say that could make up for the fact that he was not there for Manny.

"How many days since the last test?" Coop asked cautiously, knowing the recipe for the quantity of days from the test.

"Too many," Manny said quietly. It was such a struggle for him to keep this part of his life away from those that he worked with but yet, some people still seemed to understand why he wanted to distance himself from talking about it too often. His friends allowed him space, although now he appeared eager to share his thoughts and feelings; something new for him entirely.

Coop frowned deeply but then mustered up a nod of encouragement. "Keep the faith," he offered half-heartedly and began walking away.

Manny nodded in appreciation and kept walking, leaving behind an air of camaraderie and understanding that only two people who knew each other inside out could share. He felt under his shirt to check for blood after Coop was out of sight. To his relief, there was none; the stitches were still holding up after three weeks since his surgery. He placed two fingers up under his hat and felt the fresh bandage beneath it to make sure it wasn't wet. Then he activated his shield to search for any new messages from Dr. McKenna. Nothing again. He sighed in frustration as he realized he must continue waiting.

Manny took two steps at a time down the staircase to find himself in a world of noise and activity. The stillness of the tanks he left above was replaced by the chaotic racket of a thousand birds. Like an army of bugs gathering around an unguarded snack, chickens huddled together around a special station where automated arms distributed fresh food. Manny watched as robotic gates opened, ushering some of them away from their feast towards a different line—those going to be harvested. The rest stayed near their trays, greedily consuming each pellet that dropped in front of them.

As he walked along the long, narrow aisles of cages, he admired the automation and the conditions under which the birds lived. The cages weren't as spacious as those in an old-fashioned Midwestern farm, but Manny noticed how much healthier and better cared for these birds seemed to be. He reasoned that the more humanely they were treated, the tastier their meat would be in the end. Food was the bottom line, after all.

He arrived in a vast mechanical room after he walked past dozens of cages. He surveyed the scene, with pipes running along the walls and ceiling, carrying the discharge water from the above floor. The product water split into several paths, most importantly supplying fresh drinking water for the birds living in cages. Another stream of water nourished various plants and bushes within the enclosure which served as food and habitat. Yet another flowed into soil-filled planters, aiding in nutrient replenishment as well as filtering out excrement that might otherwise build up. Manny walked between the towering machines and checked several gauges, noting readings on key process indicators. All systems showed green—a sign that everything ran smoothly.

Next, he went down to the lowest floor where the large animals lived. The air grew thick as he continued down, now with a faint scent of hay and manure. On this level, large animals lived in generous enclosures to produce high-quality milk and meat. They moved in slow circles, shuffling along paths designed to give them exposure to fresh grasses and intermittent artificial sunlight and even an occasional breeze. Manny watched as they passed other cows in their circular meandering—almost seeming like they gained comfort from seeing familiar faces among the herd. At the right moment, there was a shift in the atmosphere where the automation singled out some of these gentle creatures for harvest and some of them steadily disappeared from their walking paths.

Manny meandered down the aisle of cages, eventually coming to the mechanical rooms at the end. He stopped in front of one of the bigger cages, containing about thirty cows munching on alfalfa. The little blue blooms glittered in the light streaming through the glass walls. Artificial lighting made it look like late afternoon sunshine on a summer day. On the ceiling, a projection of picturesque white clouds and a pale blue sky appeared. Manny noticed one cow with a nicked ear that twitched incessantly that seemed to be watching him carefully. Grandpa always said not to name animals on the farm, since you might have to eat them for dinner someday.

He often enjoyed the aroma of the cows grazing and eating, but today the smell was a little too strong. Manny breathed in the potent scent of cattle as he walked toward the mechanical room. He spotted yellow readouts on the control panel and knew the ventilation system was failing. Reaching up, he tapped his shield to connect with Randy Jorgenson's contact information. "Randy," Manny said, speaking sharply into the device. "We have an air filter issue at recirculating fan number three."

A moment later, Randy responded. "On it, Manny. I'll get somebody there right away. Thanks."

Manny exchanged more maintenance information with Randy, his voice nearly drowned out in the wide hallway. He kept his gaze down and clenched his jaw as he made a sharp right turn towards the harvest rooms. He paused as he pushed open the heavy door, the smell of too many actions at once clinging to the air. Beyond the steel gates stood a sea of cows, heads bowed low against their fate. Manny watched from afar, the realization of what happened here could drive some people to become vegetarians.

Manny rarely ventured down the long aisle of robotic assembly stations, where about a dozen workers attentively managed the harvesting process, looking up to acknowledge Manny as he walked by. He recognized most of them as he passed by and continued walking to the end of the process where large containers labeled with various proteins stood. From there, the workers separated the proteins into smaller portions for loading into the FOUPs. Further ahead, labelers examined each FOUP before attaching location tags to it that would direct delivery drones to the right destinations. At the end of the hallway, Coop stood at the ready, loading batches of FOUPs into van-sized delivery drones. From there, they'd be dispatched to either Chelsea Pod One or the Long Island Pod, where they were shifted onto smaller drones and sent to their final destination—the pass-throughs on people's cabin doors.

Manny and Coop made their way further down the assembly line, passing through a security gate before arriving in the quality inspection area. Here, random numbers of FOUPs were separated, opened, and inspected for quality and cleanliness. Inspectors worked to ensure that all products met health codes and food safety standards, before repackaging them with the nitrogen gas added to the FOUP for freshness.

The staff of the vertical farm took their share of these inspected FOUPs home with them because the inspected FOUPs may contain imperfections and blemishes from the inspection methods. Sunnyside also delivered some of the inspected FOUPs to group cabins for the elderly, doctor's offices, and mental health institutions that accepted donations from local organizations such as Sunnyside Farm.

At last, Manny and Coop left the building to take a look at the delivery drones, heading south with fresh protein for the New York Pod. Despite its hectic nature, moments like these seemed quiet—a time for reflection on what it meant to create something meaningful out of nothing until you had something real in your hands. As they stood there watching in silent appreciation of their work well done, they realized they already accomplished something extraordinary today: feeding hundreds of hungry people around them. They wanted more people to enjoy real food.

Roberta and James stepped into the shipping area and found Manny with his back to them, about to make his departure. Manny's presence was magnetic; the air around him seemed to hum with energy as people moved to him and went away with tasks. The safari hat perched atop his head, its brim tilting off-center, was his calling card for the other volunteers at the farm. When he turned around and spotted James, Manny's eyes grew wide in surprise, as if they did not expect to see each other there.

When they embraced in a tight hug, the air was heavy with sentiment, and James pulled away and asked, "What's with the hat?" He started to reach for it but Manny pulled back quickly, eyes wide and holding up both hands defensively. "Don't touch the hat! I know, I know."

Roberta laughed as she lightly grazed Manny's arm with her fingertip, and her gaze rested on James before he could continue his playful banter.

Manny smiled genuinely, treasuring their presence and feeling the pang of longing that came from missing these two people when he underwent the surgery. They did not know about his cancer and probably thought he was still struggling to cope with his recent divorce and job issues. "I'm out of time though so gotta run!"

Roberta grasped Manny's arm tenderly, her deep brown eyes twinkling with compassion as she gazed up at him. "You mustn't forget you are a genius! Your whole supply chain theory is working perfectly here!" She flung her hands wide, gesturing grandly.

Manny inclined his head, a flicker of uncertainty marring his features. He thanked her and they all went to work gathering food for their homes—the reward for a successful harvest day. He dashed around the room, gathering FOUPs for his cabin. For a fleeting instant, he lingered when picking a few extras for his new neighbor; was it truly wise to help someone like Theo? With hastened strides and a booming goodbye, he bade farewell to everyone clustering around him. Coop clapped him on the shoulder rather than his back this time, an understanding expression in his eyes.

Manny thought about whether he should tell Roberta and James about his cancer. Everyone knowing about it changed the way they looked at him. He didn't want to be known as "the guy with cancer." Though Roberta was always affectionate and James treated him normally, he wasn't sure if they were aware of his diagnosis yet. He asked Coop not to tell them, but juicy secrets are hard to contain.

CHAPTER 9
Some have secrets that they've kept,

As Manny strode out the front door of the farm, the chime from his shield filled the balmy air, interrupting his request for a Beeze to take him home. Only a half hour of his daily allotment of time remained on his timer in his shield. He double-clicked on the Beeze request and then double-clicked on the incoming call. "Hey, Mickey. What did you find out?"

"I'm fine, how are you?" Mickey drawled in a voice charged with sarcasm.

"Sorry about that," Manny apologized as he tapped his foot, anxious to get back to his cabin. "I'm kind of in a hurry here. I'm still at the farm."

"Just kidding," Mickey said. "More info on Theo Wiggins. Oh, and how is the farm doing? How was the harvest?" she added.

Manny stopped walking and tugged at his duffle bag full of fresh FOUPs. He knew Mickey was running low on fresh food and had resorted to eating the White Cube crap. "Fresh harvest. I've got some FOUPs for you!"

Mickey smiled, her eyes brightening in appreciation of Manny's enthusiasm. Her fingers drummed the counter as she continued. "I can swing by and pick 'em up," she said but then her expression shifted to a somber tone. "I'm afraid we are hearing more about the lockdowns. We will need all the fresh food we can get our hands on."

Manny ran his fingers through his hair, rubbing his scalp thoughtfully at the plans he must make. "I'll pick up some more FOUPs then. Have the lockdowns reached the United States yet?"

"No," Mickey answered, shaking her head slowly, a look of trepidation etching itself into her features. "But we were told to cancel all of our vacations for the whole New York Region."

"That's not good." Manny thought about spending nearly three months in his cabin a few years back. Drove the kids nuts, and his wife even more.

"By the way, I got that information on Theo Wiggins. His algorithms are going insane trying to figure him out," Mickey explained, rubbing at her chin thoughtfully. "But he is on a bunch of the Leonardo patents. Kinda walks on water. And gets away with almost everything. Sounds like a real smart ass."

Manny tapped his foot and considered this before adding, "That explains the camera."

Confusion danced across Mickey's face as she asked, "What camera?"

"Never mind. I'll tell you about it someday," Manny said evasively, almost too quickly. He thanked her profusely and they wished each other well before ending the call.

In the distance, a Beeze car pulled up to the curb and approached his location. The sound of the double doors opening with a swoosh made him turn and look when it stopped right in front of him. Manny's Beeze car arrived faster than normal, having separated itself from the massive array of similar vehicles swarming through the neighborhood when the timing of his request coincided perfectly to the algorithm working inside the Beeze. Manny stepped through the open doors, which then closed with a swoosh behind him as he situated himself in the car. He began relaxing now that he was well on his way back to his cabin, when suddenly he received a fifteen-minute time allocation notification on his shield. If he did not make it back in time, the Contros docked a time credit from his algorithms. If more than fifteen minutes late, the Contros dispatched a PoPo.

* * *

Back at the Pod Police headquarters, Mickey ended her call with Manny and deactivated her communicator shield. A mug of coffee, its heat kept at the ideal 118 degrees Fahrenheit, waited for her on a warming cradle next to her computer station. The squad room was almost empty, only the quiet tapping of keyboards from a few data analysts working late in the day filling up the space. The air conditioning hummed like an engine, white noise soothing her stress as the aroma of another fresh batch of coffee wafted through the air. She shifted uncomfortably in the uniform made of nanofiber material that tightened around her body like a second skin. It felt tighter today.

She pondered the call with Manny and had more questions about this Theo character. Why was he in solitary confinement near Manny's cabin? She also thought about the surgery her dad underwent using a Leonardo robotic-assisted surgery device, produced by the very same company where Theo worked.

The diagnosis for Mickey's father years ago was prostate cancer, something that a large percentage of men suffer from, similar to the rates of breast cancer in women. The normal incision for the surgery procedure was wide enough for three hands of doctors to fit into to manage the field of surgery. Robotic surgery allowed the field of surgery to be the size of a golf ball now, therefore recovery is much quicker with robotic-assisted surgery.

Mickey recalled the story from her father who had been a dentist for over twenty years by the time he received the diagnosis of prostate cancer. Shortly after, while working on a patient's mouth, the patient's words poured a bucket of cold water on her father's spirit. The patient discussed an upcoming project in which robotic dental tools would eventually replace traditional dentists, ushering in a new era of robotic-assisted dentistry and leaving human practitioners behind. Mickey knew her father must have felt the anxiety rising up inside him as he thought about the months of recovery he faced after his prostate surgery. That was the moment her father considered robotic-assisted surgery on his own prostate.

Mickey's father told her about when he spoke to his doctor and requested the new Leonardo surgery. His doctor sighed heavily, then replied that he did not have access to the expensive robot, then referred him to a bigger hospital that had one. The doctor's reply must have stunned her father. Was his doctor of twenty years really telling him to go somewhere else?

When her father went into surgery, he was unsure if he would make it out alive. But with the help of the Leonardo robotic system, he emerged victorious and cancer-free. Upon discharge from the hospital that night, her father became invigorated by a newfound purpose and it changed his whole career, where he eventually landed work at ARS, Automated Robotic Surgery, developing new technologies within the dentistry field. Taking on this latest endeavor, he went on to create a remarkable tooth-cleaning robot that received positive reviews from its test patients who claimed it felt like a gentle massage for their gums. Not only did ARS save her father's life, now it gave him a renewed chance to flourish professionally. Maybe he even worked with Theo Wiggins, Mickey thought.

Mickey scrolled through the file on Theo Wiggins, the details rolling past her eyes. He'd moved up the ranks at ARS due to his impeccable design and engineering skills, but his penchant for stretching those gifts too far had earned him a place in solitary confinement several times. And now he was serving sixty days of isolation. But it was this report's captivating language that enticed Mickey. The algorithms determined that Theo would reach 110 years of age instead of the 86 years his previous predictions suggested, granting him an additional 24 years to live. Everything seemed to have changed—his hobbies, his health habits, but nothing that would positively explain the jump. That unexplained adjustment must be what drew the attention of the Controllers and landed Theo in solitary until they could figure out how he did it.

Staring at Theo's file, Mickey realized that somewhere in the text were discussions of current research into time credit devices. This technology linked people directly to the ARS database to monitor their post-surgical procedures, as well as determine who may qualify for robot-assisted treatments based on their health records, transactions, and further data stored in the massive cloud. This would funnel people towards the Leonardo surgery, thus netting the company unprecedented profits. Mickey continued studying the file until the last person left the squad room.

* * *

Manny adjusted his seat in the Beeze for a more comfortable ride as the vehicle glided along the paved roads, moving in perfect harmony with the other Beezes. The occasional large transport drones broke up the otherwise monotonous journey. The transports waddled past like elephants among a herd of zebras, much bigger but seeming to fit right in alongside the smaller Beezes. Approaching open spaces, Manny watched as they passed several fences and monitored access gates, all linked to the central Controllers' system. When their Beeze paused at one of these electronic gates, it read him into the system before continuing on.

The entrances and exits of all public locations were heavily guarded with automated barriers, cameras, and scanners. Every person's RFID chip was programmed with a time limit for their visit that matched their available credits. If someone stayed longer than their allowed time, a warning bell sounded and a reminder was displayed on their shield. If the violation was not corrected immediately, security personnel were dispatched to escort the violator to their assigned punishment—usually solitary confinement in their cabin or a transfer to an individual cabin if it was an extreme offense.

The Controllers first appeared in 2020 when a pandemic reached its peak and claimed millions of lives. Since then, pandemics and lockdowns had occurred every few years, though none as severe as the original one. With strict government management, a catastrophe of that magnitude could never happen again, even if it meant giving up some personal freedoms.

The Controllers manage people's lives through intricate algorithms that predict their expenditures for years and decades into the future. The Controllers reward high-powered positions, such as chief executive officer or partner of a firm, to those who are able to score highly on attributes that pertain to longevity, health, financial stability, and time management. These leaders have more free time to spend than someone who is unemployed. The lucky few use the additional time for traveling from one pod to another or even across borders where national boundaries no longer exist.

Manny lived in a world of clusters of interconnected pods, where pods replaced countries and cities for achieving tighter control during emergencies. The new pod clusters typically consumed the city, region, country, state, and continental boundaries for their borders. A complex network of highways connects the pods to facilitate trade between them. Each pod cluster grows its own food but trades with other clusters for critical resources like raw materials and manufactured goods. Although each pod is almost self-sufficient, they need one another's assistance to sustain necessary supplies.

The supply chain links all the pod clusters together like a circuit. Bulk goods arrive at each pod and then are distributed equally among cabins there. An algorithm gives extra commodities to those with executive jobs, while making it tougher for those who lost their job and fell off the grid. These people go on a list where an algorithm calculates their chances of getting back into the loop. They find it difficult to land new employment.

While riding in the Beeze, Manny reminisced about his earlier days when he met his wife, Sarah, at the NYU Pod, a bustling city-like campus with thousands of students and faculty members. They were so young then, barely out of their parents' homes but already tasting freedom for the first time. When Manny's own children moved away to college years later, the kids were so excited to explore life far away from both of their parents. They both now attended the University of Santa Cruz Pod, part of the California Cluster. Manny lived alone in his three bedrooms, two bath cabin, surrounded by hundreds of other cabins in their high-rise structure. He knew that the algorithms would determine his future soon enough, and could almost hear the Controllers knocking on the door.

CHAPTER 10
Take the property with respect,

Theo sat at his workbench in the small cabin on the 65th floor of the Redwoods Cabin Structure, surrounded by drifting dust particles illuminated by the setting sun. He was alone on this top-floor dwelling for the last 57 days, ever since a long court battle over a credit swap. But despite his monotonous daily routines and set punishments, Theo slowly became energized by the new project sitting on his desk.

His neighbor Manny brought him more FOUPs filled with steaks and vegetables. After that first delivery, Manny kept coming back day after day with another FOUP—sometimes full of vegetables, sometimes other ingredients—and each time offering up more friendly conversation than before. Although Manny still seemed busy and distant, Theo felt like these moments were quickly becoming an important part of their daily routines.

Theo ran his fingers through his wild, untamed beard. He felt the weight of his neighbor studying him while wondering if he was wearing out his welcome. Manny was polite, and even more importantly, kept delivering regular shipments of FOUPs to Theo's pass-through door. It was a feat that left Theo both grateful and perplexed. Manny managed to procure top-notch food despite the scant details of his employer, White Cube Research, accessible over the cloud. Theo actively searched through redacted posts and research papers about Manny's work as he considered the possibility that Manny was a Contro. However, he quickly dismissed this thought after realizing the information was so outdated.

While searching for answers, he then noticed several books regarding new agriculture sciences and supply chains written by Manny. He wondered how Manny navigated the conservative environment of White Cube while publishing subversive views. With three days until public life resumed for Theo, he glanced down at his hands before impulsively scratching at his scruffy beard again.

Theo kept working at his lab desk. Rows of shelves on the wall above it housed everything from cables and tools to microchips and bits of scrap metal. His desktop was an untidy jumble of equipment, parts, wires, and electronics that were scattered over every available inch. In the middle of it all stood a vertical jig with a partially disassembled FOUP mounted on top. The shelves behind him held more than a dozen of these expensive devices, each one bearing barcodes on their surface that suggested they were used only once. He was familiar enough with PVDF materials to recognize them being applied for sanitary food handling, although he thought it was wasteful to lose track of them after a delivery. He'd developed ideas about that problem and employed every bit of his ingenuity on an experiment.

Theo worked quickly, detaching the front opening of the FOUP and carefully inserting an extremely small microchip with a sensor into a carved-out section of the material. His eyes danced across the viewer in his shield while expanding and double-clicking on the menu item labeled "Life," the name of his new application that checked for moisture, protein levels, carbohydrates, and the expiration period of the contents. This data helped track the freshness of the contents of each FOUP.

The current barcode on the outside of the FOUP only listed an expiration date and destination address for the delivery drones. This new system allowed the farm to track not only where their products were going but the content's health as well. In addition to this microchip, Theo also put in an RFID chip which would help recover lost or stolen FOUPs quickly. By his estimation, 20% of all FOUPs were unaccounted for after every delivery, which was far too high for any profit margin to grow.

Theo's eyes narrowed in concentration as he peered into his shield to study his Life application. A six-day-old piece of meat, saved from Manny's first food delivery, rested below the test chip. He carefully carved off small pieces of each fresh item he received—the habit of a scientist. Theo peered through the shield to view the FOUP and then refocused back on the results from the microchip. The readout showed 27.3% protein, 73% moisture, and zero grams each of carbohydrates and fiber. His experienced eyes narrowed in on the possibilities—filet mignon or ribeye steak? With a few more calculations and cross-referencing against his current stock at Sunnyside Farm, Theo and his chip identified the precise cut of meat. A satisfied grin spread across his face as he stroked his beard, contemplating the implications of this new delivery system.

Theo had worked hard to gain access to Greenie, Manny's treasured drone, and wanted to fly it. So, he hacked into the live feed while Manny was delivering the last FOUP. Manny had expertly maneuvered Greenie around the barriers of their patios sometimes to carefully place the FOUP in Theo's hands. Taking it a step further, Manny then performed some tricks with the joystick, making Greenie nod at Theo before returning to its rightful owner. In that moment, Theo felt grateful for this gesture and realized just how much effort and thought went into each delivery.

Theo slowly and quietly inserted a camera into Manny's cabin to see if anyone was inside. His gaze landed on the small, rectangular drone, Greenie, that rested on the kitchen floor. Theo activated the device by double-clicking its menu item in his shield. In response, the four small propellers came to life, propelling the drone forward. It glided through the open patio door and around the protective barriers toward Theo's own desk at the back of the room. With great care, Theo loaded up Greenie with a modified FOUP and two regular ones that were connected end-to-end with each other. Then, he flew Greenie back around the corner towards Manny's cabin. Despite its burden of packages, it seemed almost weightless as it moved gracefully across the air.

Finally, he set down Greenie exactly where it had been on the kitchen floor in Manny's cabin. He then released the three FOUPs and they came to rest after rolling over twice on the floor. Three FOUPs sitting harmlessly on the floor, all connected together like a straw.

CHAPTER 11
Young and old on the quest,

Maggie bounced into the room in a brilliant blue tutu, her long dark hair framing her face. She stopped abruptly in front of Manny, who sat in the waiting area of the oncology ward. His gaze was distant, worried and his hands trembled slightly. Maggie reached out and grabbed his hands gently in hers, studying each hand intently. "You got kids," she said.

Manny looked at her and saw that she already knew somehow. He didn't know what to do with his face. The girl's smile lit up the room in a way that was not just beautiful but also healing. "Well, yes, I have two kids," he said quietly.

"I can always tell," she said softly as she squeezed his hands, her eyes flickering away from his. She shifted her weight back and forth with a slight sway of her hips, the blue pants swishing about her ankles as she tugged playfully at the tutu, an unexpected but stylish addition. The scent of apple pie wafted around her in a small cloud.

Manny awkwardly let go of her hand but she quickly took it back and resumed her stare into Manny's eyes. Her eyes held him captive, and he took a moment to appreciate the delicate arch of her brows. His gaze flickered to the bandage peeking out from under her gathered hair.

She caught his glance and smiled wryly. "It's almost healed now," she said, tracing the edge of it with gentle fingers. "How about yours?" she asked.

He felt a sudden urge to lift the hat off his head, but instead, he shrugged a shoulder, hoping she wouldn't press him further. Manny forced himself to meet her gaze again. He saw something there that drew him in, much like when he spoke to his own children. "I'll be wearing a hat for a while," he answered quietly.

The air between them hummed with unspoken words as they stood together in that sterile hospital room, two strangers united by fate and circumstance. Maggie leaned in close, a mischievous glint in her eye, and whispered, "Mommy says you're a doctor too." Manny felt her stare as she looked into his eyes, and he could see tears welling up in the corners of hers. He smiled softly, taking her small hands in his. "Yes, I am. But I'm a scientist type of doctor."

She squinched her eyes in confusion. "What's that?"

Manny paused for a moment, taken aback by the question. He cleared his throat before continuing, "That means I studied a lot about food and how to grow it and how to get it to people."

Maggie thought over the information carefully before nodding solemnly. "That's okay." She let go of his hand, looking off into the distance once more. Her voice was soft when she spoke again. "I hoped you were a real doctor and could fix me."

Manny's heart melted at her words; he couldn't help but smile, his cheeks feeling flushed. "There's nothing wrong with you little girl," he said supportively, using the best encouraging words he could find.

She whirled back around to look him in the eye, her face intense, holding out her arm so that he could see. Manny saw Maggie's eyes fill with fear as she leaned in closer to him. She slowly turned her wrist and held it up before Manny, revealing a dark bluish-black irregularly shaped splotch with three mickey mouse ears extending out. As tears began to slip down her face, Maggie gave a sorrowful nod. "Mommy is pretty sad right now. I told her I wanted to be alone."

Manny turned his wrist away from Maggie, not wanting to reveal the similar-looking mark on his own arm. Dr. McKenna revealed the stage 2 melanoma diagnosis less than twenty minutes ago. He wanted to hug her but knew that was inappropriate, so he simply turned over his own wrist and revealed a similar splotch on his skin. The silent exchange conveyed pain, understanding, and sympathy between them.

Suddenly, Maggie leaped into his arms and began sobbing. Taken aback, Manny remained still as she clung tightly around his neck, her feet leaving the floor as he tried to stand upright. An attendant noticed what was happening, and quickly came to their side to try and pry Maggie away from him. "I'm so sorry Dr. Rio," she said as she kept pulling steadily, though Maggie didn't let go easily. "Maggie, let go of Dr. Rio."

"It's okay, it's okay." Manny waved the attendant away. His eyes shifted towards the door just as Rosita stormed into the room, her face streaked with tears.

"What the hell is going on here?" Rosita demanded, marching over and snatching Maggie out of Manny's grasp. "What do you think you are doing?"

"Mommy, don't be mad at Dr. Rio," Maggie pleaded, squirming out of her mother's hold and standing firmly in front of him.

"Dr. McKenna," the attendant interjected quickly. "Dr. Rio was just sitting there when Maggie jumped on him."

Maggie's fierce little face was contorted in defiance as she squirmed away from Rosita's grasp, her arms crossed over her chest and one foot stomping on the floor. Her blue tutu crinkled around her hips as if to remind everyone of how young and innocent she was. "He's my friend! Don't you dare be mad at him, Mommy," she said firmly before gently taking Manny's hand into hers, proudly displaying their matching cancer splotches. The small brown spots were a stark reminder of their shared diagnosis, both of them being diagnosed with stage 2 melanoma cancer that day. Maggie looked up at Rosita and the attendant with a mixture of fear and determination in her blue eyes.

Manny's gaze shifted from the little girl to the floor as he added, "She just wanted to talk…and I was sitting there. He lifted his eyes back up to see the small figure before him. He gave an awkward smile and glanced down at the little girl. "Maggie, is it?" He knelt down, his knees settling onto the hard floor. "Mucho gusto."

Maggie's face lit up, showcasing a row of tiny teeth interrupted by two protruding buck teeth. She stepped closer and extended her hand in greeting as she said, "Mucho gusto, yourself." A glimmer of pride sparkled in her eye as she said, "Mommy, my friend Margarita taught me how to say that."

"If we are going to keep running into each other here, you can call me Manny," he said, admiring her enthusiasm for Spanish language and culture.

Maggie smiled proudly and took a step closer to him, shaking his hand before taking hold of her mother's arm. She shyly buried her face in the folds of Rosita's blue doctor's smock. Tears began streaming down Maggie's cheeks and Rosita's eyes pooled with tears of her own.

Rosita looked between the two of them and spoke softly, "Maggie, please call him Dr. Rio."

A lump formed in Manny's throat as he looked upon them both and wondered about Maggie's diagnosis, barely eight years old—too young to be dealing with such an illness. He felt an overwhelming surge of empathy toward this little girl and the situation she found herself in. He bent down to look directly into Maggie's damp eyes and offered, "No, I insist you call me Manny. We are cancer buddies after all."

He stood there a moment looking at Maggie and Rosita, for the first time realizing they were facing a battle far beyond what he himself could ever imagine. "I've got two teenagers myself."

Manny's demeanor seemed to shift, the way his brow furrowed as he listened to Rosita's words and the way his intense gaze softened when she finished speaking. He seemed to understand, and for once, wasn't taking over the conversation or leaping to conclusions about his own diagnosis. The news of his stage 2 cancer reached him a short while ago, yet he remained surprisingly composed. Manny realized that now Maggie and Rosita had shared stories, each of them knowing the other's struggles.

CHAPTER 12
Special gifts arrive when best,

A night of tossing and turning filled Manny's night, his mind racing over the results of his tests. He got up in a daze and started digging into the research on Sunnyside Farm's desalination plant in order to distract himself from the reality of what he might be facing. Delay, Distract, and Deal—the Three D's. Manny chose to delay as long as possible before having to face the cancer head-on. His doctor scheduled the Mohs surgery for tomorrow, which was the first available appointment. No waiting for a melanoma to spread.

He knew the surgery would be more involved this time around due to the spreading mole on his wrist. Every time he looked at the little spot, he felt like it was mocking him, taunting him that it could take away his life if left unchecked. The emotions and fear were overwhelming as he looked at the half-inch wide spot that held such an immense power over him.

He pushed back from his clean white desk and stretched his arms above his head. He grabbed a mug of thick coffee, taking in the earthy aroma before gulping it down. His shower was short and efficient; focusing on the vertical farm took his mind off his worries. After throwing on his nanotechnology coveralls, he reached into a deep pocket and pulled out two small ear pods. He carefully popped them into place on either side of his head and felt the familiar tug as they molded to the callouses behind each ear—a telltale mark that everyone living in this era carried. A thought crossed his mind: what will future scientists think of the little callouses behind each ear when they look back at us?

Manny sat down at his cluttered white workbench and powered up the tools arranged on its surface. He activated his shield, which splayed a holographic image of a design for a new FOUP in front of him. With a deep sigh, he surveyed the mess that surrounded him. Shelves overflowed with half-complete projects, and video monitors displayed graphs and calculations related to various experiments. Last week alone he added two prototypes for a drone delivery system to Sunnyside Farm, but even with these new advancements, Manny was struggling to get the farm to turn a profit. His journals, patents, and books provided some income, but not enough to sustain himself or his work on the farm. He did not miss working at White Cube, but he missed the income.

He headed to the kitchen, still cradling his cup of coffee, when he stumbled over a straw of FOUPs, a long, thin line of them strangely out of place. He frowned in confusion, glancing around the room. His neat stack of FOUPs was still in its place against the wall, but he couldn't remember if it had been that way before he left for his biopsy appointment. He stepped to the refrigerator and opened the door, peeking inside. His heart sank as he saw how few FOUPs were left, barely enough food to share with his neighbor today. He sighed and ran a hand through his hair. How would he explain that there wouldn't be any more FOUPs for a few days? It felt strange to think about distributing produce like one might sell drugs.

Manny tapped his shield, today the coloring of a futuristic, blue-tint, and brought up Theo's name. He double-clicked on it, and Theo's face shimmered into existence. "Hey, Theo," Manny said warmly.

"Hey Doc," Theo replied. "Long time. I know you're busy so I didn't want to bother you."

Manny shifted his attention from the shield to the fallen strays of FOUPs scattered along the floor. "Sorry, but I don't think I'll be able to help you out for a few days with the food. My supply is pretty low," he added as he stooped down and began carefully collecting the ones on the floor.

"I see you got my package," Theo revealed as he saw that Manny was picking up the FOUPs. His face in the shield widened into a Cheshire cat grin; there was something about the delivery of that sentence that made him look very pleased.

Manny looked at the FOUPs in his hand and then back to Theo's face in his visor. "What do you mean? How did they get here?"

"I couldn't resist," Theo said while still grinning. "Delivered them this morning. Take a look inside."

Manny held one of the FOUPs up to get a better look, noting its intricate markings in one spot that shone like stars on a clear night sky, definitely different from the normal FOUP. "I don't understand. How did they get here? What did you do?"

"Greenie delivered them."

Manny felt uneasy as he stared at the FOUPs in his hands, then looked at Theo. "I don't understand."

Theo shifted his weight back and forth, and Manny could see the beginnings of a sweat break out across his forehead as he realized that this conversation wasn't going too well. "I had them delivered," Theo said. "Greenie flew around the barriers, loaded up the FOUPs, and dropped them off."

Manny slapped his palm against his forehead in anger. "You took Greenie?" He instantly went over and picked up Greenie, resting on the floor quietly, and protectively set Greenie down on his parking and recharging slot. Walking quickly back to his desk, he rotated the FOUP with the funny colors to try and get a closer look.

Theo tried explaining but Manny wanted to hang up. Manny tried to double-click on Theo's name to disconnect, trying and failing so hard that it hurt his eyeballs. But he missed and there was Theo's face still on his shield, still trying to explain. Manny was fuming. How could he trust this guy? He should call the PoPos. "And what did you do to this FOUP?"

Theo pleaded, "Be careful with that end one, I modified it."

"You what?" Manny questioned angrily. "To the FOUP? What did you do?" Manny held up the end FOUP and detached it from the others.

"I added some AI," Theo answered. "Only a small chip and an RFID."

Manny held the FOUP and continued rotating it in front of him. "AI? Where? Why? What are you up to? What do you mean you added artificial intelligence?" Manny's eyes widened as he realized what the other man was saying and began to examine the FOUP more closely. He strapped it into a jig on his bench and peered into the magnifying scope connected to his visor. A shiny speck near the hinge of the front opening confirmed Theo's words—inside the FOUP was a miniscule chip, with colors reflecting from the white lights.

Theo began talking animatedly, gesturing at the FOUP in Manny's hands. He explained how the device was modified with a chip that would indicate its contents and an RFID chip which would allow it to be tracked no matter where it went. As he spoke, Manny looked carefully over the FOUP, his brow furrowed in concentration as he tried to understand what Theo accomplished and the implications of this work. Theo added, "I suspect the waste is high on these FOUPs. I don't understand how you can make a living with such a high rate of losses from your deliveries."

"Thirty-nine percent."

"You lose thirty-nine percent of all of your FOUPs?" Theo replied in disbelief. "How the hell can you make a profit that way?"

"We don't," Manny acknowledged, shaking his head in resignation, then added, "That's why we need so much funding."

Theo animatedly tapped the touchscreen of a tablet as he spoke, explaining that with the new AI-enabled system, they could track and identify each food product within the FOUPs. He discussed how this automated system would reduce waste, breakage, and returns, allowing them to recover an estimated 99% of those FOUPs. His enthusiasm for the technology was palpable.

"Why only 99 percent if this is so good?" Manny mocked while starting to grasp the significance of this moment.

"Breakage," Theo replied. "We have to account for material and workmanship losses."

Manny shook his head in amazement, trying to take it all in. He couldn't believe this was real! It was an incredible year of hard work with some very lean times. His muscles relaxed a little bit, and he realized how tight he was recently; his whole body was sore in fact. This would make the farm profitable! Manny ran his hand through his hair, trying to process it all. So many thoughts were spinning through his mind—tracking materials, making sure there weren't any losses—when suddenly, Theo's comment hit him like a bolt of lightning. "You said, "we." What do you mean?"

"I'm joining you," Theo announced with unwavering certainty. "I can supply the chips. I already started working on the design for mass production to twelve-hundred chips per 300-millimeter wafer. It shouldn't add much in terms of cost to the FOUP."

Theo's explanation showed confidence in his ability to repeat the chip fabrication process, and he knew someone had to feed data into the machine-learning database. Through each successful identification of food in a FOUP by the chip, the accuracy would gradually improve over millions of iterations.

Manny examined the data with his keen intellect, calculating and recalculating as if his brain was a computer. This was both his greatest asset and his biggest weakness. It helped him solve complex problems but also made him difficult to understand. He felt Theo's gaze on him, but he refused to acknowledge it and instead kept on crunching the data in his head. "Will this even work?" he wondered, feeling a mixture of excitement and apprehension.

"Go ahead and test it," Theo challenged with an eyebrow raise. "Put some food in it and see what happens."

Manny quickly glanced at Theo before darting to the kitchen. His hands trembled as he grabbed two pieces of food within easy reach and returned to the desk. He carefully placed one of them inside the contraption and nervously shifted his weight while he waited for something to happen. Manny paused, waiting for some kind of reaction. His heart raced, urging him on as he secretly prayed for this experiment to succeed.

"Flank steak," Theo said confidently.

Manny quickly switched out the scrap for a carrot and waited for a reaction. His heart pounded in anticipation, and his palms grew clammy as he silently prayed for success.

"Carrot!" Theo exclaimed triumphantly.

Manny's eyes widened in amazement. He again ran calculations through his mind, imagining all the possibilities this technology could bring. Suddenly, he remembered something else. "And what did you say about the RFID?"

"This uses the radio frequency identification technology that's present at all entry points," Theo stated. He noticed, however, that the last gate failed to detect the FOUP in Manny's hands. He stopped and wondered aloud, "That's strange—the chip says it never left your room?"

Manny gave a quick and smart response, "There's no gate on the balcony. The readings are still from when I first brought it home through the front door."

Theo looked as if he considered this new information and a spark of understanding formed in his eyes. Transporting to and from a cabin using a drone would not register on the Controllers' radar. Even more interesting was the possibility of being able to track exactly where a FOUP was located if it passed through a gate. "That could reduce loss significantly," Theo declared, excitement entering his voice.

"We can trade a full FOUP for an empty one. That way, no one loses anything," Manny concluded. He thought about it and the numbers kept checking out. If this worked out, he'd be able to work at Sunnyside. He did the math in his head over and over again; the answer was always the same. This may be the solution.

Theo began to speak, breaking the silence between him and Manny. He gave Manny a meaningful look, letting him know that his words were important. "Manny... I have decided to move on from ARS and join Sunnyside as the CTO."

Manny snapped out of his daydream, his face creasing with worry. "We don't have money for that kind of position. We can barely pay the bills now."

Theo smiled reassuringly. "Not anymore. And to show you my commitment, I'll take the same pay as you."

Manny scoffed. "That won't be much."

"I know," Theo replied softly.

"But...maybe this is the answer to our problem too," Manny began, thinking aloud. He paused for a moment before continuing. He spoke to the air. "What other high-cost operating expenses do we have? We were ready to pull the plug from the utilities, right? So, I figured why not go all in—we just installed a solar and battery system so that we don't need to be dependent on anyone else for power. Plus, our desalination plant is running at peak efficiency, so we won't have to worry about paying for water either."

"You mean self-sustaining? Off the grid?" Theo asked. Manny watched him rub his beard in anticipation and then raise an eyebrow. "What about waste treatment?" Theo asked.

Manny watched him trying to do the mental calculations to understand how Sunnyside was suddenly in a much better financial position than it had been only days before. "One hundred percent recycling. No discharge at all," Manny answered confidently.

Theo nodded and glanced down at his watch, and must have been thinking about his last days in solitary and his first day as a vertical farmer. Theo stated, "We're ready then."

Manny, on the other hand, felt a wave of unease deep in his stomach. He thought about his first day as a full-time employee of the vertical farm, and potentially his last days on earth. He looked down at his wrist and studied the dark stain in the shape of Mickey Mouse ears—the cancer threatening to take him away from this world. He swallowed hard and looked up again, determined to make the most out of his days.

CHAPTER 13
Man and woman oft collide,

Roberta rolled onto her back and placed one slender arm behind her head after first moving her long black hair to the side. She turned her face to James as he rolled onto his back, both arms behind his head, and the bed sheets down to his waist. His skin looked like polished onyx in the soft lighting, a beautiful man with a sculpted body. Her heart melted when she saw him smile back at her. Although now she kept thinking about work again after this wonderful distraction. Roberta's mind wandered as she thought about adding Manny permanently to their staff full-time. "We have to get Manny to join."

Roberta watched her man let out a low laugh and looked over at her while he studied her body and face. She knew he marveled at her beautiful curves and the fine details of her body. The two were tucked in tightly between layers of sheets, barely covering her breasts. His eyes followed down to the dips of her waist and hips, and she felt her heart flutter as he took it all in.

James asked, "You think of Manny right away after that?"

A coy smile spread across Roberta's face as she draped an arm over James's chest and traced circles around his muscles with her finger, sending shivers up his spine. "That was beautiful, James," she murmured in a soft voice. "You know that. But it just popped into my head. That's all."

"Always thinking of Sunnyside," James replied with a smile and rolled back towards Roberta. His hands slid from her tiny shoulders, tracing along the curves of one side of her chest until it met its counterpart on the other side. His fingers continued their journey southward to her waist where they found comfort in their favorite spot, the point where her pelvic bone protruded slightly from the perfect canvas of skin surrounding it. He held the moment. "But I love that about you."

She smiled and brushed her fingers over his temple, her touch as light as butterfly wings. "Oh James, you are the best," she whispered. She entwined her leg around his, feeling his skin warm against hers, smooth and supple to the touch.

They both stayed silent for a while, savoring the sensation of being wrapped up in each other's arms. As they relaxed into their embrace, the dampness from their powerful lovemaking began to evaporate, leaving cool patches on their skin that made them shiver with pleasure. Their eyes met for a moment before closing again in peaceful contentment. They lay together like that for a long time, lost in their own private world of warmth and tenderness.

After a few moments, James spoke up, his deep voice cutting through the silence, "You're right about Manny, by the way. He needs to get his mind off of things."

Roberta smiled and playfully pushed him away before pressing her lips against his in a passionate kiss. She pulled away after a few seconds and let out a laugh, "Besides, he's your boyfriend." She felt herself blushing and jumped off the bed. She looked back with a mischievous grin on her face and kissed him quickly on the lips again before running out of the room.

"It's a bromance!" he retorted playfully. His gaze never left Roberta as she ran to the restroom without any clothing on.

When Roberta reached the entrance to the bathroom, she propped herself up against the doorframe with one breast on either side. She raised her leg and delicately drew circles in the air with her foot like an exotic dancer entertaining the crowd. "You love him like a brother from another mother," she joked.

Roberta watched as James laughed and sat up in bed, effortlessly lifting his knees as the sheets slid down to reveal the tanned muscles of his torso, sculpted from thousands of precise sit-ups. He made sure the sheets were tucked in neatly at the waist before replying, "He's got the time now, let's get this farm moving. We're almost there."

Roberta stood naked in the open door. "What's with all the hats?"

"I know, right?" James chuckled softly. "But I do have to say that I like his Indiana Jones one. It's quite the fedora."

"You are such a metro-sexual." Roberta added, "Especially for an accountant."

James' cheeks flushed, and his lips curled into a shy smile. He combed his fingers through his hair, and they came to rest behind his head, his biceps flexed as he leaned back and watched Roberta with admiration. "You have a point there. I guess there is more to life than numbers," he chuckled.

Roberta noticed everything beneath James' nerdy accountant persona, which gave him confidence and showed that she appreciated everything he did at the farm. After all, James held both full-time jobs—White Cube during the day and CFO at the farm in the evening. While Dr. Manny Rio busied himself with advances in technology, it was up to James to keep things running smoothly in the finance department. And thanks to that, Roberta could focus solely on her career as a scientist without having to worry about anything else.

Roberta grinned and disappeared behind the door. "Let's talk to him today, then. It's time."

CHAPTER 14
One sets out on a wild ride,

Coop climbed into the cab of the long-hauler, his hands trembling as he activated the shield to engage the assisted driving system. He glanced back at the vertical farm and looked towards the first-floor windows where he knew Naoko was working. He heaved a heavy sigh and fired up the motor, his eyes lingering on the place he now called home, and began another trudging trip delivering FOUPs to neighboring pods. The money was good and Sunnyside became his haven, but he grimaced in dread at the pandemic news from Russia blaring away in warnings from the Contros. "Stay there you fucking pest," Coop thought with a sneer.

As the hauler pulled out of the driveway, the electronic leashes that kept the autonomous vehicles in check came into play. The smaller Beezes moved cautiously around him while the long haulers and delivery drones quickly changed lanes to make way for his brutish vehicle. Meanwhile, the built-in charging system under the road began to charge his truck's internal batteries, making up for the energy-heavy farm work used earlier. Coop could tell the farm was well on its way to achieving total autonomy, but they still needed occasional boosts from external sources. He imagined it like a flywheel rotating slower and slower over time until a shot of energy was added to get it up to speed again.

Coop revved up his semi-trailer long hauler, called "Betsy," and drove out of the farm, picking up speed as he moved out of the Long Island Pod and later past the Bronx Pod. The large truck easily weaved past the few Beezes that were scattered around the pod's circular pathways, while most seemed content to stay within the more heavily populated areas within the pods. Other vehicles crowded the roads leading out of the pods—transport drones whizzed by, shuttle buses stopped at regular intervals, and delivery trucks zoomed along the road. All powered by AI bots that constantly updated the road conditions and transportation habits. Coop's job took him around Chelsea Pod One and beyond; his long-hauler carrying packages from one pod to another. Most of the Beezes stayed within the pod, which was the primary method of transportation now for most people.

The inter-pod trains wound their way through the subterranean tunnels created by large drilling machines. High speed trains for cross-country trips linked the pods together and Coop could see the trains appear through the walls of the pods and gently slipping below the surface. He looked up to the sky occasionally and saw airplanes that still flew in the azure sky above, but only wealthy travelers could afford to take them, usually for intercontinental journeys over bodies of water.

Coop activated his shield and selected a menu item for the path he laid out the previous day. A long drive lay ahead of him—through the New York, Ohio, Indiana, and Illinois regions before reaching the Wisconsin area in under ten hours. He activated the autonomous driving option so he could rest up for the remainder of the trip, having sacrificed sleep on the farm in preparation for the long journey ahead. Coop slid out of the driver's seat, stepped away from Betsy's blinking lights of her dashboard, and deactivated his shield. Stretching his arms, he climbed into the sleeper cab in the back that was fitted with a queen-sized bed and plenty of storage space. He pulled a blanket up to his chin and felt the soothing hum of Betsy's motor as she drove while he slept.

Coop was not driving alone. His traveling companions lay stacked neatly in the cargo bay, each five-gallon bucket stocked with wriggling worms and sweet-smelling manure, a byproduct of the farm. The worms broke down the manure produced by the farm animals into compost, which in turn helped fertilize the livestock feed, thus creating more manure that spawned even more worms. The worms helped create a nutrient-rich environment by leaving behind worm casings, which served as delicious food for the fish hatcheries back in the Midwest. It was like feeding the fish a filet mignon every day. Coop knew he was helping to support a closed-loop system, in more ways than one.

Betsy drove from the highway onto the ring roads around Madison Pod Four—there were too many pods named Madison in the world, so the Contros used a numbering system to differentiate them. As Betsy drove closer to the pod area, the speed of the long hauler slowed to a crawl due to the overwhelming amount of Beeze vehicles in the area. People were leaving their jobs and heading home to their cabins after a long day's work. Coop controlled the vehicle in driver-assisted mode when suddenly, a warning message flashed on Betsy's shield and she immediately tapped the brakes. Coop inspected his shield and discovered that Madison Pod Four went into lockdown mode. A new illness was discovered and Controllers initiated protocols to control its spread. Until further notice, no shipments, food, water, air or people could enter or leave the pod.

Coop looked over the digital pages on his panel, scrolling through the containment requirements of the lockdown. He sighed and clicked off the screen. He would sleep in Betsy tonight. Surviving through lockdowns before, he knew they rarely lasted more than a few weeks. This Madison Pod Four lockdown was predicted to last only six days unless the virus reared its ugly head again and extended it further. Coop shuddered as he recalled the pandemic of 2042—too many lives were lost because of lax rules in place, which drove the Controllers to take command. Ever since then, Controllers in all the pods banded together to prevent viruses from escaping to other pods, even if wealthy travelers insisted on traveling. This was taxing on personal freedoms, but the good of the many outweigh the good of a few.

Coop expertly guided Betsy away from the main thoroughfare, University Avenue, that connected to the entrance of the University of Wisconsin Pod One, thus avoiding the entrance and being trapped in lockdown. He zigzagged across and around some side streets and drove with a purpose, not wanting to waste time or to become caught in a tether, a type of electronic leash. As Betsy left Madison Pod Four behind, the faint smell of fish hatcheries grew stronger and more pungent in the air. He noticed the odor from the soil and worms in his cargo hold that was surprisingly more complex than the fish hatcheries when combined. He briefly contemplated investing in nanotechnology coating that would reject odors, but then quickly turned his attention back to his driving.

Coop pulled up to the fish hatchery and surveyed the area, looking for the entrance to the loading docks and a path between the light traffic. He carefully navigated the long hauler around to the side of the building, keeping his distance from any structures. As he passed one of the tanks filled with water, the sun's rays caused the liquid to sparkle like a million diamonds as the fish came alive in a frenzy. Betsy moved smoothly and gracefully as if she were dancing along the road. Her white body curved into aerodynamic scoops on both her front and back and her almost-invisible wheels weaved between electromagnetic plates that absorbed energy from chargers in the roads. She looked like a long, white, hot dog that had begun to melt. The only time Betsy completely drained her batteries of energy was during a particularly lengthy lockdown when Coop got stuck in a pod without her. With no one to talk to, her battery slowly diminished until it ran out.

Coop activated his communication shield, searching for Katherine's contact information at the fish hatchery. The familiar face of his friend pulled up on his screen as he double-clicked. "Hello, Katherine."

"Coop! Good to see you!" Katherine replied with a bright smile that seemed to illuminate her entire face. Around sixty years old, she was beautiful inside and out according to Coop—an attractive older woman who always made him feel special.

"Nice to see you too," he returned the sentiment with a boyish grin and added a playful comment. "You look gorgeous as ever."

Katherine laughed softly but playfully put a hand to her mouth. "Aw,

Coop, don't let Bill know about us!" Coop knew she married her college sweetheart nearly forty years ago and was loyal through and through. But flirting was also fun.

He chuckled lightly in response. "That's a deal. So, I've got 300 buckets of worm poop stinking up my truck. Where can I deliver it?"

"Loading Dock 3 today," Katherine said. Her light green eyes sparkled with enthusiasm as she gestured toward the mammoth structure at the far end of the dock. "We got a lot of hungry Steelheads waiting for you!"

As Coop looked at Katherine, his expression changed from amusement to concern. He questioned whether it was a good idea to be around people who may have to go into lockdown suddenly. The last time he encountered a lockdown, he learned not to take everyone at their word; not even those on the inside knew what was going on. "What do you know about the Madison Pod's lockdown?" Coop asked, incredulous that somehow the virus spread all the way from Russia to a relatively small place like Madison, Wisconsin.

"Hang on, I got a report right here." Katherine frowned as she scanned the words on her shield, her face grew pale and her lips thinned. "It looks like this virus is the same one as in Russia." Taking a deep breath, she straightened herself and continued, "According to the news, a rich guy flew from Moscow and didn't know he was already infected. His kid attends the University of Wisconsin Pod."

Coop winced knowing how Controllers hated people who skirted around their rules. Coop added, imagining their fury over someone daring to break their stringent rules. "The Contros must be pissed!"

"Yeah, they locked down the Okrug Pod in Moscow and then locked down the Madison Pod right away," Katherine replied. "But they missed this guy." A sly smirk grew on Katherine's lips. "They confiscated his private jet. The sonofabitch deserves it."

Coop laughed and then thought about their proximity to the Madison Pod. "Are you safe here?"

"Yes, as long as you don't go past the entrance gates," Katherine warned.

Coop understood that if he did, the RFID readers would record his presence immediately. She added, "Stay inside Betsy and don't get out. You might want to activate the self-containment mode too."

"We can dump the batch robotically," Coop stated as he studied the controls on the dashboard specially built to keep the driver inside a protective bubble while making deliveries. Betsy approached the loading docks as Coop studied the hatchery for signs of life, almost empty except for a few workers who committed to sleeping there overnight with their families in makeshift dorm rooms. "Thanks, Katherine," Coop responded. One of the many reasons Coop liked delivering to this hatchery.

Katherine sighed; her face looked drawn with worry in the harsh light of the LED bulbs in her office. She straightened her hat and adjusted a new mouth covering before turning back to Coop. "No problem. I guess we better all get used to wearing masks again." Katherine looked straight into the visor and added with a forced smile, seen only in her eyes now above the mask. "At least we have plenty of fish to eat!"

None of that White Cube gelatin food here. And Coop still had about a dozen FOUPs filled with fresh food in the fridge in Betsy's sleeping quarters. But it would be lonely days and nights ahead until he could get back to his Sunnyside Farm. If he can get back to it at all; these lockdowns tend to expand rapidly.

"Katherine," Coop added. "Do you mind if we unload now so I can put some distance on?"

"I see what you mean. Let me round up the staff and we will have the port open at the loading dock," Katherina said. Coop hoped she understood why he wanted to hightail it out of there. She added, "Don't get out of the hauler at all, okay? We can run the unloading through our shields."

With a few clicks on the control panel, Coop activated the isolation protocols and initiated Betsy's air system for the upcoming self-containment. The main cabin began recycling oxygen from outside air through its oxygen generator, reducing it to an optimal concentration for sustained life. The long hauler could operate on this mixture for an extended period of time, but restocking food and water was a critical aspect of any operation. Fortunately, Coop had enough provisions stored away for his needs in the next few days.

Betsy obeyed several commands as she backed up and a portion of the tube on her bed started to rise. Its content began to siphon out into the conveyor belts of the loading dock below. Coop heard the orders given by the hatchery workers, and Betsy moved and unloaded in response.

After the last of the worm casings dumped into the holds of the fish hatchery, Coop immediately activated the escape route from the hatchery grounds. As Betsy moved quickly around the front of the hatchery and passed through the gates, an eerie light switched on and a cacophony of metallic clangs announced that all gates were slamming shut. The lockdown had begun.

"I'm past the gate!" Coop screamed back at Katherine. His heart raced as he saw the gates slamming shut in his rearview screen.

"May the virus miss you!" she replied, in a desperate attempt to keep the traditional words present even in such dire moments.

"And also miss you!" Coop replied in the way of the pandemic.

Betsy drove a little too slowly out through the roads leading to the exit of the region's pod gates. Coop instead gripped the wheel and floored the accelerator. A few Beezes scurried out of his way as he navigated tight corners and a gate with an electronic tether that tried to stop him. The red lights and sirens of rotating beacons blared ahead, warning signs popped up in his shield, and a physical barrier was replacing the electronic tether as he flew towards the Winona Pod exit gate. Sweat beaded on his forehead as he double-clicked away the override popup, and Betsy glided into the closing barrier. This was a risky move, but there was no way he was going to get stuck in a lockdown in another pod.

The barrier's sliding gates, each fifty feet wide and ten feet tall, closed foot by foot. Coop calculated his chances and kept his foot firmly on the accelerator before switching off his shield to block out any distracting warnings. Betsy barely managed to slip through the gates in time. Once through, he slowed to his usual speed and let Betsy take control while he navigated his way around the pods. And then suddenly, his shield reactivated and a warning came on from a PoPo requesting that Coop accept their call or be taken over by an electronic tether.

The face of a stern-looking young woman lit up on his shield. She had short, spiky hair and her eyebrows wrinkled as she studied the screen in front of her. Her eyes darted back and forth between Coop's information and the logs on her screen. "Long Hauler 7Z577324IBEX, prepare for a tether," she commanded with a hint of suspicion in her voice.

"That won't be necessary, Officer," Coop calmly responded as he shifted his weight nervously. He peered into her eyes in search of some understanding, but they only darted back and forth as she studied her screen. He added, "I'm in self-containment already."

"Amadeus Thaddeus Cooper, I presume," the officer looked up at him with a slight tilt of her head.

"Yes, Officer. I have not been in physical contact with anybody for 27 hours. You can see it in the RFID logs." His gaze followed hers as she reviewed the data on the screens. He exaggerated, hoping she didn't see the log, and added, "And I was in self-containment mode the whole time."

She squinted at the screen, biting her lip as she looked like she was trying to understand what was the logs said. Her inexperience was obvious in the way she searched for answers and looked frustrated when she could not find them. After a few moments, she finally looked up with a deep sigh, the wheels in her mind looking like they slowly turned before she conceded, "Yes, I see by the logs that you are right. It'll take me a few minutes to override this, so just hang on."

Coop breathed for the first time in a few moments, unaware that he held his breath to make sure he heard every word from the young PoPo. He knew if he'd done something wrong, or had gotten out of the truck, he would already be in their pod and locked up for the duration of the pandemic. His thoughts went to Naoko at the vertical farm, and he wished he could be there with her.

The young officer stood up, her slight frame straightening with resolve. "Okay, Mr. Cooper, you are free to go." She met his gaze and smiled, though the corners of her mouth kept twitching in an effort to contain her emotions. "Good luck to you, Sir. All signs point to a long one this time."

"Thank you, Officer. Good luck to you too. May the virus miss you and your loved ones," Coop said the customary goodbye during all quarantines. He'd no doubt tire of hearing this phrase once the pandemic passed.

The officer nodded, reciprocating the sentiment with a polite smile on her face. "And also miss you," she added before she scrunched up her nose with another double-click.

"Well, Betsy," Coop said, patting her dashboard. "Looks like it's just you and me for a while."

As Coop and Betsy plotted the course home on the map, they watched in dismay as pod after pod along their route locked down, like cells in a prison, trapping the occupants within. The sound of steel doors clanging reverberated through the journey. Families were split apart; hours were cut short; shipments no longer arrived, yet there was still the steady rhythm of White Cube food being delivered. Amidst it all, the need for vertical farming became more apparent than ever before.

Coop wove his way around Chicago, always just ahead of the lockdowns. He checked his shield anxiously as he neared a factory where his shipment of FOUPs awaited. The airport and train station nearby was already closed off, leaving him little room for error if he wanted to get back to his Sunnyside Farm before the lockdown reached them too.

CHAPTER 15
Controllers present, one bad, one good,

The six members of the Governing Body of the New York Region entered pensively, eyeing each other as they approached. Three doors opened into a large chamber, with video screens and cameras arranged along the walls. In the center stood a conference table framed by two monitors at each high-back chair, while at the far end, a bank of monitors and cameras aimed towards the gathering. As everyone took their seats, face shields activated and bathed the room in a cool blue light, slightly distorting their facial features. The remote attendees appeared on both the wall-mounted monitors and on the screens in front of each participant.

Brock Masterson, Director of the Governing Body, walked towards his seat at the head of a long table in the center of the room. He looked out of place with his large glasses, small stature, and shiny bald spot, but the authority in his step made it clear he was not to be trifled with. He took his usual seat at the far end of the table from the large monitors mounted on the wall and softly cleared his throat before beginning promptly at 10:00 a.m. "Welcome everyone to this week's Governing Body review for the New York Region. For those joining us virtually, please keep your shields on and stay on the icon for this meeting. Now, if we all pay attention and stick to the agenda, I think we can get through this in 30 minutes."

As the attendees of the Governing Body meeting sat around the large, wooden table, Brock scrolled through the exceptions cases on the large screens and in their shields. The virtual members watched from their consoles and sent in their votes as well. The algorithms once again carefully analyzed each situation, made swift recommendations, and most times were accepted without dispute. But now and then, a situation popped up that the machines couldn't quite handle. In this case, an extra bit of scrutiny was required, and it was up to the team to decide how to proceed.

The members of the table watched with rapt attention, and as soon as Brock's voice broke through the silence, they turned to him in unison. He stood a few feet away from them and looked at one of the many monitors that lined the walls of the room. A few seconds later, he announced the name of the assigned person for this case, "Claudia Rosenberg." He pointed to a bright green box that appeared on all the screens and said, "You have a case highlighted for a special vote."

Claudia glanced at Brock, her colleague and mentor, who gave her a small nod before she began. She cleared her throat nervously and looked out over the group of scientists and executives in the room. "We have a case here where the algorithms determined a 40-year-old man, let go from his job only a few months ago, his marriage ended recently in a divorce, and is diagnosed with a poor health prognosis shortly after that. The algorithms reduced his lifespan to 62 years."

Andrew Bagsund, a large figure with curly red hair, sat up straighter in his chair and looked around the table. He spoke in exasperation and disbelief; this wasn't the first time Claudia had pleaded a case for the weak. "Sounds about right."

Claudia took a deep breath before speaking. She looked like she needed to prove her point in order to win back their attention as they all began to agree with Andrew. "At first glance, you may be correct," she started slowly, "but this man, Dr. Manuel Rio, was a renowned scientist at White Cube Research until recently." The audience began to review the details on the screen as Claudia continued.

One of the members asked, "Why was he let go?"

Her delivery was quick and calculated as she responded. Claudia blinked; her face illuminated by the glow of her visor's hovering display. "He is the current CEO of Sunnyside Vertical Sustained Growth, or VSG as most of us call them. They are a startup formerly funded by White Cube that went awry. Despite their ambitious approach, they have yet to turn a profit and directly challenged White Cube's own interests." She paused briefly then swiped her finger across her visor, projecting an image of the vertical farm onto the screens around the room and causing a collective gasp from those present. The image brought into focus what exactly was at stake.

Brock watched as Claudia spoke, her hands forming grand gestures and her words leaving no room for dissent. She spoke of the need to override the algorithms for a sensitive case and Brock saw how her passionate advocacy swayed the members in favor of her argument. He didn't have any particular qualms with Claudia, but he knew that if she wanted something, she usually got it. "Go on," he said.

Claudia shifted in her seat and stuttered after seeing the disappointed expression on Andrew's face as she continued to lay out the facts. Brock wondered why Andrew was always the one to disagree with Claudia. She must have spent hours poring over Dr. Rio's medical history and looked confident that she would prove her point.

Claudia continued, "Although he is in excellent physical condition, he has stage 1 melanoma, which is very treatable with Mohs surgery."

Andrew spoke up, incredulous. "Treatable? Most people die of that one."

"Stage 1 is treatable," Claudia reaffirmed. "And regarding the divorce, I should note that it was not a surprise to anyone—they were separated twice prior to it. That would have prepared Dr. Rio for the eventual divorce in a calm and measured way, thus minimizing any effects it might have on his lifespan."

Brock's gaze shifted over the data on the computer screen as he pointed out something else. "I see that the algorithms also want to move Dr. Rio out of his three-bedroom cabin," he said.

"I think leaving him there is a wise decision," Claudia said. She went on to explain that it would allow for his twin children to be around during their college breaks, as well as give him a place to keep running Sunnyside

VSG from his workshop.

Most of the members agreed, but Andrew couldn't help but ask why this one individual was so special in comparison to others. He squirmed anxiously in his seat, awaiting a response.

Brock previously agreed that Claudia did not need to mention she was a customer of a vertical farm in the Harvard Pod. The refrigerator in her home probably contained FOUPs full of fresh veggies, waiting to be cooked up for dinner tonight.

Claudia cleared her throat before responding. "Because vertical farming systems are becoming more and more common throughout the world. I know of at least ten pods with vertical farms just in the eastern region alone."

Data does not lie — Claudia presented the correlation between six months' of FOUP deliveries and longer lifespans attributed to healthier choices. The algorithms awarded a longer lifespan to those same people due to an increased healthy life. According to the Algos, people who ate healthier also became more active and began logging increased hours in healthy activities. Surprisingly, even though the algorithms calculated the connection, they did not report it on their public dashboard. She concluded it was because White Cube held a vested interest that might be compromised by its disclosure.

Brock hesitated and glanced around the room. A dozen Controllers in their custom-tailored uniforms sat at the long table, their stern faces illuminated by the bluish light of the video monitors flickering on the wall. Claudia studied them, her lips set in a determined line. Andrew sneered as he crossed his arms over his chest, unimpressed with her suggestion. "What do you suggest?" Brock finally asked.

Claudia glanced around the room, taking in everyone's expectant expressions before speaking with confidence. "We maintain residency as is, but reduce the lifespan calculation by only five years. We have to override those algorithms on both residency and life expectancy."

Andrew scoffed, "Nonsense. Why do we even have the algorithms then?"

Brock interjected before anyone else could speak up. "The algorithms are a guide to the Controllers, not the bible," he said, then called for a vote that ended up nearly unanimous in favor of Claudia's motion. After a pause in the murmuring and all their votes were cast, Brock moved the meeting forward. "Next."

The room buzzed with energy as the video monitors blinked and whirred to life, displaying case after case of other uncontested cases. Once again, everything came to a screeching halt when an anomaly showed up among the algorithms. Brock saw the Controller's name associated with the case, looked around, and said, "Andrew."

Andrew stood and began reciting the case of Theodore Wiggins from memory. His voice punctuated each fact with dramatic flair and he leaned over the conference table to emphasize his plea for an override to the algorithm. "This individual did everything exactly according to protocol— exceptional performance, participation in all extracurricular activities, and good health. All perfectly executed manipulations of the system to his own advantage. And four, I say four, separate stints in solitary confinement as a reward!"

The audience members began to chatter loudly amongst themselves, discussing the various points of the presented discussion. Meanwhile, Brock scanned the room with a stern gaze, trying to bring back their focus to the vote at hand. "What do you recommend then?" he asked.

Andrew stood up and raised his voice to be heard over the din. "Reduce the lifespan from 110 years down to 96 years," he said firmly. "That is sufficient for most people. The algorithms are rewarding this man for trickery instead of doing their job."

The vote was nearly unanimous in support of Andrew's motion.

CHAPTER 16
Father and children in the brood.

Manny glanced at the clock on his cabin wall and calculated the time difference in his head. It was 4:00pm in the University of Santa Cruz Pod, where his son Alex Rio was probably studying right now. He activated his shield and opened the menu of options. With a quick movement of his eyes, he double-clicked "Twins," and waited for the shield to buffer. Soon Alex's face appeared in the glass screen of his shield. Manny smiled at seeing his son who was tall like him but kept his mother's more feminine facial features. He looked much younger than 17—his age upon graduating high school along with his twin sister, Amy. "Hi there, kiddo," Manny said warmly. "Is Amy around too?"

Alex nodded and stepped back as if to allow someone else in front of the camera. Soon enough, Amy appeared on the screen with her signature mischievous smirk, a stark contrast to her twin brother's more reserved demeanor. Her video feed bounced slightly as she spoke, perhaps due to movement within the cabin she shared with Alex.

"Just got in from classes. They are going really well!" Amy said confidently, her bright green eyes exuding pride for graduating high school early alongside her brother. Her light brown hair hung down beyond her shoulders. She applied too much mascara for a young girl, and a hint of blush enhanced her cheeks. She wore patchwork jeans, a white tank top, and mismatched socks. "How's the farm going?" A safe topic since the divorce.

Manny gave a small smile, his lips barely curving up at the edges. "We have a new harvest going right now. We are ahead of schedule."

In the video screen in the shield, Alex and Amy stood near each other, their images overlapping every few moments like watching a holographic projection on an old science fiction movie. Then Alex's expression changed suddenly. His jaw clenched angrily and he broke his gaze away from the camera, and characteristically jumped to the subject on his mind. "White Cube doesn't know what they are missing," he said through gritted teeth. Manny taught him every inch of Sunnyside Farm and its potential like the back of his hand. And Alex knew exactly how White Cube tossed the farm, and his father, aside like trash.

Amy rolled her eyes, crossing her arms. "We wouldn't have gotten this far without them. They got us started."

With a determined look on his face, Alex declared boldly, "That's why we're going straight to the University for funding. No private equity stake here."

Manny nodded in agreement, a hint of knowledge in his eyes. "Smart choice. Go with university funding right away. You know, NASA is also looking into vertical farms for their space voyages. I've been applying for grants with them too. So, how's your farm doing?" He was aware that the twins were part of the University of Santa Cruz's vertical farm to which Manny had already supplied over one thousand FOUPs. They had adopted this standard delivery system too in cooperation with several dozen vertical farms outside of pods all over the country. If each farm had developed their own systems, it would decrease profitability and make deliveries more complicated, but if they all adopted the same supply chain requirements, such as shipping container sizes and material handling devices, it would simplify the process.

Alex and Amy glanced at one another, their faces beaming with pride, and then they turned to Manny in unison. "Dad, we did it! We got the funding! Now we can finish building the aquariums!" He explained how the management at the farm was ecstatic to finally have the key element needed to get the system in motion. The most productive vertical farms are the ones with a constant source of freshwater for the aquariums, sourced from desalination plants harvesting saltwater from the surrounding sea.

"Fantastic!" Manny exclaimed. Both children's faces glowed as they responded to each query, an exchange only three agricultural and science nerds could possibly understand.

Finally, Amy glanced up at her father. "Dad, could you come out and help on the desalination plant? We don't have any experts here—not like you anyway." Her voice was timid yet hopeful, and Manny couldn't resist; he always held a soft spot for his little girl.

Alex chimed in, adding a bit of subtle persuasion, "I don't think we can get the aquariums going without you." Their eager faces turned to Manny in anticipation; it was obvious that his presence was vital for their success. He thought back to when the kids were young and remembered how his heart would swell when they looked to him for guidance—a feeling he missed experiencing in what seemed like an eternity. He couldn't deny them this opportunity. Alex added, "You know NASA is right next to us out here."

Manny's heart raced as he weighed his decision. He contemplated purchasing a ticket and hopping on the nearest flight, but the distant vision of cancer cells multiplying brought him back to earth. Stage 2 melanoma cancer was no joke. If he didn't act now, it could metastasize and spread to other parts of his body like an insidious fog. He became practiced at tracking changes in the spots scattered across his body, and then scheduling biopsies for any suspicious ones.

Even though skin cancer is fairly common, this particular type of skin cancer is the number one killer, claiming over 100,000 lives each year. Before researchers began using the mRNA vaccines in response to the Great Pandemic of 2019, there was not enough research on reliable treatment options for melanoma. Now researchers began knocking off each cancer, one at a time, but began with the most prevalent ones that affected the largest majority of people. With all these cutting-edge medical advances, Manny prayed that science would focus on curing melanoma and give him an opportunity to keep living.

Manny looked tenderly at his children as he spoke, their faces reflecting the deep love that bound them together. He opened his mouth to give them the bad news about his recent diagnosis, but thought better of it—there was no need for them to worry any more than they already were with their studies at the university. Instead, he changed the subject. "I'll think about it, kids. The Algos are making adjustments. They might make us move out of our cabin."

Alex immediately screamed in outrage, "Those bastards! They can't take our home!"

Seeing the distress on his children's faces Manny quickly offered some reassurance. "Don't worry, I filed an appeal. I'm not going without a fight."

Amy looked directly into her shield, her eyes wide with determination. Normally more reserved in her wording, and unless she became emotionally charged, she reverted to calling him Daddy instead of Dad. "You can do this! I know you can," she said firmly. "Don't let them take our home."

Manny replied in a comforting gesture. "I won't, kids," he said confidently, pumping himself up with an internal mantra: be strong like the river, Rio Constante; always pushing forward and wearing down the banks of the river, no matter how long it takes.

"Dad, you should come out here before the next lockdown starts," Alex suggested, undoubtedly recalling the last time they were confined in their cabin during a quarantine. Manny and Sarah endured weeks of close confinement, and it was one of the last things that eventually pushed them to divorce. Although some couples manage to grow closer together under these circumstances, it can also be very damaging for some relationships. Alex continued. "It's already spreading through the Midwest."

Manny contemplated the idea of being alone for an indefinite amount of time. He weighed being with his children versus staying at the peacefulness of Sunnyside Farm, the only two places he could see himself enduring such a long period of solitude. Thoughts of his friend, Coop, crossed his mind in the midst of the chaos. "It's going to be a battle. This Russian strain is spreading like wildfire."

CHAPTER 17
Medicine needed for young and old,

Dr. Rosita McKenna stepped into the waiting room and immediately noticed Manny, perched on the edge of a couch near the doctor's station, his foot tapping anxiously against the carpeted floor. On the other side of the room sat an overweight woman in a wheelchair, a tube sticking from her neck and IV fluid dripping from a pouch hanging above her right shoulder. She wore a faded floral blouse with stains spotting its fabric, and her face was still without expression until she met Rosita's gaze and smiled weakly. Holding an electronic writing pad in one hand, Rosita glanced at the woman before addressing Manny.

"Good morning, Dr. Rio," she said, not looking up from her scribbling.

"Please call me Manny," he replied nervously. "Oh, and good morning."

Rosita smiled briefly, nodded her head, and motioned for Manny to follow her. "We like to keep things professional here, so if you don't mind, let's stick with Dr. Rio."

The woman in the wheelchair chuckled mockingly and yelled out, "Give 'em hell in there, Doctor Reeeohhh!" with emphasis by singing his name. She then held up her hand and gave Manny a big thumbs-up signal for luck.

"Will do, Henrietta!" Manny responded energetically as he rose from the couch and stretched his legs and back as if getting ready for a race. Manny marveled at the woman's attitude as he moved across the waiting area. This would be his sixth surgery, so his anxieties lessened each time. However, this was the first time he was facing a stage 2 diagnosis and whatever the complications that it would bring.

"Follow me and we will get you into the OR prep." Rosita swiped her arm past the electronic RFID reader which emitted an audible click like a prison gate being opened. Manny followed her down the hallway lined with operating rooms and into a larger room with curtains separating the patient beds. His eyes took in the various pieces of equipment laid out on long tables at one end of the room like waiting soldiers, some tucked away behind curtains where they attended to various patients in preparation for surgery.

Rosita's shoes squeaked against the linoleum as she and Manny approached the fourth bed in the center of the long room. Electronic equipment glinted along one wall, and several patients emerged on hospital beds out of the alcoves, like an assembly line of medical care.

Manny grabbed the folded blue hospital gown and two paisley-colored socks from the top of the hospital bed. He felt the chill of the vinyl flooring through his soles even before changing into them. Rosita promised that the block team would arrive soon and started to move back towards the door, but Manny stopped her with a question before she could leave. "Excuse me, Doc, what is a block team?"

Rosita hesitated for a moment before replying in a cool voice. "Remember we have to do a block anesthesia for your shoulder and arm due to the severity of the melanoma. The team will be here to explain it all."

Manny tried not to think about what that meant or how it would feel. He stripped down further, donning the awkward robe with its ties that refused to cooperate. Finally, he slipped on the old-fashioned but surprisingly comfortable socks. He tucked his valuables into a bag and surrendered himself to fate.

As he lay down on the cot, he clung to the familiar weight of his earbuds in his pocket, knowing they wouldn't be allowed during surgery. They were a small comfort in a sea of uncertainty. The cool metal of the bed sent shivers through his body as he tucked himself under some blankets just before a young male doctor entered the room. The doctor wore a blue smock and had an electronic pad tucked under one arm. "Good morning, uh...oh, Doctor Rio," he said politely after seeing Manny's title.

"Please call me Manny," he replied.

The doctor grinned, looked around, and whispered, "I'm Chuck. Nice to meet you." His dark eyes twinkled with amusement when Manny tried saying "mucho gusto" before remembering that he wasn't wearing his earbuds with the universal translator. Embarrassed, Manny quickly changed his response to "Nice to meet you."

Chuck then held out his electronic pad for Manny's thumbprint and retina verification on the risk form.

Confused, Manny asked, "What is this for again?"

Chuck explained that it was a nerve damage risk acknowledgment form and began describing the block anesthesia process. But still unsure of what was going on, Manny kept questioning until Chuck answered all of his questions. Treating the situation like an experiment in his lab, he removed variable after variable until everything made sense.

Chuck continued patiently while explaining each section of the form to clear up any confusion until Manny felt comfortable. Pulling back the pad, Doctor Chuck's expression became more serious as he informed him of the risks associated with the Mohs surgery. "The risk of nerve damage is fairly high for this procedure due to the depth of the invasion. We have a 5 percent chance of having to remove the tendons and the hand from the wrist down." Manny paled while processing this information.

Manny slowly lifted his right hand up to eye level and stared at his trembling fingertips, his gaze far away, as if picturing what life would be like without his hand. Chuck must have understood the gravity of this moment and waited patiently until Manny finally looked back up at him, his resolve solidified. Manny pressed his thumb into the scanning pad and gave one final confirmation with the retinal scan.

Chuck smiled as he said a courteous, "Thank you." He began to gingerly probe Manny's shoulder with his fingers as if searching for something deep inside the tissue. He spoke as he worked, explaining that the rest of his team would be joining them shortly. They would administer a nerve block designed to lessen the amount of sedative needed by flooding the three nerves located around the shoulder with an anesthetic. If Manny wanted, he could be put under for the block procedure. Chuck explained the procedure would deliver only minor pain, but some patients preferred no pain at all. Instead, he asked if Manny would stay awake and help pinpoint the exact location of each nerve while injecting the block.

"What do you recommend?"

"Oh, I prefer the patient to be awake, then they can help us find the right nerves and guarantee the minimum amount of anesthetic is used. Less is better for the recovery." Chuck waved for two other doctors to come through the curtains after they peaked inside. Several pieces of equipment on wheels trailed the doctors.

One of the new doctors pulled a type of scope with a metallic glint. She propped it up against the bed and looked up at Manny. "Yes, that helps a lot," she said gently. "It only hurts a little but it helps us a lot."

Manny took a deep breath and nodded slowly in acceptance. "Okay, I'll stay awake and help," he said calmly.

The second nurse put her hand on his shoulder and squeezed it lightly while smiling. "That's so brave of you!"

Manny had his doubts about the decision, but the doctors kept on going, removed his gown, propped up his arm on a tray, and added mini-blankets to cover him up while leaving entry points for the needles. He felt the sting of each needle puncturing his skin and also a burning sensation of the topical painkillers. As the doctors inserted the catheters one by one, and with Manny's feedback, they hit each nerve perfectly on each first attempt. Manny watched on the scope as the doctor guided each one to its proper place in his shoulder. He felt nothing but pressure and warmth, his nerves quickly numbing until he could no longer lift or feel his arm at all. Soon enough, three bags of fluids hung above his head and slowly drained into his veins. First his shoulder became numb and then gradually worked its way down until even his fingers could no longer move. All he could do now was watch helplessly as control over his arm left him. It was like watching a movie of himself.

He watched the block team walk away and two other attendants come to take apart his bed and gather his things. They worked methodically as they packed him up, before pushing him feet first down a long hallway. Finally, they stopped at an operating room door, where they looked over their electronic pads before pushing him feet first through the doorway. He squirmed uneasily as he felt a chill in the air. Were they supposed to have already given him anesthesia to knock him out now?

He held his breath as they moved his bed towards an overhead boom with lights, medical air, medical oxygen, and some strange exhaust snorkel attached to it. It wasn't until later that Manny found out what it was, "WAGD," or Waste Anesthetic Gas Disposal, a method used to keep doctors from breathing in too much anesthesia. As four attendants or doctors circled his bed to lift him onto the operating table, Manny asked nervously, "Would it be easier if I just lifted myself over?"

A female doctor smiled in relief and stepped back with the rest of the circle, leaving him to try and move himself over onto the operating table. Despite his best efforts, his dead arm would not cooperate and so one of the doctors stepped forward, and gently lifted the arm up before helping Manny slide safely onto the sterile medical operating table. His intravenous bags were quickly replaced by others, and a small, clear mask was fitted over his nose. Above him, a large robotic device moved into place; its four arms resembled something out of a science fiction movie, and scrawled beautiful handwriting along its side declared its name: "Leonardo."

Manny recognized Rosita as she inspected each arm of the device, making sure each one was correctly aligned. He could hear her low, confident commands echo in the vast room. The Leonardo resembled a four-legged spider waiting to strike its target, his arm, at any moment. Its sleek steel limbs glinted under the fluorescent lights as it shifted into position.

In a low voice, Rosita gave instructions for someone to start the drip and

Manny felt himself slipping away. The last thing he remembered was seeing his arm floating above the other parts of his body like a small boat in the middle of an ocean. He closed his eyes and silently pleaded for this strange contraption not to take his hand away from him.

He awoke in the recovery room of the hospital, a place that he became begrudgingly familiar with over the past couple of months. With a groan, he mustered up enough energy to move his arm just enough to see if his hand made it through surgery. After some effort, he managed to lift his head and take a peek at the end of his arm. A large oven-mitt-sized bandage was wrapped around it. Letting out a sigh of relief, he fell back onto the bed with a huge smile on his face.

Manny's vision slowly adjusted to his surroundings. He was in a different hospital room. A kind-faced woman with a friendly smile and stark white lab coat stood beside his bed. Her glasses reflected the light from the LED lamps above, and her long fingers hovered gracefully around an electronic tablet that she glanced at from time to time. "Dr. McKenna will be here shortly to explain the results," she said softly as if speaking to a child.

"Everything went fine, right?" Manny tried to sit up, but his numbed arm tugged heavily on his shoulders.

"Yes, it went well," she reassured him calmly, "and don't worry about that arm. It may take a couple of days for the feeling to come back." She nodded one last time before moving on to her next patient with delicate steps. Manny heard her calming voice with the next patient, who sounded like a little girl, only a few beds over.

Rosita emerged from around the corner then, her gaze catching Manny's. Her typically stoic expression softened slightly into a faint smile as she spoke. "Welcome back, Dr. Rio," she said lightly, then moved closer and explained what happened while Manny was under the robot.

"We got all the cancer, but had to take quite a bit of tissue and a portion of the lymphatic system with it," she said methodically. "Your hand should be alright though; it will survive." She paused for a few seconds then, observing

Manny's reaction before nodding in confirmation.

"My hand is okay then?" Manny pressed for clarity, attempting to move but unable to due to the heaviness in his arm.

"Yes, your hand is alright but we will have to wait and see about the mobility," she explained patiently. "The melanoma was quite deep. There are no signs that it metastasized yet but we cannot be sure until we do some more tests. And maybe immunotherapy treatments."

His eyes widened at the realization that this time, it was going to take more than surgery—immunotherapy with an effective rate of just twenty percent, to be precise. But it was still less invasive than chemotherapy; those highly toxic chemicals tended to kill both cancer and a little bit of the person along with it.

Rosita turned to leave as Manny asked, "When do we start?"

Without looking back, she answered firmly, "Two days."

"What about the hand? You said there could be some side effects?"

Rosita stepped forward and stared at his bandaged hand closely as if seeing through the thick wrapping. "There could be some limited mobility with the middle three fingers," she answered, holding up her own middle three fingers to imitate the possible effect.

Manny saw the doctor display her three fingers at him and couldn't help but let out a chuckle.

"What's funny about that?" she asked incredulously.

"The last time someone showed me three fingers like that, they told me to read between the lines," he replied, holding his own three middle fingers up for emphasis before shaking the middle one.

Rosita fought a smirk as she rummaged in her bag and pulled out a small bag of circular bandages. She tossed it onto his lap.

"What's that for?" Manny asked, staring at the tiny bandages in confusion.

"That's for the new spot for your RFID chip," Rosita replied. She pointed to Manny's left forearm and he tugged his sleeve back to reveal an identical round bandage already affixed to his left arm. He flexed his wrist tentatively, aware that somewhere underneath the gauze was a tiny chip in his left arm that had been with him in his right arm since he was two years old.

Rosita's gaze remained glued to her electronic pad as she tapped away at it with practiced ease. "Your chip is working perfectly," she said after a few moments passed in silence. "You're officially back on the grid."

Manny stood up after a while and moved to a soothing recovery area with comfortable chairs and gentle illumination. A fabric sling around his neck held his large bandaged arm, but he still felt the substantial weight in his alternate shoulder that carried the weight of both arms. He leaned back and shut his eyes until the anesthesia slowly dissipated. When he opened them again, Maggie stood in front of him wearing a pink tutu over her outfit and with her arm in a similar sling across from Manny's own.

"Manny!" Maggie cried out and tried to jump into his lap, but her oversized bandaged hand taped in a sling around her neck prevented her from doing so. She settled for leaning against him until their foreheads touched. "Cancer buddy! How ya doing?"

Manny smiled, relieved at the sight of his friend. "Did you get rid of your big one?" he asked with hope in his voice.

"Mommy said the doctor got it all!" Maggie exclaimed as she spun in circles with joy. "Mommy was in the room with me the whole time!"

Manny gazed towards the entrance, trying to make out Maggie's mother through the glass doors. "Where is your mommy now?" he asked, partly wanting Maggie to be with her mother and partly because he was supposed to talk more about starting immunotherapy.

Maggie leaned towards Manny and whispered, "She's still inside." She glanced at the entrance too, sadness suddenly washing over her face. "She cries a lot, you know."

At that moment, Dr. Cheryl Blanding appeared in the doorway and smiled warmly at the two patients who were becoming friends with similar circumstances. "How are we doing now, Dr. Rio and Maggie?" she asked kindly.

"I can't feel my arm and it's all squiggly," Maggie answered with a mischievous smile and moved her shoulders in a little dance.

A grin tugged at Manny's lips as memories of his own daughter at that age flooded him with nostalgia. He played along with her joke, saying, "Mine is squiggly too!"

"Dr. McKenna will be right out for you, Dr. Rio," Cheryl said before turning to Maggie. "And as for you little girl, come with me to the other room so that we can have a little talk." She reached out her hand to Maggie and they both walked together to one of the other rooms. Maggie turned back and smiled at Manny.

After about ten minutes, Rosita emerged from the room, totally transformed into casual attire. Her jeans were loose and comfortable with a white blouse that stylishly created a sleek figure. Manny couldn't help but stare at this unusual sight of his doctor wearing something other than a blue smock. He cleared his throat before asking, "I have more questions about the surgery."

Rosita tried not to roll her eyes and looked up from her electronic pad. "Are you up for seeing some of it yourself?" She moved the pad slowly into Manny's hands and his eyes widened as he took in the view of an open surgical wound centered on his wrist. His exposed skeletal structure and bare tendons leading to his fingers was clearly visible, illuminated by the bright hospital lights. Manny noticed Rosita had a slight smile as she watched Manny's grip tighten around the pad.

"You took a lot of material around it," he said tentatively as if he was afraid of what else the video revealed.

Rosita nodded. "Yes, it wasn't normal for this kind of procedure. We had to make sure we got all of it before it spread through your lymphatic system. It might have already, which is why we want to start the immunotherapy right away."

Manny forced himself to look up from his bandaged wrist and met Rosita's gaze. This stuff was trying to kill him but with her help, he'd make it through this. "When do we start?" he asked quietly.

CHAPTER 18
Friend's distractions often bold,

Manny stepped out of the Beeze ride and made his way to the entrance of his cabin building. After a few awkward attempts at the main entrance, the door finally recognized his chip and opened to welcome him into the familiar lobby, a warm and inviting area, and he walked calmly down the hallway to the waiting elevator. After watching the brightly lit numbers climb to 65 on the ride up, he expected the door to open as always, but it stayed closed.

He tried to move his dead arm up to the electronic reader, but the sling kept his arm still. The red light blinked but nothing happened. He realized that the RFID chip did not read on his shield, and barred his exit. He tried to step out of the elevator but the door wouldn't open. Then he remembered the RFID chip was now implanted in his left arm instead, and moved it closer to the scanner. It beeped and lit up green as it recognized him, unlocking the door with a satisfying click. He stepped out into the hall and made his way to his cabin. A pair of burly men brushed by him, carrying some bulky items in large black bags as they headed toward the elevator.

As Manny trudged down the hallway, he noticed that the ominous solitary confinement attachment on Theo's cabin door was gone. When he looked up, his new friend Theo emerged from inside and jumped back slightly when their eyes met.

"Theo!" Manny called out in surprise. His friend looked different somehow, but then again, Manny only saw him in the visor of his shield before.

"Oh my God, Manny!" Theo cried out in surprise, then peered at him more closely, seeing the sling and boxer glove bandage wrapped around him.

He moved awkwardly and debated whether to shake hands or give a hug. "It's so good to be out! But what the hell happened to you?"

"Never mind that," Manny happily replied, disregarding his surgery for the time being. "You're out!"

Theo let out an exhausted breath and gave Manny a relieved smile. "Glad that is done. They just took the locks off," Theo replied. "Another couple of days in solitary and I would have gone mad."

Manny smiled as he saw the familiar face in front of him, for the first time, in person. He motioned for Theo to follow him. "Come on, I want to show you something."

Manny fumbled with the doorknob, a clumsy effort from trying to use his left hand instead of his dominant right. Theo offered Manny a reassuring pat on the shoulder, and after several attempts together, the door finally opened. They stepped inside and the warm familiarity of home washed over them.

"Wow!" Theo exclaimed, his voice echoing off of the tall ceilings, numerous doorways, and large windows along the far wall. "I knew it was big, but damn this place is something!"

"I knew you would like it," Manny said with a proud smile. "Raised the kids here, but they're away at college now."

"Married?"

Manny laughed and shook his head. "Naw."

Theo again noticed the sling and the boxer-glove bandage. "And what happened? Why the bandage?" he asked, gesturing to Manny's arm.

Manny hesitated before responding, his eyes darting from the wall to Theo's face as he deliberated whether or not to tell him the truth. He stretched out his left hand and waved it over a reader panel on the wall. The view screen lit up and Manny watched as the readings of his RFID chip registered on the screen. After a few moments, he spoke quietly, "It's nothing, just an old sports injury I needed to have repaired."

"Interesting." Theo studied Manny's expression for a few seconds, then gave him a warm smile. "Wanna go out? I have to get some fresh air."

Manny opened a small door in the wall and he grabbed a FOUP from inside. He passed it to Theo, who examined it with curiosity, spinning it around and inspecting every corner before opening the little door at the end to find something amazing. His face lit up. "Cake!"

Manny grinned. "Been saving it for you."

Manny and Theo stepped out into the crisp twilight air of their street while Theo enjoyed the last few bites of the cake. The row of cabins along their walk was interrupted by the occasional mixed-use building with shops, restaurants, and offices beneath. A central gate at each building checked everyone's RFIDs as they passed, scanning people's arms for entrance. The buildings had an unmistakable waffle shape to them with protective barricades extending from balconies to protect against cross-contamination in the event of an emergency.

Rumors circulated about possible lockdowns in central regions, although it was impossible to tell how much was fact and how much was fiction. Manny and Theo discussed this and many other topics as they strolled down the street together. Manny steered the conversation away from his surgery earlier that day, whereas Theo was just glad to be out after his solitary confinement. They both spoke excitedly about Sunnyside Farm, a topic that brought enthusiasm and joy as Manny described more and more of the details of the vertical farm. "Any particular restaurant you have in mind?" Theo asked.

Manny smiled at the memory. "The Lafayette," he said proudly. "They've been around for 150 years, and they serve up some real food!" Manny spent many evenings there when his ex-wife was still in the picture, and they enjoyed the refined atmosphere. Set across the Houston Street divide in NoHo Pod, it was the perfect spot for a romantic evening. Now it was home to Sunnyside Farm deliveries at a pace of thirty FOUPs per day.

The NoHo Pod bustled with activity; theaters, performance halls, and art schools filled the district that he loved so much. Today, however, he walked, talked, and worried about the ominous lockdown looming and whether it was wise to cross over to another pod. He also worried about the posting in his shield stating the Algos removed another 6 years from his forecasted lifespan. But despite this jarring news, Manny felt oddly at peace because the Contros did not remove him from his cabin. This was one of the better days for him, aside from cancer surgery.

Theo squinted at the building in front of them, a curious combination of a rustic cabin and Victorian architecture. A line of people snaked down the block, patiently waiting for a free Boule bread, the chef's signature daily creation from this renowned bakery.

Manny and Theo edged their way through the gate and stepped into the Lafayette. The rich scent of freshly baked goods and roasted garlic immediately filled their nostrils. Somewhere outside, an electronic beep indicated they had entered the No Ho Pod.

The Lafayette was lively and bustling, with people milling around the entrance. Most wore their shields extended partway down, but some were completely extended, with their fans whirring quietly. The effects of the impending lockdown were visible in the crowd. No one seemed to be taking any chances and began wearing their shields down everywhere they went. Manny and Theo approached the host station and asked for a table, but a tall and slender young man behind it replied they were all booked. He offered them a seat at the bar instead.

The host led them to the bar, a dark wooden, extraordinary bar—an artifact of a bygone era. Its murky wood shone in the low light and fine scrolling ran along the rails. Inlaid brass footrests added a subtle flair, and tall brass chairs, each with a posh red leather seat and backrest, lined the bar. An aroma of something old yet sophisticated filled the air as they took their seats at the end of the bar. Their eyes scanned the other patrons—suited businessmen, young women in evening gowns, and even some more casual locals.

Just as the bartender came to them to take their order, a man tapped Manny on the shoulder. Manny felt nothing due to his numb arm which hung inside the sling. Suddenly, Manny's chair spun around to face a tall, stocky man with reddish hair, wearing a fine suit. The abrupt movement caused Manny's arm to fall out of its sling and dangle limply at his side.

"What the hell are you doing here?" Gary Thornton asked. He squared up in front of Manny, ready to throw down at any moment. His gaze shifted between Manny's eyes and then down to the useless limb that swung from Manny's side. The last time they saw one another, Gary arrested Manny under false pretenses during the first days of Manny's divorce.

Without warning, Gary swung at Manny's jaw, which although Manny's shield was good for acting as a computer and looked solid, it did nothing against a fist to the jaw. With the force of the blow, Manny felt a sharp jolt in the side of his neck and his bar stool spun him around in a 360-degree circle. His hat flew off his head and across the room, while his limp arm flung wildly like a helicopter, sending every item on the bar top flying as if in slow motion. Glasses shattered, condiments splattered, napkins fluttered and containers clanked against the wall behind the bar.

Manny's chair stopped spinning, and he viewed a sight he had not expected. Theo stood above Gary, who lay crumpled in a puddle of spilled beer on the floor, his legs splayed awkwardly, like broken twigs beneath him, and his eyes wide open with shock. All this happened so quickly that everyone in the room stared in confusion.

Theo slowly stepped forward; his fists still clenched. In a menacing tone, he glared down at the man and warned, "Get up again and I'll beat you."

Before Gary attempted to stand, two men rushed over from behind and grabbed Theo firmly by his arms. They swung him around and pushed him face down onto the bar counter with such force that the bar glasses clattered loudly in protest.

"Gentle now, PoPos!" Theo said calmly as he was pinned against the bar top. "I'm not going anywhere."

Gary slowly pushed himself off the ground and wiped away the blood dripping from his lip. With a smirk on his face, he watched Theo squirm against the bar. "Damn right you're not going anywhere," he sneered. "Assaulting a Pod Police Officer is a regional offense."

Manny stood up but the PoPo's eyes were immediately drawn to Manny's limp arm hanging at his side like a wet noodle, with blood seeping through the bandage around it. Gary stepped forward and looked Manny in the eye with an expression of revulsion. "And what the hell is wrong with your arm?"

"Nothing, just a motorcycle accident," he said to deflect the questions. Theo looked at him strangely, hearing yet another excuse for Manny's dead arm. Manny then glanced at the two other PoPos who tightened their grip on Theo. Manny said with authority, "You're all out of uniform and in the wrong pod. You have no jurisdiction outside of the Bronx Pod."

"We have positional authority no matter where we go," Gary retorted.

"Bullshit, Gary," Manny said firmly. He locked eyes with each man before continuing, "And let go of my friend before I call Captain Michelle Killian."

Theo looked away from Gary, blinking slowly in surprise at Manny's bold words. A few tense moments passed before Gary gave a slight nod and his cohorts released Theo, who rubbed gently at his sore wrists. Gary glanced away, avoiding Theo's gaze as he spoke, "No need to get the captain involved."

Manny slowly swung his right arm, which remained hanging limply at his side, towards the sling draped across his shoulder. His left hand shakily found its way to the opposite elbow in an effort to guide the dead arm into place. The other two men watched in bewilderment as Manny calmly put his arm back into position in the sling. Manny shifted his steely gaze from one man to the other before finally settling on Gary. His voice carried a sternness that reminded the men of their fierce captain, who wouldn't be pleased with a drunken brawl in another pod. "Gary, go home and work this off," he said, his tone dripping with authority.

Gary bent down and began scooping the scattered items off the floor, avoiding Manny's gaze. He muttered, "Well you can have her." With a quick tug, he drunkenly pulled his jacket back to its original shape and looked at Manny with understanding before leaving. He muttered something else under his breath that Manny did not understand.

"What do you mean?" Manny replied while steadying a few glasses back upright on the bar top with a shaky hand.

"She's back with you now." Gary replied while rubbing his unshaven jaw. Although he wore a fancy suit and a polished watch glinting on one wrist, most everyone knew he was a PoPo.

Manny shook his head vigorously while taking a step back. "Sarah? No, she's not. I haven't seen her in months."

"But she said..." Gary started before he realized he was being manipulated once again. He glanced at his two buddies, then Theo, and lastly Manny. They all realized how foolish Gary looked. "Let's leave," he murmured to his friends as he motioned toward the door. The three of them marched forward, three out-of-uniform PoPos in a foreign pod. It was a sad sight. The entire scene was rather sorry.

After the fight, Theo sat back down quietly and glanced up at the bartender who was now holding a steel rod with a heavy golf-ball-sized weight on the end. The weapon had a strange blue electric light emanating from the end. A tense moment sat between them and the bartender, until he lowered his weapon, knelt down to pick up Manny's hat off the floor, and handed it back to him. He then nodded towards Manny's bandaged head. "You're bleeding there too."

Manny gingerly touched the bandage and felt for blood before placing his hat back over his head slowly.

Theo looked at Manny still facing away from him before commenting to the bar top, "Nice friends you got there."

Manny was about to answer when a trickle of fresh blood started rolling down his outstretched fingers protruding from the sling. Grabbing some paper towels from the bartender, Manny tried to clean up the mess while flexing his jaw with his free hand and checking for more bleeding.

"You gonna tell me what that was all about?" Theo asked after a few moments of cleaning, taking in the details of Manny's injury and glancing at the door where the goons had exited earlier.

Manny didn't know if Theo was asking about the PoPos or about his arm. "Someday." Manny tried to deflect the conversation by asking Theo where he learned to fight like that, but all he got from him in response was an uncomfortable silence. The bartender still stood there, watching them with interest, and Manny realized they needed to get out of this conversation quickly. "Two rye whiskey Manhattans, please," he said shortly.

Theo smiled, a touch of sadness behind his eyes as he slowly shook his head. He stumbled upon this unlikely friendship that seemed to be blooming, and it gave him hope for the future. "Fight Club in the Bronx Pod," he replied in response to Manny's inquiry about his fighting skills.

Manny's face lit up at the mention of his old stomping grounds. "Really? I know the place," Manny said.

Theo pointed to Manny's scalp and then to his arm; the marks of his recent surgeries were unmistakable. "Skin cancer, right?"

Manny fixed Theo with a disbelieving stare and then yielded to the question. "How did you know that?"

Theo didn't respond right away, silently taking a sip from his drink immediately after the bartender set it down. Eventually, he lowered the glass and gave Manny a solemn look. "Lost my dad to it a few years ago," he said.

"Sorry to hear," Manny replied instinctively, and he instantly felt a connection with his new friend. They both sipped their drinks and stayed quiet as the bartender continued cleaning up around them, no doubt aware of what was being discussed.

"Scalp, nose, cheeks, shoulders, hands, and feet, right?" Theo asked eventually, gesturing to Manny's hat now covering the surgery on his head, and then to the hand wrapped in a makeshift bandage.

"Missed my nose." Manny shot him a half-smile as he pointed towards his oversized nose without an answer. "Amazing, huh?"

Theo chuckled and took another sip of the cool brown beverage; the clinking of ice cubes resonating in the room like tiny bells. "What kind?"

Manny sighed and nodded toward the empty glass on the table.

"Melanoma," he said softly.

Theo turned instantly to Manny and said, "Shit. Same as my dad."

A death sentence, is what Manny wanted to say.

CHAPTER 19
Medicine is a father's guide,

John Strunk, Manny's energetic and carefree university roommate at NYU, enjoyed a wild freshman year. He'd stayed up all night with his buddies, drinking and playing video games, then managed to get a straight "A" in classes the next morning—an impressive feat that Manny never matched. The partying was fun for John, but the realization hit that it could not last. After a few transformative semesters of hard work and dedication, John gained the knowledge and confidence necessary to move on to Stanford University's graduate program and eventually become a professor there. Now he is Dr. John Strunk, head of Cancer Research.

Manny double-clicked on John's name in their virtual shield and within moments his old friend appeared on the viewer. His formerly shaggy hair was impeccably trimmed and shaved, adding elegance to his crisp navy suit. "Hi, John!" Manny said excitedly.

"Manny, you old scoundrel," John replied warmly. "How did the surgery go?"

"Dr. McKenna said they got it all, but it was definitely in the lymphatic system."

"How far?" Dr. Strunk asked, his brow creasing with concern.

"Don't know." Manny breathed deeply. "That's why they want to start the immunotherapy right away."

"Do that," John said firmly before continuing, "but first send me a blood sample right away. I want to see if you qualify for a Phase 2 clinical trial we have going here at the lab. We have this mRNA vaccine that can be tailored specifically to each person."

"What would that do?"

"Only save your life, that's all," John explained as condescendingly as possible to his old friend. "This is powerful, and it really works!"

Manny smiled, his eyes twinkling with hope. "What are my chances?"

"The Phase 1 trials showed a 75 percent cure rate in 250 people with Stage 2 and 3 melanomas," John explained, his voice softening with compassion. "You have to get this treatment before it's too late."

Manny's eyes lit up with hope and his mouth curled into a smile as he heard John's words. "That's amazing!" he exclaimed, not having expected such promising news. He remembered reading about mRNA vaccines before, hearing that scientists have achieved great success with them against a variety of cancers.

John nodded gravely. "The immunotherapy only has a 15 percent cure rate. You need to get me a blood sample and come here as fast as possible. That melanoma can be fatal in four weeks if they don't treat it properly."

Manny thought about all that would have to happen—getting a blood sample, traveling, shots, and doctors. "I'll go to Dr. McKenna and get a blood sample for you."

"She may not be willing to cooperate," John said slowly. "It's a cross-pod diagnosis. That might not be accepted by the system out there. Let me see if I can figure out how to get the blood sample through an outsourced lab."

Hope blossomed in Manny's mind and he began to see a future beyond this cancer treatment. He continued, "Would it be possible for me to send two samples?"

"What do you mean?"

"Dr. McKenna's daughter is going through the same cancer as me."

"Manny," John replied doubtfully, "I'm not sure if I can even get *you* into the trial program."

"Please, John," Manny begged. This mission to save Maggie felt almost as important as saving himself. "She's only eight years old."

"Damn," John cursed softly, knowing how rapidly early-onset cancers take innocent children. Manny watched him glance over at the electronic chart posted on his wall filled with names of those in consideration for the program. John explained it had one thousand spots already taken and nearly five thousand more still being evaluated. After a few moments of contemplation, he said to Manny, "Okay, I'll see what I can do."

Manny respected John and knew that at its core, his job was about saving lives—especially a child's life—and he could not turn away from trying to help.

CHAPTER 20
We all go for another ride,

The government-enforced lockdown in Wisconsin, Illinois, and Indiana was as strict and absolute as ever. Coop, in his long-hauler Betsy, wanted to avoid being caught up in the quarantine net at all costs. He'd managed to circumnavigate three of the locked-down pods, but no option existed other than to drive straight through the gates of the fourth pod at its eastern entrance. Keeping a wary eye on the news, Coop steered Betsy towards the Gary Industrial Park Pod at the far end of the region without being tethered with an electronic leash. As they approached, he saw that traffic was sparse, likely due to the impending lockdown, so he took a chance and drove straight through the gates. Once inside, the roads were almost deserted, and only a few other long-haulers were traversing its expanse.

When they arrived at the loading dock of his pickup point, Coop was relieved to see the loading of two-thousand FOUPs would be a breeze. The FOUPs lay connected together in long straws measuring twenty feet in length, each bundle stacked securely for transport. This innovative design maximized space efficiency and made it easier for drones to speed up the loading and unloading process. Thanks to this setup, Coop wouldn't have to interact with any people while remaining inside the protection of the main cab.

Coop watched from inside Betsy, as a squadron of lifter drones carried piles of cylindrical tubes from the loading dock to the rear hatch of Betsy's cargo area. He squinted and tilted his head when one of the drones passed by. The tubes were so long, they looked like thin straws in comparison to the large white "hot dog" shape of Betsy. Suddenly the drones stopped, and Coop quickly pecked at buttons on his control screen before being interrupted by a voice coming through his earpiece. "Coop, this is Charlie. Do you have solitary containment on?"

"Yes, I do. You never know with these lockdowns," Coop spoke into the shield as his gaze darted across the readouts displayed on the monitor.

"Good. We have an unknown case of something with one of our people," Charlie said gravely. "You never know with the Contros what is going to happen next. You got enough food to last?"

"Yeah, I do." Coop relaxed a bit as the drones started loading again. "Let's get this load on and I can get out of here."

"Will do," Charlie replied and was about to sign off. "May the virus miss you and your family."

"And also miss you," Coop replied.

Soon Coop finished loading and headed for the pod gate, hoping it would still be open when he got there. His heart raced a bit while driving slightly over the normal speed limit, but the swarm of Beeze vehicles responded to his pushy attitude and cleared the way. The gate, with massive brick posts, loomed over him like guardians as he passed through. He peered into the block gate posts as he drove through, knowing he would register on the gate and be open to a tether for another few miles.

Once past the tether detection area, Coop exhaled slowly and turned his attention toward Sunnyside Farm, which was still twelve hours away. He activated his shield and made a call to Naoko, hoping to get an update on the status of his home base. He really wanted to hear her voice, double-clicked on Naoko's contact information, and nervously waited for a response.

Moments later, Naoko's beautiful face appeared in the viewer of his shield. "Konnichiwa, Cooper-san."

"Hello, Naoko," Cooper barely breathed as he wondered if he overstepped his bounds with this call. Coop the driver and Naoko the brilliant scientist.

"I've got two thousand FOUPs and am headed your way."

"Watashi was anata no koto o totemo shinpai shite imashata!" Naoko replied sympathetically. "I was so worried about you!" is what Coop heard from the translator.

Coop couldn't believe his ears when he heard the words of affection from Naoko. The sound of her voice was melodic and higher-pitched than normal. "I'm alright," he replied. "I was worried about you too."

The two stared into each other's eyes, their hearts swollen with emotion but unable to vocalize it previously due to their professional situation. Finally, Naoko spoke up again. Her voice sounded like any other Japanese-speaking person at first, but soon the syllables shifted, morphed, and rearranged into the proper syntax of Coop's language. It was a curious side effect of the shields that prevented both of them from exposing their true feelings too soon. She asked, "When will you return?"

"About ten or twelve hours, depending on the lockdown situation."

She asked him if he had enough food and water. Maybe it was fear that brought them together, but Coop couldn't help but feel like there was something special growing between them, something that could carry them through this uncertain time.

"Luckily, my family at Sunnyside keeps me in FOUPs for each trip," Coop added.

"Did you see FOUP number 21 yet?" Naoko asked, her cheeks turning pink from embarrassment.

"No, not yet," Coop replied with an inquisitive glint in his eye.

"I made a chocolate cake for you," she said eagerly, her smile radiating joy. "Fresh eggs harvested the other day."

CHAPTER 21
Man and friend on a quest,

Theo knelt on the floor, eyes scanning the intricate mechanisms and components of the drone, Greenie II. His experienced hands adjusted the latching arm to fit perfectly into a pass-through designed for a White Cube box. Next, he reached for the bundle of four straws of two FOUPs each and carefully fastened them securely within the structure. Satisfied with his efforts, Theo sat back and admired his work: a simple modification that increased the strength of the latching arm of Greenie II.

Theo glanced up from the drone he was studying, memories of his time at Advanced Robotics Solutions flooding back. He worked on a tiny robotics suite of products and remained proud of his accomplishments, including the completion of one final project prior to leaving. He'd accepted that it was time for something new.

He remembered what it was like to maneuver the small fiber-optic connectors, how his hands seemed so large they would snag when he tried to plug the connectors together. The task became tedious for him and he felt stagnant, but now, he stared with admiration at this larger version of the same technology. Previously, his work helped people during critical surgery. Now, his work will help people live longer and be healthier. And it would form a resistance against the oppressive Controllers. Algorithms be damned.

Theo flew Greenie II around his cabin, navigating the bundle of FOUPs with ease courtesy of the new horsepower. Greenie II's final task was lifting the straws into the pass-through door. She flew towards the monitor of the door, activated it by beeping out a tiny signal, and then carefully delivered the FOUPs into the compartment before signaling for the door to close.

A satisfied smile appeared on Theo's face as he watched Greenie II complete the task forty times in a row with barely a hitch while using its machine-learning technique with its AI chip. It was time to show Manny. Theo quickly activated his shield and double-clicked on Manny's name. They agreed to meet in the hallway to start the trip to the Sunnyside Farm and present their work.

Manny entered first into the shared hallway when something small, but powerful, flew out of Theo's door and raced past Manny. It carried a load of FOUPs and looked like Manny's own Greenie except stronger. "What is that?" Manny asked in disbelief.

"Meet Greenie II," Theo answered, stepping out of his doorway and into the hall. "I wanted to show you what I've been working on." Manny watched in awe as Theo explained how he modified his original Greenie drone to carry more FOUPs than ever before.

"That ain't the half of it. Watch this," Theo continued and closed the door behind him. He then steered the modified drone around both men tightly in the narrow confines of the hallway and drove it to the monitor on the door. The drone's sensors detected the pass-through door, activated it, and carefully set down its bundle of FOUPs before closing the door again. "Fini."

Manny's eyes lit up as soon he heard the explanation of the invention, and his mind raced through calculations of potential profits and applications. He pressed his hands together in amazement, a wide smile breaking out across his face. "That is really fantastic!"

"I've been working on a few other things too," Theo said as he noticed Manny's arm swing easily by his side, the sling replaced with a white, new-looking cast. "What's that on your arm?"

Manny held it up for Theo to see, rotating it so that he could get a good view of the top. "I've got the feeling back and changed the cast," Manny explained as the Greenie II drone hovered quietly nearby above his head.

Theo leaned in closer. A curved piece of plastic protruded from the top of the cast. As Theo reached out to touch it, he realized it was a broken FOUP fitted into a perfect curve along the top of Manny's cast. The piece kept the cast elevated off of Manny's skin and allowed air to pass through while still protecting the stitches from the recent surgery. "Clever. You should patent that thing."

Manny flexed his fingers to show off their mobility. "Now I can get back to work again," he said with relief. Theo asked him for more details about the surgery, but he stopped when he realized Manny did not want to talk about it.

Manny and Theo summoned a Beeze to take them to the farm. The self-driving automobile arrived with a metallic whoosh and stopped gracefully near the sidewalk next to them. As they climbed aboard, Theo's excitement was palpable, as if he were a little kid going to an amusement park for the first time. He fidgeted with his seatbelt and talked non-stop about how he couldn't wait to assemble hundreds of Greenie II's as part of a major expansion of Sunnyside Farm.

Manny felt a twinge of concern about the investment, but he also knew that this drone and the new FOUP design could be the key to making Sunnyside VSG completely self-sustaining financially. As they traveled between pods, Manny couldn't help but think this could be his new job, along with working with the brilliant and oddly cunning man sitting beside him.

Manny and Theo watched as their Beeze communicated with its swarm-mates before heading to the farm. They crossed out of the Chelsea Pod One, passing through the steel gates that marked the entrance into Long Island Pod. Both men glanced at each other apprehensively as they thought about the rumblings of a potential lockdown in their region.

"This is the place to be if that happens," Manny said, breaking the silence.

"I don't have anyone to worry about," Theo answered cryptically. "So, I might as well be where there's great food!"

Manny kept quiet but nodded in agreement, glancing out the forward-viewing windows as he pointed towards the farm. He gestured towards a tall glass building with sporadic patches of green vegetation growing along its walls. "There it is."

Theo gazed in awe at the Sunnyside vertical farm before them. Its walls stretched up into the sky and its colossal size barely fit in his vision. "Wow, it's massive! And beautiful!"

As their Beeze pulled closer, Theo bombarded Manny with questions about how the farm operated. Manny smiled and gestured towards the backside of the farm. "The best part is we have a shelled-out area in the back for expansion. That whole backside is empty. For now."

CHAPTER 22
To the farm they'll invest,

Manny motioned for Theo to take control of the Greenie II delivery drone as they weaved through the security gates and into the lab. The drone descended and perfectly placed the bundle of FOUPs on a lab table. All eyes in the room rested on Theo, his posture stiff with nervousness. Roberta, looking especially intrigued, fixated on him as Naoko and the other scientists examined and discussed the drone at length. Manny stepped forward and introduced Theo to the group.

James Ceglia, the farm's finance manager, today wearing blue coveralls splattered with glue and caulking, entered the room from the back. He approached with a quizzical expression, his gaze fixed on the hovering drone, "What is that thing?"

Manny smiled and greeted James enthusiastically, "Meet Greenie II." He then motioned for Theo to demonstrate how it worked. The drone picked up and placed a bundle of FOUPs into James' hands.

James' face lit up with amazement and joy as he watched the drone float back to Theo's side. "This is incredible!" James said. Manny assumed the look on James's face came from immediately thinking of increased profits with speedier deliveries.

Roberta nodded with admiration. "This might be the answer we've been looking for," she said.

Manny stepped forward. "There's more," he offered, lifting one of the FOUPs from the stack James held. He asked James to bring it over to the jig on the far side of the room.

James hesitated, confusion etching his features as he reached out and grabbed the FOUP from Manny. He carefully placed it in the frame of the testing jig as Manny asked Roberta to take a piece of food from the lab's sample refrigerator. She approached with caution, hands cradling something small and white.

"Don't let anybody see it," Manny cautioned. Roberta nodded silently and tucked her unbuttoned lab coat tighter around her body, concealing a delicate navy dress she chose to wear that day instead of her normal scrubs. She opened the FOUP's door and dropped the food inside before gently closing it again.

"Chicken," Theo commented after inspecting it through the visor in his shield. "Three days old by the look of the moisture level."

"How did you do that?" Roberta asked in amazement.

"Moisture, carbohydrate, and protein sensors aligned with the farms harvest data," Theo explained pointing to each one in turn. "There is also an RFID tracking sensor and I threw in an inexpensive AI chip." His explanation drove more questions from the gathered scientists, falling on Theo like rain on an apple tree. As groups took turns inspecting the FOUP and Greenie II, unsure which was more interesting, James pulled Manny aside and whispered, "Where did you find this guy?"

Manny smiled slyly. "My neighbor. He was at ARS as the Chief Technical Engineer." He left out the solitary confinement part.

"Impressive," James confirmed, admiration reflected in his eyes. He paused thoughtfully before continuing. "I don't know a lot about the technical aspects, but do you understand what this means financially?"

Manny looked his friend in the eye and slowly nodded. "Profit may be just around the corner."

James grinned widely and smoothed out the wrinkles of his blue coverall as if preparing for a presentation. "No, my friend, profit is already here," he replied confidently. "The solar went active today—eight Megawatt-hours produced just today! We are officially off the grid." He extended his hand to shake Manny's, aware of Manny's injured arm and retracting it quickly. Manny reached with his left hand instead and gave an awkward backhanded handshake.

"That is amazing!" Manny exclaimed, his voice ringing out in joy throughout the farm. He noticed Theo looking their way with a smile on his face. Meanwhile, Roberta stopped asking questions and strode towards them, her beautiful skirt billowing as she moved.

James smiled at her approach and grabbed her hand in his own, as he spoke animatedly about how each panel engaged its own micro-inverter to produce enough power to feed the farm. He explained they still needed to activate the battery system so they could run all night without taking energy from the grid.

He gestured animatedly. "The best part is, I've been calculating delivery losses and packaging losses, and with this type of drone, plus the tracking we'll do for every FOUP, we should be able to minimize our losses down to about five percent."

Theo stepped forward, adjusting the visor of his shield. "Actually." He felt suddenly very aware of the other faces in the room. "From my calculations, I believe it could be less than a two percent loss. Of course, I defer to you all to establish that."

A deep laugh rippled through the room, causing Theo to relax. Manny patted James on the back and gave him an encouraging smile. "Maybe you can get a little help with the accounting department too."

James smiled widely and chuckled along with them all. "Damn right, I could!" He turned to Theo and asked, "How expensive are the sensors and the chips?"

Theo reached into his pocket and pulled out a handful of the sensors. He poured some into James' hand as if they were sand and said, "I would guess less than two percent of the FOUP cost. Chips are cheap, that PVDF plastic is the main cost driver."

Stunned by this news, James took a moment to register what he heard, did another mental calculation, and turned to Manny. "I think we have a viable business now. This was our last loss leader. We better start reformatting the whole business plan."

Roberta stepped up beside James, gently placing her arm around his waist and pulling him closer. She added with confidence, "No more reliance on outside funding and no more restocking during shortages." Then she looked across at Manny, her eyes filled with admiration, and said, "You need to come on board full-time as the CEO. Enough of this part-time business."

Manny took in everyone's expressions in the quiet room. He was involved in almost every aspect of their work: from his fifteen years of studying technical agriculture, his writings, his training manuals, and his supply chain studies, to helping build the White Cube research algorithms. He looked down at his cancer-stricken arm while a weak smile tugged at the corners of his mouth. He lifted it up slowly and declared firmly, "I'm in."

He held up his arm again and proposed James to take on the CFO role as a full-time position. Everyone agreed. Manny speculated that James was thinking of the consequences, including leaving his finance position at the Controllers.

Manny raised his hand once more into the air and captured their attention. "And one more nomination—I would like Theo to come on board as Chief Technical Officer." They all glanced toward the drone hovering above Theo's head. Roberta exchanged a doubtful look with James, but their reservations faded as the group erupted into cheers.

Manny beamed confidently. "We may not have much money until we get it going, but I think we just solved the last-mile delivery problem." He thought fleetingly of the cancer in his arm and the looming lockdown. "God forbid there are no macro-forces to stop us."

James and Roberta linked arms and grinned at each other, both thrilled that three years of hard work finally paid off. The group splintered into smaller clusters; some surrounded Theo and Greenie, while others crowded around video monitors displaying an array of graphs. Their energy intermingled and crackled, infusing the air with electricity.

Manny lingered with James and Roberta, chatting about trivialities. Suddenly, James pulled Roberta closer and planted a kiss on her cheek before rounding on Manny. "Alright, partner. Spill it."

Caught off-guard but knowing exactly what James was asking about, Manny tried to deflect.

Roberta didn't let him get away with this as she stepped back from James and moved swiftly to Manny, her hand wrapping firmly around his bandaged one as she gently flipped his hat off his head with an agility that seemed almost effortless. Her voice was firm yet gentle when she spoke again, "Start explaining right now, mister."

Only a few people around them noticed the commotion, but their attention soon shifted back to their own conversations. Manny politely asked for his hat back, which Roberta allowed him to take, and he slowly placed it back over the bandage on his scalp all while keeping eye contact with both James and Roberta.

"Alright," Manny finally agreed, his tone one of resigned acceptance. "Can we go somewhere private first?"

Roberta clasped hold of James' hand and pulled him along after her towards one of the side conference rooms. As soon as they went inside, Manny told the story, breaking down each emotion as he revealed the details. Roberta's tears welled up in response and James threw an arm around his bro, feeling similarly overwhelmed. Even Manny fought back tears—acceptance seemed to be the only viable option left at this stage—he experienced denial last year, anger quickly followed, bargaining was almost nonexistent, and depression lasted for what felt like ages. But amidst all of these emotions lay a glimmer of hope, perhaps in the form of a vaccine thousands of miles away.

Roberta wrapped her arms around Manny in a motherly hold, nearly swallowing him up whole. James surrounded both of them like a bear. Maybe acceptance was not so bad after all.

CHAPTER 23
Remedy might the answer be,

Three days went by after all of the happenings at the Sunnyside Farm, so Manny had little time to focus on the doctor's checkup scheduled for this morning. His stomach felt like a sack of rocks while taking a Beeze to the hospital, traveling on the same path taken many times before. The glass doors of the Beeze opened with a whoosh and Manny made his way down the familiar hallway, passing patient rooms filled with those suffering from malignancies. He checked in with the same desk attendant as before, steeling himself against whatever news this appointment might bring. He'd already gone through eighteen procedures—biopsies and surgeries—looking for either a negative result or cancers in any of its four stages.

Once inside, Dr. Cheryl Blanding greeted Manny with a polite, "Good morning, Dr. Rio." He reminded her once again she could call him Manny. She smiled and promised to do so, asking him to call her Cheryl as well.

"Okay, Cheryl, please tell Dr. McKenna I'm here for the checkup," he said while holding up his bandaged hand. The wound from his last surgery healed but still itched relentlessly. He moved his fingers along the scar on his scalp where he used to wear a hat and bandage.

Cheryl smiled again and waved him in the direction of a waiting area outside one of the exam rooms. "Have a seat, I'll let her know you are here."

Manny sat down and set his bag on the seat next to him before taking in his surroundings. After several minutes passed, Rosita finally poked her head through the door and beckoned him into an exam room. Small talk did not work very well again, so Manny resigned himself to going through the motions with his stoic doctor.

The room was smaller than other OR suites containing robotic systems, but it held its own set of intricate equipment attached to the walls and ceiling: high-intensity lights that shone down from above; gizmos that hummed softly as they worked away; and a cast that Manny built himself for inspection by Rosita with her expert eye that appreciated the thought put into every material within it.

Rosita pulled her glasses down from her forehead, studying closely the PVDF material on Manny's cast. She ran a finger along its surface, feeling for any irregularities before inspecting the stitches. "Pretty good," she muttered. Then, spotting a whitish streak, she leaned in closer. "But I'm seeing a rhizomatous streak here." Her voice held a note of concern as she pointed to it.

Manny leaned in, but he couldn't see what Rosita was pointing at. He asked, "And that means?"

"It could be melanoma trying to reestablish itself. We took out a lot of tissue during the surgery, including your RFID chip, but I think we may have missed some cells." Moving on to inspect Manny's scalp from the previous surgery, Rosita felt an underlying tension absent moments before.

She moved to the wall and grabbed one of the gizmos to extend a reddish light over Manny's head, then dropped her shield to inspect in closer detail. "I see the rhizomes here, too. It's spreading."

He gazed up into Rosita's eyes as she continued. "The Cancer Board may have been right the first time. Two of them wanted to rate your melanoma as stage 3. After checking your algorithms, they decided to rate it a stage 2 instead."

He shuffled nervously in his seat, close to tears yet unable to speak as he processed what he had heard. Finally, he gathered his courage to ask her, "What's next?"

"Chemotherapy," Rosita answered confidently, her eyes dropped to the floor, rarely seen from her normally stoic demeanor. As Manny studied

Rosita's face, he noticed how the past year took its toll on her, though she appeared much younger than the forty years he estimated her age to be, there was a weariness around her eyes not there before. He tried to ask more questions but he already knew the answers. That which doesn't kill you weakens you beyond recovery. Manny saw the other cancer patients, their bodies frail, their skin a pasty gray hue, hairless, with brittle bones, and deteriorating mental health—the cost of chemotherapy. "I thought we were going to do immunotherapy?"

"That's only got a fifteen percent chance of improvement," Rosita clarified. "We need to get this out of you faster." She pulled up a stool and sat down directly in front of Manny, her body radiating determination.

Manny pondered that and then replied, "But chemo isn't much better."

"Forty percent or so." As she spoke, Manny noticed a tear drop from her cheek. Quickly, she wiped it away and glanced nervously at Manny, as if afraid he noticed the emotion. Manny did not recall seeing Rosita show anything other than complete professionalism before this moment. Reaching for a wrinkled handkerchief from the pocket of her lab coat, Rosita delicately dabbed at her eyes and cheeks, taking care not to smudge the thin layer of eye shadow that perfectly accentuated her blue irises.

Manny sighed heavily. A forty-percent chance of improvement was not much better than before. It was not much hope at all.

Rosita began crying uncontrollably, and out of shame she quickly turned away from him and leaned against the side desk, pressing her head into her hands as tears kept flowing freely. He knew that there was nothing more than a professional relationship between them. In fact, Manny found Rosita very attractive but respected her too much to think about her otherwise.

"I'm so sorry," she said into the wall between sobs. "This is so unprofessional of me."

Though he was expecting a stoic response, Rosita looked up at him incredulously before finally succumbing to tears. Her sadness seemed beyond what the diagnosis would bring; something else clearly struck a chord with her.

Manny mustered up the courage to pry further, Manny decided to be bold. "Rosita…Rosita, what's going on?"

She hesitated for a moment before answering one word—a name that sent chills through his spine, "Maggie."

In that moment, Manny knew exactly why she cried and could only drawl out a soft "oh shit" in response. He quickly stepped forward to steady her, wrapping his arms around her shoulders as she racked with sobs. "We'll fight this," Manny said, doing his best to comfort her as she swayed.

But Rosita stepped away from him, looking confused and uncertain. "You have your own problems, Manny," she said pointedly, using his first name deliberately to show that she trusted him enough to share such intimate details about her daughter. She respected Dr. Rio despite his stubbornness, impatience, and straightforwardness; after all, they'd known each other for two years already.

Manny realized the significance of Rosita finally addressing him by his first name. He suggested it numerous times before but Rosita never felt comfortable breaking protocol, until now. His heart sank as he looked into Rosita's eyes and saw the fear so familiar to him. This news of Maggie came unexpectedly. His cancer buddy, Maggie, was just a little girl and was diagnosed with the same disease. He felt the emotion swelling up inside him, but he managed to stay composed and asked in a soft yet determined voice, "How bad is it?"

"No worse than yours," Rosita replied bleakly. "She's got the same rhizomatous tubers as you. Stage 3. We're looking at four or five weeks before it spreads to her organs."

The reality of what this meant for Maggie hit Manny hard: Early onset cancer is tougher on young bodies. Manny let that sink in for a moment and asked, "Surgery?"

"No," Rosita said flatly. "You can't remove the lymphatic system. I must use directed chemotherapy to attack the systems."

Manny considered this option for a few moments before taking a deep breath and deciding to address what he thought about all along—clinical trials at Stanford. This was initially supposed to be a long-term goal, but now it was an urgent necessity. "There is another option," he said determinedly, taking a step forward. "For both of us."

As Rosita began inputting information into her tablet, she paused and glanced up at her patient. Manny recognized the hint of skepticism. "What do you mean?" she asked.

"They developed mRNA vaccines."

Rosita couldn't help but snicker. To a doctor, Manny's plan must have sounded like something from a science-fiction novel. An intelligent man facing mortality. "That's too far in the future. You need help now," she reminded him.

But Manny new the past six months transformed him: empathy replaced the old him. He stepped closer, his gaze penetrating her eyes. "Let's get a six-pack of our blood samples," he said firmly. "I already called my friend at Stanford, Dr. John Strunk, we went to NYU Pod together. He works in the cancer research lab and suggested that we rush the blood samples for Phase 2 clinical trials."

Rosita stared intently at Manny for a moment before grabbing him and shaking his shoulders in disbelief. "You know Dr. John Strunk?" she asked excitedly. She bombarded Manny with question after question, her mind desperately piecing together the puzzle. "And he said he would take Maggie?" she asked eagerly, her voice trembling slightly with hope and fear.

Manny's eyes held an intense seriousness as he watched Rosita process his words. "Yes, but we have to hurry and get on a plane," he declared. "John said we should send him the blood samples, and they'll take a week to prepare the vaccine. We get four shots over two weeks."

Rosita entered the data into her electronic pad as Manny spoke, and when she finished, she looked back up at him. He had let her take the time to absorb all the information without interruption. "I've been studying his work for two years now, ever since Maggie…" she trailed off sadly.

"Me too," Manny quietly confessed. "When I was first diagnosed, I thought I was a goner. So, I scoured the databases looking for my own cure."

Rosita remained thoughtfully quiet, her gaze shifting between Manny and the floor. Finally, she raised her head and looked directly into his eyes with an expression of determination. She reached for the buttons of her blouse and began to undo them, one by one. Manny was stunned, yet Rosita's gaze carried no hint of seduction or flirtation. When she finished unbuttoning the top two buttons, she stretched out the collar of her blouse, tucking some strands of her long black hair behind her ear to uncover a faint scar along her collarbone. "Stage 2 melanoma. Ten years ago."

Manny gasped in shock. Everything made sense now.

"Melanoma runs in families," Rosita said, her voice thick with tears. "My father had it, and I have it, and now I gave it to Maggie...I'm the reason she's sick."

"No," Manny said fiercely, shaking his head. "That's not how it works. It's not your fault."

But even as he spoke, the words felt empty compared to the weight of her guilt and terror. Science can be a cruel master—and Rosita had already seen its ability to rob people of their futures. She wept softly into his chest, and Manny gently held her until she was ready to look up at him again.

"My father and I were lucky, because we had it late in life," she sniffled. "But when you miss the early warning signs, it's...it's too late."

Manny recalled the photo in the lobby of her office. "Your father?"

Rosita was quiet at first, debating the desire to share personal information, then explained how her parents started a prosthetics company that donated their products to those who needed them most. But as she spoke, he noticed her eyes wander away from him; what must have been pride for her family became shrouded in sadness before she began to speak again about her daughter. "Yes, he and my mother live in Berkeley."

"Well then we better get those blood samples going and book our flights to Stanford," Manny said soothingly, wanting nothing more than to help

Rosita find some hope in this awful situation. His words seemed to shock her out of the depths of despair as he mentioned the phase 1 trials results—seventy-five percent cure rate—results not available to the public.

Manny stared into her hopeful eyes, knowing that if the public saw the results of the clinical trial, the chance of getting into the trial would be gone forever.

Just then Maggie strutted through the door, wearing a bright purple tutu and neon green sneakers. Her eyes grew wide when she saw her mother and Manny standing so close together, both their faces damp with tears. She stopped and waited for them to move apart before quietly asking Manny, "Mommy cried when she told me. You got it too, don't you?"

Manny ignored the question and let out a slight chuckle. Rosita smiled as her face softened and spoke to her daughter, "Maggie, we are going on a trip."

Eagerness filled Maggie's face as her eyes darted from her mom to Manny. She excitedly asked, "Really? A trip?"

Manny moved to where he set his bag down before and fumbled through it to pull out a present for Maggie: an oddly shaped cylinder with some black contents visible through one side. He handed it over to Maggie. Rosita looked on cautiously. Manny said, "I brought this for you."

Maggie took the cylinder in both hands and turned it over curiously. It was cold to the touch but felt strangely light compared to its size. She asked, "What is it?"

Rosita spoke up, recognition in her voice. "Is that one of those FOUPs?"

Manny was surprised she knew what it was. He supposed she must have been studying food sciences recently. He nodded and said, "Yes, but what's inside is what I think you'll like."

Maggie fiddled with it, eventually finding the latch and opening the container. "Pull it out," Manny instructed. Maggie obliged, her eyes widening at the sight of two baggies filled with food. She looked up at Manny with curiosity.

He smiled tenderly at her curiosity as he explained what was inside each one. "The dark one is a cake we made yesterday at the farm," he said fondly. "Chocolate cake."

"Really?" Rosita asked with disbelief in her voice. "Real cake?"

Manny realized these were White Cube people, unfamiliar with eating real food due to doctors receiving fairly low pay in the Contros-run system. "Yes, real cake. And the other bag has two fresh eggs, some chocolate, and a bag of instant-cake mix. You can make your own cake tonight!"

Maggie eagerly plucked out a piece of the offered cake and lifted it to her nose. She inhaled deeply before turning it around in her small hands to examine its unique shape and texture. Finally, she popped it into her mouth, eyes widening in amazement at its flavor. Quickly grabbing another piece, she rushed over to her mother and offered it eagerly. "Mommy, you have to try this!"

Rosita enjoyed the cake, savoring each bite while rolling her eyes back in bliss. "I've had real cake before, but nothing like this." She gazed at Manny adoringly as she inspected the eggs with reverence. "Fresh eggs, oh my."

"This is what I do," Manny said dramatically as he gestured with his bandaged hand.

Maggie swallowed her mouthful of cake, the chocolate frosting smeared across her lips. With a full mouth, she asked, "So, where are we going?"

CHAPTER 24
Devices fight with constant glee,

The tension crackled as two Board of Controllers members squared off at either end of the elongated meeting table. Words flew between them, each sentence heavy with aggression. At the head of the table sat Brock Masterson, Director of the Governing Body of Chelsea Pod One, his face an impassive mask of authority. His tie-breaking vote held enormous power in this room, where decisions made by the algorithms every second directly impacted the lives of all citizens within the pod. The wall-mounted monitors beside him calculated algorithms requiring no human oversight, unless something set off a warning flag. Brock listened to these two bickering for fifteen minutes now. It was exhausting, hearing them argue day after day.

Brock's gaze shifted to Claudia Rosenberg and Andrew Bagsund, two Board members of opposing views arguing passionately over the fate of one citizen. But Brock was very proud of his group and grew accustomed to the frequent debates.

Claudia summarized her point of view after this lengthy discussion. "We have a case here where a previously perfectly healthy child contracted melanoma cancer and is being treated by a wonderful doctor's office using the latest Leonardo surgery," she said with conviction. "The algorithms are wrong to give her only twelve years. We know this will inevitably become a self-fulfilling prophecy—her credits would be limited, her time allocations would shrink, and she'd be doomed to an early death. We cannot let this happen to another child."

But Andrew couldn't contain himself any longer. He rose to his feet, towering over everyone else in the room like an angry bear. "This girl went through seven Mohs surgeries already!" he bellowed. "The algorithms are correct once again. She's going to die from this disease no matter what we do."

The tension in the room was palpable as Claudia and Brock exchanged glances. They both knew that this conversation was not over.

Claudia continued arguing, emphasizing certain words for dramatic effect. "Her surgeon is one of the best robotically-assisted surgeons in the world! That doctor is a genius at the Leonardo tool!"

Andrew paused, scanning each person's expression before making his final point. "And she is being treated at her mother's hospital, and that still hasn't cured her." Andrew collapsed back into his chair with finality, running his fingers distractedly through his wild red hair.

Claudia took a deep breath and shifted her gaze to Brock. "We have got to change the algorithms' responses to stop being so drastic. They are not taking into consideration all the mitigating factors. Each case and each citizen is unique. We cannot dump them all into tight compartments of generalities and apply them to everyone within the group!"

"That's why the algorithms exist!" Andrew interjected.

Claudia's nostrils flared and her hands balled into fists as the words shot out of her mouth. "And that's why we exist! To stop the algorithms from controlling the outcome. They were designed to predict the outcome, not fulfill them!"

Brock's face was unreadable, but his body language spoke loudly. With a slow and steady movement, he held up his hands in a universal sign for silence. "Okay, that's enough. This is the same argument you have every time there is a disagreement." The tension hung heavy as lead in the air around them, an uncomfortable reminder that this had happened before and would happen again if no one did anything about it. Brock stood up with a single graceful motion and cast an icy stare to each person in the room, a look that said "Don't even think of talking back to me or else." He walked towards the large video screens at the end of the room.

He paused in front of each monitor, feeling the gaze of countless cameras and sensors watching his every move. His voice echoed through the room as he spoke, emphasizing each word with a flourish. "We have been given a great responsibility…to use our advanced technology to ensure that our citizens can live full and happy lives."

"Although I recognize your points, Andrew," Brock said, leaning forward and folding his hands together on the conference room table. "I cannot ignore the fact that our algorithms are linked to an increased risk of premature death. We must find a way to adjust our formulas to reduce or eliminate these risks."

Andrew nodded slowly, a glimmer of hope in his eyes that perhaps he did not lose his case after all.

Claudia opened her mouth to ask a question before Brock held up his hand, stopping her in mid-sentence. "This will take time to implement," he spoke.

Relieved, Andrew sat upright and gave a slow smile.

"But what about this child? Are we to simply accept her early death as a data input?" Claudia asked, raising her voice in disbelief.

Brock motioned for her to be quiet again, but not before she had already registered the tragedy of the situation. She slumped back into her chair and looked down at her electronic pad, which showed a picture of little Maggie McKenna smiling up at her mother.

"I will propose an override that allows us to modify the outcome of this case while still protecting other users," Brock continued, bringing up a menu on his shielding display. He paused for a fraction of a second then spoke firmly: "Set the lifespan of Margaret Anne McKenna, Chelsea Pod One, at sixteen years old."

CHAPTER 25
Children know what occurred so far,

"How did it go, Dad?" Alex asked into the shield. His father's voice was unusually low and sad, making it unbearably clear that something went wrong with their father's cancer surgery. The twins held their breath, their eyes glued to the video screen waiting for their father to tell them the outcome.

"Tell us the truth, Daddy," Amy demanded sternly. "Otherwise, you wouldn't be calling so soon. Tell us how the surgery went."

Manny closed his eyes as he spoke, unable to look his children in the eye. "Well, kids...the cancer is spreading." He paused and ran a hand over his scalp where surgeries left small red scars. "In my arm and on my head."

Amy gasped and tears welled up in both of the twins' eyes from behind their shields. Manny felt helpless in the face of his children's pain. Alex held back his tears and tried to ask more questions as Manny filled them in on the details of the rhizomes reaching into his lymphatic system like bamboo shoots trying to go under the neighbor's fence.

"But I'm coming out to see you," he promised them before more questions could be asked. "My friend from college is working on an mRNA vaccine. He says it has a seventy-five percent cure rate." Amy nodded and released a sob while Alex wrapped an arm around her shoulders.

"Can you get it? The vaccine?" Alex asked.

"At Stanford," Manny explained. "That's why I'm coming out to see you."

The twins at first remained speechless as they absorbed the information. Then with an impulse, they could not contain their excitement as more questions came pouring out. They explained how they regularly delivered FOUP's to Dr. Strunk at Stanford as Manny suggested.

Manny listened to the excitement in their voices. "That's not all. I'm sending a load of another thousand FOUPs to Slug Farm. And wait until you see what we've done to them!"

The three of them felt hope mixed with fear.

CHAPTER 26
Engage a flight to reach afar,

Manny typed away on his laptop, confirming blood test details with Rosita before sending them to Stanford. He placed the call to Dr. John Strunk, expecting a rush of excitement and relief as he relayed the news that the samples were on their way. Instead, he heard a tinge of worry lacing John's voice as John explained the complexities of administering this medicine.

"Really? I didn't realize they expired so quickly," Manny said in response to John's warning about the limited shelf-life of mRNA vaccines.

"And these things are bloody expensive," John clarified. "Our funding only covers one vaccine recipe per patient. That's four doses in a two-week period. If we miss our window for this batch, it would cost more than a year of your salary to replace it."

Manny knew all too well the value of money. He was employed by a startup, and his pay was meager now, and may stay low for the next couple of years. He glanced up at the plain ceiling in his cabin—the Contros had not kicked him out yet. They also did not shorten his lifespan as much as he'd expected, considering the small amount he noticed on his algorithms. "I'm booking the flight with Rosita and Maggie in a few minutes," Manny finally said.

"It looks like someone in high places is looking out for Maggie," John remarked. "The universe put her in the right spot at the right time for her to get into this clinical trial." John didn't seem satisfied with the comment as he cautioned, "Just don't celebrate too soon. We don't know what comes next."

Manny replied, "I'll let you know our flight times once I book them. We're planning to stay somewhere close to the twins when we get there."

John asked one more question before they parted ways. "Do you think the lockdowns will spread?"

Manny nodded his head slowly as he read the latest reports on how quickly the virus was spreading through various regions in pods. The thought made him anxious for his own health, as well as where he would be if the lockdown did happen. "Looks like it's just a matter of time," he concluded grimly.

"I know. Looks like it's going east from the Chicago region. At this rate, it could hit New York in days."

Manny thought of being stuck in a pod during an outbreak and it made him anxious and uneasy, especially since he recently read the reports of what happened when the pandemic first struck the nation back in 2020. Hospitals became so overrun with pandemic patients that other types of patients barely got any treatment for their issues and ended up dying while waiting.

The two men parted after sharing their grave concerns about the situation, and Manny began preparations for his flight to the west coast. He activated his shield and double-clicked on Dr. Rosita McKenna's icon to confirm the last details before tomorrow's flight to New York but instead of her cheerful voice, he heard nothing but heavy sobs.

"Rosita?" Manny asked, confused. "Are you okay? What happened?"

"Manny...they changed the algorithms for Maggie!" she managed to get out between uncontrollable tears. "They adjusted her lifespan down to sixteen years! I just checked all her files and credits. It's true. They are trying to kill my little girl!"

Manny was stunned at the news and questioned its reality. But he must take action quickly. He tried to reassure her they would figure something out. "We will get this fixed! But first, we have to get our asses out to the Stanford Pod! Let's go!"

Rosita nodded, her face pale and drawn but determined. "You're right. We can do this." She paused, her voice turning quiet. "Just don't tell Maggie anything about this, okay? I don't want her to worry."

Manny agreed that it would be better for Maggie not to know. Taking a deep breath, he opened his menu and logged into the travel site he used every time he flew out to visit the twins in California. As soon as his screen lit up with the booking site, a warning flashed across the top of the screen: JFK Airport Pod just went into lockdown. Contact tracing also revealed someone traveled from the O'Hare Airport Pod to the New Jersey Pod, and it went into lockdown too.

Panic ran through Manny's body and he quickly dialed Rosita again. When she answered, her voice rang high with emotion—She'd just heard about the lockdown too. She was frantic and all attempts at calming her thoughts were futile.

CHAPTER 27

Power steps in with all their might,

The World Health Organization, known commonly as the WHO, held the driving force behind all of the pandemic-related forecasts, and as a result of the Release from Pandemic Act of 2045, CATACS—the Controllers of Agriculture, Time, Authority, Credit, and Substances—became the fourth branch of government in nearly every country. This interconnecting network quickly superseded local, regional, and national powers, allowing executive, legislative, and judicial branches to remain in place, but relinquish first place to the new branch. The Pod Police meted out punishments to those opposing such measures.

Years passed since the world had witnessed a pandemic on this scale. Thus, each lockdown announcement caused trepidations among people who feared that 2020 might repeat itself. The authorities used contact tracing methods, such as RFID technology, to quickly trace potentially infected individuals and prevent huge catastrophes from occurring. It created an ethical struggle between individual interests and the collective good, but it was a necessary sacrifice for protecting humanity.

Dr. Curtis Fauci, the Chief Medical Officer of the World Health Organization, a distant relative of his famous namesake from the 2020 pandemic, stepped into the President's Oval Office at the White House. The Chief of Staff summoned Dr. Fauci on short notice as news of a worldwide lockdown spread like wildfire. With his petite frame, Dr. Fauci stood confidently in a perfectly tailored three-piece suit, complete with a matching kerchief that echoed the color of his extended shield – a rare touch many other medical professionals overlooked. As always, he was the most informed and intellectually on-point in the briefing. But while Dr. Fauci was brilliant, he sometimes struggled to express himself using layman's terms instead of scientific language when he spoke. The President gestured to him, signaling it was his turn to speak, and his piercing gaze landed on the scientist.

Dr. Fauci said, "Mr. President, we are looking at a growing lockdown situation that may or may not be nearing containment."

As he cleared his throat to speak, the Chief of Staff shifted in his chair, his lips pressed into a thin line, an unmistakable furrow between his brows as he squinted at the numbers in front of him. He looked up from the papers and spoke, "You are suggesting this may grow farther?"

Dr. Fauci hesitated for a moment before responding in a slow and measured tone, "It's rather hard to predict with any degree of accuracy."

The Chief of Staff, an accountant by trade and well-known for putting large teams together quickly, appeared uncharacteristically grim. An aide suddenly informed him, "We have surpassed the 72 pod lockdowns we encountered during the Miami incident fifteen years ago. That figure is now up to 79 pods after we locked down 4 more airports and 6 more pods following the contact tracing."

Dr. Fauci frowned and mused worriedly, "The New York area is what I am particularly worried about. We already imposed lockdowns on all the major airports and three of the surrounding pods. But unfortunately, I fear we may need to take even stricter measures soon."

CHAPTER 28
Friends get back to their delight,

Although Naoko spoke basic English, the communication shields were able to process her complex Japanese words and accurately translate them for Coop. As they conversed into the night, their relationship strengthened from the months of him delivering FOUPs and harvests for Sunnyside. Naoko helped guide him through the maze of pods that entered into lockdown. The virus already spread throughout Wisconsin and began spreading to the other states to the east. Thanks to her knowledge and hours of conversation, Coop was near his destination: Chelsea Pod One in the New York region.

He knew that if he kept moving, he could avoid the lockdowns. Food was not a problem either; every 40 miles along the inter-region highways were White Cube Centers where he could purchase the ever-so-familiar gelatinous food pouches if needed.

The last time he went this long while avoiding a lockdown was during the big pandemic five years ago, when the pandemic swallowed up Indiana, Iowa, and Illinois whole. But now, with this lockdown looming over him, Coop wanted nothing more than to settle with Naoko at Sunnyside Farm, his new home.

Naoko punched the coordinates into the GPS and a route appeared on Coop's screen. As she zoomed in, Coop saw smaller patches of yellow creating figures like stars across a dark sky. These were the pods that Naoko tracked since he left Chicago. New York already glowed red on the screen. Coop quickly directed Betsy onto the highway, towards Scranton, Pennsylvania. For the next few hours, he flew down long stretches of road clear of traffic, took exits past small towns, and navigated around Bridgeport to finally reach the Port Jefferson Ferry terminal late in the day. As they rolled towards the dock, every vehicle seemed to be heading for the same destination. Coop drove Betsy closer to one of the larger haulers at the back of the queue and stayed seated inside his cabin.

Coop watched as people got out to stretch their legs while waiting for the ferry to finish docking, but most stayed inside their vehicles to avoid close contact with anybody. Everywhere he looked there was a reminder that self-containment was an absolute if he was going to make it home before lockdown, a proposition that seemed more inevitable by the minute. Finally, with a deep shudder, Betsy moved onto the Atlantic City Ferry and started crossing Long Island Sound.

The ferry churned through the choppy waters of the harbor. Coop remained in self-containment but ventured out onto the rear platform of Betsy where he could breathe in the briny air while still staying in self-containment. As they drew closer to Long Island, he made out the shapes of buildings in the distance, their glass facades glinting in the sunlight.

The Long Island Pod loomed ahead of them; a sprawling mass of glass buildings surrounded by a shimmering sea. To its west lay JFK Airport Pod, a vast metropolis centered around one of the busiest airports in the world. The Controllers separated the two pods years ago to reduce the spread of the viruses during lockdowns.

People and vehicles packed the ferry to capacity, every inch of deck space taken up by long haulers continuing their routes or people trying to reach loved ones before the pandemic lockdown took effect. Despite the crowd, the ferry swayed only slightly in the breeze. Coop clung to the railing of his private platform and marveled at how something so massive could move so smoothly through the waves.

He tapped on his shield, sending Naoko another message while squinting at a small square off in the distance.

"I'm still on the ferry, but I can see Sunnyside now," he said.

Her face lit up with a smile and she replied in Japanese, "Kisushitai, Cooper-san." He smiled back and heard the words that echoed around him. "I want to kiss you," she said.

CHAPTER 29

Code for escape but 'tis too late,

Manny strode across the length of his cabin, his hand occasionally running through the mess of hair atop his head. His thoughts looped around a single idea: that every day of this lockdown was another day for melanoma to spread inside his body and leave him one of the many victims of the overburdened hospitals.

He felt helpless until a ping went off in his shield, signaling an incoming call. He stopped pacing, arms crossed against his chest, and took a deep breath before accepting the call.

"Manny," came the familiar voice of his friend, Captain Mickey Killian. She asked, "Have you been watching the news?"

He heard the tension in her voice and, with her call coming in an hour after the news of a possible lockdown dropped, Manny knew why she called. "Of course," Manny replied. "Do you know if the Bronx and Chelsea Pods are going into lockdown?"

"Listen carefully," she began quietly, glancing around her nearly empty Pod Police station to make sure no one heard her, even though shield calls were all monitored by AI bots anyway. "I think I'm pregnant."

Manny let out a heavy exhale. "Shit," he muttered under his breath, realizing that this was their code for when something dangerous like a lockdown was impending. "Am I the father?"

"Yes." With the one-word answer, Manny understood that the Chelsea Pod was about to go into lockdown. Contact tracing must have followed somebody out of the JFK Airport Pod. With this knowledge, he pushed further and asked, "How far along are we?"

"Eight months." From Mickey's response, Manny knew it was very close. Any day or hour now a harsh bubble of protection would lockdown Chelsea Pod One.

Manny looked at Mickey, his oldest friend. He needed to tell her the truth. "I have stage 3 now," he said. His voice cracked, and he dropped his gaze to the floor as he explained the biopsies, surgeries, and heartbreak he'd gone through for the last few weeks. He finished with a soft voice, "I wanted to tell you, but I…"

Tears streaked down Mickey's face as Manny spoke; she knew of the previous surgeries, but not about this recent diagnosis. Manny remained strong like the river—too proud to ask for help when he knew it was available. She wanted to both hug him and strangle him at the same time. Softly, she said, "You should have told me. I could have helped you, you know."

Manny nodded slowly in understanding as the tears threatened to fall from his eyes too. He knew that she would always help him if he simply asked. Now that lockdown was imminent, he realized how much trouble he was really in. "I thought it would be over quickly, but now I'm in trouble. I need your help."

Mickey spoke, her words gentle yet firm. "Anything. What do you need?"

Manny sighed heavily, realizing how much he previously underestimated the danger of the situation. "I need to stay out of lockdowns, I need to know which ones are happening so I can avoid a tether—if I don't get to a vaccine fast, I'll die in lockdown." He looked at Mickey pleadingly. "I have to get to Stanford as soon as possible."

She paused, gauging the risk involved in helping him. The AI systems already heard too much of the conversation. "That's quite a feat considering how far along I am," Mickey replied guardedly, continuing to use the code words they both understood. The shifting attitudes of this woman according to the AI bots' previous readings must be totally confusing by now. Married to a woman for fifteen years and now pregnant with a man's baby?

"I better get back in time," Manny said, using language tailored for the AI bots surely listening to the conversation.

"In four weeks then," she replied coolly.

"Updates every day until then?" Manny asked.

* * *

As Manny signed off, Mickey let out a deep breath and turned around to face the chaos of the police station bullpen. The fluorescent lights flickered overhead as Gary out in the squad room motioned for her to come over. She made her way through the maze of desks and officers, trying to ignore the growing pit in her stomach. He spoke into his communication shield with furrowed brows and a pinched expression, motioning for her to wait until he finished the conversation. "I just talked to my friend in the Controllers," he said, looking around to see if anyone else heard him. "He thinks we are going into lockdown tonight."

"I think you are right," Mickey replied, her gaze lingering on Gary. She knew all too well how Sarah slowly drained away his enthusiasm and ambition with her icy grip. A great effort broke him free from her clutches. Mickey asked, "Listen, I've got an important job to do. I'm going to need your help."

Gary nodded eagerly, relieved to finally feel part of the team again. The dark clouds hovering over him seemed to be lifting. "You name it, Captain."

CHAPTER 30
Change of plans with family's fate,

Rosita felt her heart drop as she listened to the news of the lockdowns, knowing it changed their plans instantly. Manny's voice cut through the air over their communications shields. "Head to Sunnyside right now! The airport is closed!"

Rosita's eyes widened in disbelief and desperation as she looked around for an answer. "I know, what are we going to do?"

Manny could tell what was going through her mind and quickly said, "I have a plan. Grab your stuff, but make it light because there won't be much room. Get to Sunnyside Farm fast!"

"Why the farm?" Rosita asked anxiously.

"I'll send you the link. Get a Beeze and get out of Chelsea Pod before it goes into lockdown tonight! It should buy us another day or two." Manny shouted, desperation thick in his voice.

"I don't understand, they closed the airports," she protested, fear for her daughter lacing through her words. "How is that going to help? We'll just get trapped there."

Manny met her eyes and nodded reassuringly. "I told you, I have a way out." He double-clicked on the address and added softly, "Please get there quickly. We will use the ferry."

Manny's voice remained steady as he explained his plan: they would take a ferry out of town, but they needed to get there fast. Manny rushed back to his cabin and loaded up a dozen FOUPs filled with food, slinging them over one shoulder. He also grabbed Greenie, his faithful drone, and the bright blue backpack from an unforgettable trip taken with the twins before everything went to hell. The backpack seemed to weigh him down more than the food as he hurried around the corner to Theo's place. On his way there, he activated his shield and double-clicked to call Theo for help, knowing he could explain the rest of the plan once they were already on their way. "Theo, you home? I'm coming around the corner, I need your help."

When Manny arrived at Theo's cabin, he threw open the front door and rushed inside like a force of nature. He wore a patchwork of clothes, FOUPs bulging from his bag, and a knapsack slung over his shoulder while Greenie flew overhead.

Theo heard the panic in Manny's voice. "What's going on? Why the rush? I don't understand."

"We're going into lockdown tonight," Manny replied. The whole scene was like a Tasmanian devil swirling through the door and coming to a stop in a cloud of dust. "We have to get to Sunnyside as fast as possible."

"Shit," Theo mumbled under his breath as he registered all of this information. Manny mentioned rumors about going into lockdown before, but now it was really happening.

Theo had already been in preparation mode, prepping for a last-minute escape to the farm just in case. He grabbed a bag and started packing his work from his desk. Then he snatched some random gadgets, tools, and equipment off of a shelf, and added them to the bag. As he had no family or friends to worry about leaving behind, he figured why not go to Sunnyside?

He went back to his desk and collected a handful of miscellaneous components and machines. With Greenie II hovering over him in follow-me mode, Theo gathered up all the chips, tools, and electronic pads that seemed useful. Who knew how long this lockdown would be? He was already working on improving existing ideas; perhaps this would give him the time he needed.

Manny watched with amusement as Theo went about packing up his work desk, marveling at the priorities Theo placed on his work versus what most people would have focused on—toiletries, mementos, and legal documents for instance. It was almost a video replay of Manny's own mad rush just moments before.

"Five minutes?" Theo asked Manny as he slung another bag over his shoulder.

With a deep breath, Manny explained the plan as Theo continued shoving odds and ends into his large carrying case. Manny said, "I'm heading out for the Stanford Hospital Pod," he said.

Theo shook his head. "The airports are closed."

Manny smiled. "I've got another idea." He zipped up the bag and flung it over a free shoulder as both men marched through the front door.

CHAPTER 31
All destined for pastures away,

Manny and Theo looked like two Pacific Crest Trail hikers as they left to take a Beeze to Sunnyside. Above their heads, Greenie I and Greenie II hovered with FOUPS in tow. Both men carried large duffle bags with other smaller bags consolidated over their shoulders. As they traveled, Manny briefed Theo on the details of their mission. Manny's heart raced as he thought of how quickly the gate could close, trapping them in an endless cycle of quarantine and travel restrictions.

Theo began making plans with someone at the farm, holding several shield calls end after end. Manny took a break and checked in with his fellow traveler, Rosita. He double-clicked on her name in his shield and asked, "Where are you?"

"I'm on Long Island Pod," came her quick reply. Relief flooded through Manny, knowing Rosita and Maggie escaped the Chelsea Pod before it locked down, but they both knew the lockdown could come at any moment for the Long Island Pod too.

The Beeze they rode in roared through the Chelsea gates and into Long Island Pod. A shiver ran up Manny's spine as he thought of the fate of those who were still stuck inside. Coop, their ticket out of here, awaited their arrival to take them across the ferry.

Manny remained connected to Rosita's call. She shared a view of Maggie, sitting comfortably with her hands clenched tightly together in her lap, eyes wide and unblinking as she stared out the window. Questions about the unknown that lay beyond the city limits must have filled

Maggie's head. Rosita nervously asked Manny if they would make it to their destination safely.

Manny calmed her worries and then disconnected from Rosita quickly, his fingers flying over the list of names in his visor as he searched for Coop's contact. Theo spoke quietly in the background, giving directions and instructions to someone else as Manny finally found the name in his visor. He double-clicked to contact Coop, waiting for a response as his stomach churned with anticipation. "Coop, are you at Sunnyside?"

"Yes, just backed up to the loading dock," Coop replied. "What's this thing they want to load up? Randy said he has a housing cube to load."

Manny frowned and shook his head in confusion. "I don't know what you're talking about. What housing cube?" Then he heard Theo's voice, thanking Randy before disconnecting the call. He turned to look at Theo with a question on his lips.

Theo just smiled and explained, "Randy has an isolation housing pod in case of a lockdown. And you're taking it for a ride. Perfect timing for a test run."

Coop nodded in understanding, then replied that they would finish loading the cargo into his truck, Betsy, right away. He reminded Manny that they must stay inside the hauler's isolation chamber for the journey ahead, and must avoid any contact with the hundreds of passing pods. As Coop continued speaking to Manny, a soft tapping sound came from Coop's door, and a figure in a full bunny suit came into view wearing a thick white protective suit covering the person's body from head to toe. The person was on the ladder next to Coop's truck, peering into the side window. Coop and the stranger both reached up to tap their protective shields twice to be able to speak with one another. Manny recognized Naoko right away and clicked to activate his viewer.

"Cooper-san," Naoko said. Then she saw Manny join the call. "Manny-san."

Through the viewer, Manny could see Naoko's almond-shaped eyes locked onto Coop's with an unwavering gaze. Coop was about ready to open the airlock, but then Naoko spoke again in perfect English, this time more sternly, "Do not open the lock."

Coop looked deflated. His hand wavered over the release button, but he put it back at his side and pleaded, "But, Naoko…"

Naoko continued on with her demand, but with loving eyes that sought out Coop's soul. "Our love can wait two more weeks, Cooper-san," she demanded, yet with a hint of tenderness mixed in there as well. "We must help Dr. Rio first."

The conversation now shifted into uncharted territory. Manny wanted to disconnect and allow his friends to discuss their longing in privacy.

Still looking into Naoko's eyes, Coop replied, "I'll be back in two weeks."

Naoko stayed at the window and her gaze softened somewhat as she added very seriously, "Take care of that little girl and Dr. Rio."

"I will." Coop nodded and stepped away from the airlock.

Naoko started to turn back towards Sunnyside but paused mid-step and swiveled back to look at Coop one last time. "This is why I love you, Cooper-san," Naoko said softly, pointing one finger at him gently.

Coop smiled softly in response. "I love you too, Naoko."

"When you get back, Cooper-san," Naoko stated emphatically. "You are going to get more than just unlocked-down," she said, arching an eyebrow mischievously before finally turning and marching determinedly towards the entrance to Sunnyside.

CHAPTER 32

All have plans it seems today,

Manny's heart raced as the seconds ticked by and he anxiously shifted his gaze from the massive Sunnyside Farm in front of him to the interior of the Beeze where their belongings lay stacked to the ceiling of the passenger compartment. "Change of plans," Manny barked into his shield to redirect the Beeze.

The Beeze hastily followed Manny's new orders, quickly traversing around the large building and arriving at the loading dock moments later. Manny saw Randy operating the lift, which slowly lowered a cubicle-shaped housing unit into Betsy, Coop's long hauler parked immediately adjacent to the loading dock. The hatch that allowed the unit to fit inside opened wide, and when it cleared the limits of the tube, it vanished into the hold. Immediately, Theo rolled his shoulders back and activated Greenie II, who then followed him as he approached Randy with an overabundance of gear firmly in his arms.

Manny pulled his backpack onto one shoulder and crossed the tarmac, with Greenie buzzing around him like a faithful pup. He rounded the massive hauler truck and caught sight of Coop in the cab, hands pressed to the window as he stared at Naoko walking away from the truck. Her bunny suit concealed her almost entirely, but with just enough of her edges exposed to show the diminutive frame and slender limbs beneath the fabric. A fond smile spread across Manny's face as he felt happiness for his friends.

At that moment, a voice called out from behind him, "Manny!" He turned to see Maggie running towards him, her arms flung wide open. "Are we going on a adventure?" she beamed up at him.

Manny smiled down at her and said, "Yes, you and Mommy." Manny looked over and saw Rosita walking quickly towards them, smiling, though the worry in her almond-shaped blue eyes was unmistakable.

"Dr. Rio," Rosita acknowledged formally, no longer concerned that her daughter was hugging a new person in their life but still wanting to keep it professional. "We are ready."

Manny saw James and Roberta struggling to carry more gear, yet both wearing odd smiles. He lowered Maggie back to her feet but hesitated when he met Rosita's gaze—he became tempted to hug Rosita too, but froze with the awkwardness between them.

Rosita met Manny's gaze for a brief moment before turning away to help James and Roberta with the weight of their backpacks and bulging bags. At that same time, James broke the tension by rushing up to Manny, throwing his arms around him in a tight embrace, still carrying items in one hand. With his forehead pressed against Manny's, he looked into his eyes and said, "God bless you, my friend. Do what you have to do to fix this."

"Thanks, James," Manny replied, voice quiet but resolute.

James added, "You better get going. We are loading up the FOUPs right now."

James smiled and headed for the truck. Roberta dropped her belongings and hugged Manny too, her face softening as she gently ran her fingers through his hair like a mother sending off a child. Tears streamed down her cheeks, full of love and pride, not sadness or fear. She pulled away abruptly and began barking orders at James before turning back to Manny. "Manny, you got this. You get your ass to Stanford now," she said firmly.

Manny received the hugs graciously and tears began to well up, realizing he was leaving his new family and may not live to see them again. Roberta continued stroking Manny's hair with one hand while motioning toward the truck with the other. James smiled and headed for the truck. He silently mouthed, "Love you, Man," to Manny.

Manny and Rosita looked at each other once more to signal their departure, so he kissed Roberta lightly on the cheek and suggested they should start making their way to the truck. He smiled warmly at her one last time and said, "May the virus miss you, my friend."

"And also miss you," Roberta replied as she wiped away tears with her blouse like a child would. She took a deep breath, stood up tall, and said, "Now get going! Get out before the pod closes! And you keep an eye on that little girl!"

Manny smiled again and quickly walked toward the truck. He paused for a moment as he tapped his shield to connect with Theo. "Coordinate with Captain Michelle Killian directly. She has a code worked out for the pod closures. Remember the code."

"Will do," Theo replied, adding that Randy and he had some surprises for them in case of an emergency.

Then Maggie ran up to grab Manny's hand, and Rosita grabbed Maggie's other one, and they gently began swinging Maggie as they walked. The trio remained side by side until arriving at the ladder leading up to the living pod of the long hauler. Coop anxiously awaited their entry into the living pod so they could get out of Long Island before they became trapped.

Manny lifted his shield to Coop, "Nice to see you!" he called out.

"Hey, Manny," Coop replied from his seat in the cab above them as he looked at the trio. "Hello, Dr. McKenna. Hello, Maggie," he added.

Maggie was already tugging at Manny's arm. "Can I drive? Please, please, please!"

"No, sweetheart," her mother said softly. "We have our own place in the back where we can stay during our journey. See? Up there," she said as she gestured towards the second ladder leading up into the cargo area.

Rosita waved sheepishly at Coop, who peered out the window of the driver's compartment high up in the front of the truck. He tapped his shield as a motion for Rosita to activate a proximity link, which she did. Suddenly, Coop appeared on her shield screen from his viewpoint in the cab.

"Nice to meet you, Dr. McKenna," Coop said with a friendly smile.

"Please call me Rosita," she replied candidly, studying his face intently as they spoke. "We're going to be traveling together for a bit so might as well be less formal." She looked over at Manny and said, "You too. Please call me Rosita."

Coop smiled even more broadly as he thanked Rosita. She stood tall, statuesque, and striking in her long black boots, blue jeans, and flowing burgundy blouse that fluttered in the breeze. She carried a variety of bags and jackets, ready for a big trip. "Call me Coop," he said in response.

Manny scooped up Maggie and grabbed onto the ladder while Rosita froze for a moment before following. The three made their way up to the outdoor platform where Manny opened the door to the living pod inside the long white tube of the long hauler. Rosita paused before entering, wanting to make sure she kept protecting her daughter. Lastly, Manny stepped through and glanced back at Sunnyside Farm one last time.

All of the staff stood at the loading dock; James waving emphatically, Randy holding his hand high in the air to wave goodbye, Roberta covering her mouth with her hands, and numerous staff members smiling and waving. Theo stood motionless with his arms crossed at his chest, his shield hovering over his face as he spoke urgently into it with last minute instructions for the long hauler. But Naoko's gaze fixed on Coop as she blew him kisses, no longer afraid to let everyone know how she truly felt about him.

Manny waved one last time to his beloved friends, stifling his own emotions as best as possible before slipping through the door of the living pod, their new home for the journey.

CHAPTER 33
Escape is the mission they seek,

The living pod looked comfortable and cozy, with its interior designed to imitate a sleeper car on a passenger train. Two sets of bunk beds lined the walls: Maggie sat perched atop the top one on the left side, and bags and boxes spread over the top two tiers of the stack on the right. Video monitors mounted on the walls on each side resembled real windows, allowing views from actual exterior scenes outside through video cameras. The artificial light from above created a bluish glow in the interior. Manny watched his friends in the window on the right as they slowly began filtering towards their work, not realizing the three inside the living pod could see them all. All except Theo and Randy, who remained standing and waving goodbye to the long hauler, knowing they appeared on the image on the inside on the windows of the living pod.

Manny tapped his shield and Theo appeared, smiling in his visor. Manny greeted his friend, "Nicely done."

"That's all Randy's doing," Theo explained. "He made this for himself for transportation to and from Sunnyside. All we did was quickly add a few modifications." Manny and Rosita exchanged puzzled looks, neither expected such a thoughtful surprise.

Manny looked around the capsule and noticed two doorways at the rear. Rosita opened one and peeked inside. "Nice bathroom," she said while looking back at Manny. "It even has a shower!" Excitedly, she stepped in for a closer look.

Theo added through his shield call, "There's also a changing room with a backdoor into the storage area. We loaded it with the smart FOUPs, enough food for two weeks, and all the other essentials."

"I can't believe you did all of this!" Manny exclaimed in awe. He looked up towards the ceiling and saw a hatch of some sort.

"If you press that blue button on the wall there, it should open up," Theo said.

Manny obeyed without pause. The hatch opened and a ship's ladder unfurled to the floor. With her bandaged hand, Maggie rushed eagerly onto the ladder, not allowing the injury to hinder her enthusiasm.

Once she made it to the top, Maggie squealed with delight. From her perch in a one-person seat that rotated around 360 degrees, she was able to see far out into the surrounding area in the shadow of the Sunnyside vertical farm. "I can see everything!" she shouted.

Theo and Randy laughed as Manny shouted instructions for Maggie to open the window in the glass tower. When she did, Maggie poked her head out of the window and yelled out, "Hello, everybody!"

Theo smiled and explained he wanted her to feel the fresh air. Rosita became overwhelmed by the thoughtfulness that she teared up and touched Manny's shoulder while silently thanking him. Theo then reminded everyone they needed to stay inside to avoid detection.

Manny was curious about that comment but let it go for now.

CHAPTER 34

Next stop over by travel unique,

The long hauler rumbled along the road towards the ferry, its electronic signals clearing the path through the numerous Beeze vehicles carrying people to their eventual homes to survive the lockdown. The swarm of Beezes buzzed around them, but Betsy deftly navigated through them using her priority shipping protocol. Despite Betsy's steady progress, Manny and Coop could not shake the uneasiness that crept over them as they rolled toward the ferry to take them off Long Island Pod.

Manny pulled himself up into the observation tower of the living pod and watched for any sign of activity or obstacle from outside. His heart raced as he listened intently to Coop's conversation with the Contros at the gate. Thankfully, no alarm sounded and the Contros gave them passage— prompting Manny to let out a deep breath of relief.

"We are out," Manny reported quickly as he climbed down the ladder and saw Rosita and Maggie waiting anxiously in the cab. Rosita ran forward and threw her arms around him in a tight hug while Maggie, not fully understanding what was happening, hugged both him and her mother.

"Thank you, Manny, thank you, thank you...a million times!" Rosita exclaimed and cupped his face between her hands before planting a kiss on his cheek. She thought about that for a moment, then quickly moved to the bunk beds, where she rummaged through one of the bags until finding the FOUP filled with its mysteriously dark contents. "Here it is!"

"What is that Mommy?" Maggie asked with wide eyes.

Rosita grinned and opened the FOUP door as if revealing a hidden treasure—square pieces of delicious chocolate cake glistening inside. She held up one piece triumphantly. "Roberta gave us a cake!"

Manny was about to reach for the cake when he paused, his dark eyes searching through the contents of the FOUP. He grinned impishly and asked, "How much do you have?"

Rosita smiled and happily took out more pieces of chocolate cake from the FOUP. "Enough for everyone," she said before taking some and quickly closing the door on any remaining cake, shielding it away from prying little hands.

Manny thought of a way to get some of this delicious treat to his friend Coop, then immediately remembered the pass-through in the back of Coop's cabin. He carefully picked up the FOUP and stepped outside into the crisp air between their cabins. With a double-click on Coop's name, he explained what was coming through the pass-through.

He remained outside in the airy night, its crispness tinged with the smell of saltwater from the Long Island Sound snaking its way through the land. As Manny set the FOUP into the pass-through for Coop to collect, he heard Coop's voice informing him that the Long Island Pod snapped into lockdown moments ago. He froze in place as images of previous lockdowns filled his head: mandatory self-containment, closed highways and roads, and contact tracing systems identifying and quarantining anyone who encountered an infected person.

Manny released a deep breath when he saw an alert appear on his shield from Mickey saying "Long Island Pod. Betsy successfully logged out." Relief flooded through him; they managed to get away in time. Being locked down in another pod could mean being stuck there for weeks or months on end and missing the mRNA shots so desperately needed. The highways were their only home for now.

CHAPTER 35

The winding road brings doubts ahead,

Betsy, with Coop at her helm, had traveled for over 200 miles since the ferry ride, skirting the edge of each pod they passed. The artificial intelligence within Betsy helped plan the most efficient route while maintaining a safe distance from any signs of life. The Contros investigated his long hauler each time, granted them passage, and waived him on without requiring him to lockdown in the pod. They recognized his self-containment logged him in for one week already. His cover story of delivering food to the University of Santa Cruz's vertical farm was enough to keep them safe as they drove along. The three passengers inside Betsy remained undetected inside the living pod, allowing for less scrutiny each time they passed a pod.

Inside the living pod, Manny watched as the distant landscape shifted with each passing mile. Maggie sat at a hand-carved desk near the back of the cabin, playing a three-dimensional video game that projected into her shield. Rosita monitored which games she played. The current version of *Worldcraft* allowed people to build all kinds of characters and entire pods, and passed Rosita's litmus test.

The Controllers no longer allowed children to play violent video games, ever since the lessons learned in the early 2000s when violence and personal liberty levels skyrocketed to a point where society rebelled. This led to fertile ground for the Controllers taking over as a fourth branch of the government. The debate continues whether or not this new governing system went too far. Nonetheless, no one can deny this group successfully prevented the spread of subsequent pandemics, like what happened in

2020 through 2035 that killed millions of people.

On the opposite side of the living pod, a bright light from Maggie's screen illuminated her face, as her hands swiftly worked the game controller. Meanwhile, in the anteroom, Rosita stood over Manny, seated in a chair, while Rosita delicately parted his soft hair with her gloved fingers. An attachment on her face shield emitted a low hum and cast a thin beam of yellow light across his scalp.

Rosita stepped around to face Manny and he noticed her jet-black shirt tucked in neatly, accented with a small crest on the right pocket. She wore old-fashioned jeans tucked into high western boots. The delicate scent of her perfume filled the room as she used an attachment on her safety shield to send a specific type of light into his skin. He smelled the subtle fragrance of her perfume and guessed she applied makeup during her morning routine in the bathroom. She looked beautiful.

With a satisfied mumble, Rosita pulled away and deactivated the light, pausing to make some notes on her electronic pad. She turned and faced Manny. "The rhizomatous veins are getting worse."

"How much worse?" Manny asked even though he already knew the answer, he recalled a book he read years ago, *All the Things You Already Know, But Just Need to Hear Out Loud* and its words seemed particularly relevant now.

Rosita paused before responding, going over to a desk to set down her special lighting tool. She turned back to him and said with finality, "If we were back at the hospital, I would do another surgery. This could end up as stage 4 cancer in a few weeks. Who knows where it will show up next? Your lungs probably. Maybe your liver."

Manny's stomach dropped as he absorbed what Rosita reported and began mentally going over their days and the travel ahead, desperate for minimizing obstacles and seeking solutions. He thought of the vaccine nearing completion two thousand miles away, but his mind quickly jolted back to reality when he glanced over at Maggie playing her video game before speaking to Rosita. He stood up and walked over to Rosita, lowering his voice to a whisper, "How is Maggie's?"

Rosita glanced lovingly at her daughter before slowly turning her gaze back to Manny. "Even worse," she replied while wiping away a tear.

CHAPTER 36

Mistakes are made that must be shed,

Manny looked out the video window to see another regional pod in the distance. Highway 70 was their path coast-to-coast but it took them too close to several major pods like Indianapolis, St. Louis, Kansas City, Denver, and Salt Lake City. One wrong turn or detection of the three hidden passengers, and the journey was over. They would waste away locked down in a pod. Immunotherapy and chemotherapy treatments could do nothing but delay the inevitable outcome. Maggie's early-onset cancer would likely claim her within a few more years, or even in only a few months.

Manny turned again to the viewing window to see a distant cluster of pods on the horizon, recognizing it as the Columbus, Ohio region. He fumbled to tap his shields with an unsteady hand, and Coop's groggy voice replied in response.

"Thanks, Coop. Well done on the route," Manny said.

"How are our friends?" Coop asked.

"Settling in for the long haul," Manny replied, watching as Rosita stood at the window and stared warily at the passing pods.

"Good," Coop replied sleepily as he grabbed a mug from the shelf and filled it up with hot coffee. "The Contro towers tried to tether us in the Grove City Pod, but they let us go when they saw I was in self-containment for this long already."

"You are a lifesaver," Manny replied gratefully as Rosita spun around quickly at the sound of his appreciation.

"Well, isn't that the point of this trip?" Coop asked as he stirred a teaspoon of honey into his mug. He stood up in his cabin and looked out the window.

Manny let out a loud laugh and then immediately regretted it when he saw Rosita's worried expression morph into one of sadness. He coughed to cover his mistake and disconnected from Coop. With an apologetic look, he gestured for Rosita to join him in the anteroom again.

Rosita sat down next to Manny on one of the chairs in the little room and looked at all of the FOUPs filled with fresh food. She crossed her arms and raised one leg to graciously fold it over her other leg as she looked pensively out the window. She looked sideways at Manny and bumped his shoulder with hers. "Maybe we should stop."

He looked worried and confused. "Stop what?"

Rosita moved her hand to Manny's shoulder and looked deep into his eyes. He felt her breathing on his face as she spoke slowly. "Maybe we should go to a hospital and do surgery on the both of you. I can easily travel with my residency and find a hospital with the robotically assisted tools."

Manny shot up from his seat at this suggestion. "No! That's not going to happen!"

"Who are you to tell me what to do with my daughter?" Rosita shouted, voice reverberating through the room.

Maggie jerked her head around from her video game, eyes widening in surprise before quickly switching off her shield. "Mommy!" Maggie said sternly from the other side of the room. "Do not yell at Manny!"

Rosita's face shifted from anger to understanding as she remembered that her role was that of a kind mother. She rushed over to Maggie at the desk, placing an assuring hand on her shoulder as she said softly, "It's okay, Maggie. We were just having a discussion."

"We were talking about who was going to get that last piece of cake," Manny interjected. He smiled at both Rosita and the child in front of them, giving a little nod as he did. His eyes met Rosita's briefly, conveying their mutual realization that it was going to be tricky being with a child in such a small space.

Maggie stood up firmly in her pink tutu, arms crossed and eyes narrowed at the two adults. She lacked the size of either one of them, but there was no doubt who held the power in that small room. She questioned Manny skeptically with a simple statement, "Manny, did you take the last piece of cake?"

Rosita interjected then, knowing full well Manny was covering for her, "Mommy wanted it, but Manny said he was saving it for you."

Maggie's face lit up and she ran to Manny and threw her arms around his neck. He chuckled and lifted her up with his good arm while she hugged him tightly. "Thank you, Manny! That's the best cake I ever had in my whole life!"

"Run along then and eat your cake," Rosita said softly as she took Maggie from Manny's arms and set her back on her feet. Holding her hand, she guided the child towards a door on the left side of the room and opened the door to the anteroom and kitchen area, the walls painted bright white with fluorescent lights beaming down from the ceiling.

Several FOUPs lined the shelves, filled with an array of treats, including Maggie's favorite—cake! In one corner was a small kitchen complete with stovetop, sink, and microwave which surrounded a tiny table with two chairs tucked neatly beneath it.

But what caught her attention most was the "skylight" above, instead of a glass and wood frame, this window-like feature was another video screen displaying an image of a bright blue sky filled with puffy cumulus clouds typical in the midwestern states. That type of cotton-ball-looking cloud often meant changing weather in the forecast.

Rosita fetched the cake, plate, and fork for Maggie. But instead of using the provided utensils, Maggie grabbed the cake with both hands and took a huge bite out of it. Chocolate coated her cheeks and lips while she savored every yummy mouthful. Finally, she licked her lips like a dog eating peanut butter.

"You stay here and I'll come get you in a bit, okay?" Rosita said as she opened the door to leave.

"Okay, Mommy!" Maggie squeaked out before the door had even shut completely. Then, just as Rosita was about to close it all the way, Maggie yelled one last thing: "No more yelling at my cancer buddy!"

Rosita's gaze met Manny's, both were fighting back laughter at Maggie's comment. "Thanks for that," Rosita said sheepishly.

"No problem," Manny replied with a smile.

Rosita stepped up to Manny, her chin jutting out defiantly. Round two. The air between them crackled with tension as she spoke. "I'll do what's best for her," she stated.

Manny responded without hesitation, "Then you will be killing us both," he said gravely.

Rosita scoffed in disbelief and spun around, facing away from him. Her gaze settled on the vastness of Ohio's countryside visible from the window next to them. Cows lazily roamed wide fields littered with haystacks and trees while birds swooped across the horizon. "You can't know that," she argued embitteredly. "You don't know if the vaccine will even work."

Manny offered a fact-based rebuttal. "The clinical trial showed a 75% cure rate," he reminded her. "Immunotherapy is 15% and chemotherapy is 25%. I'll take the 75% any day."

"But what if it doesn't work for Maggie?" Rosita implored. She went straight up to Manny and grabbed his shoulders while shaking him. Manny stood still while Rosita's hands rested on his shoulders. She moved slightly but she kept a firm grip on Manny. She looked him straight in the eyes and added, "Early onset cancer is worse on a child. I say surgery is the best for her."

Manny inhaled sharply and tightened his grip on Rosita's shoulders. His forearms were taut and muscular beneath the rolled-up sleeves of his shirt. He remembered the words of Rio Constante again: be strong, be guiding, and push forward with all of your strength. "We have to try something else. We can't just keep cutting this out of her. The mRNA vaccine at Stanford is the answer. We have to hurry there. It is our only hope," he said urgently, pulling her closer into an embrace as she began crying.

Rosita's sobs became uncontrollable against his chest, and Manny felt a deep sense of helplessness wash over him. But he pushed it aside and spoke with conviction another time, "Let's give her a chance at life. I know this will work. We have to change tactics. We can't keep doing the same thing over and over and over again and expect different results."

Rosita pulled away slightly and stared into Manny's eyes, their faces only inches apart. "Are you sure this will work?"

Manny looked deep into her blue orbs, glimmering even under tears. "I'm certain of it. I am completely positive this will work."

Manny could feel Rosita's breath and soft curves still pressed against him. Uncontrollably, his instincts got the better of him and he moved the last two inches and kissed her lips. Immediately after, he felt embarrassed. However, before he could apologize, Rosita stepped back quickly and crossed the room to look out at the cows again, not saying a word.

Manny stood in silence for a moment before finally mustering up the courage to speak. "I'm sorry," he said quietly.

CHAPTER 37
Trouble looms in offshore bays,

Strained interactions between Rosita and Manny marked the following day. Whichever was there, the other would promptly leave in order to find some relief in the restroom, kitchen, or on the deck outside of the long hauler. Breathing the crisp air out-of-doors proved soothing for Rosita as she talked with her confidantes, relatives, and coworkers over shield calls. In particular, Dr. Cheryl Blanding, who stood by Rosita through this tough experience, and always lent a hand when it came to rescuing Maggie. Manny overheard Cheryl's comments about whether surgery should happen now. He also overheard one side of a secretive conversation with her sister that ended up with Rosita hanging up quickly when she did not like what her sister said.

After passing through Limon Pod in the Colorado region, Manny caught sight of Rosita and Maggie climbing the ladder to the observation deck. He quickly stepped outside and tapped his shield to summon Theo's face into the video screen. His fingers were shaky as he double-clicked on Theo's name, and without waiting for a response, he asked, "How's it going on the farm?"

Theo gave Manny a knowing look, as Manny's eyes flickered up to the familiar olive-green fedora perched atop Theo's head—a relic commandeered from Manny's office at Sunnyside no doubt. "Good place for a lockdown, I'll give you that much. Damn, the food is good here."

Manny could tell there was something Theo wasn't saying. "Theo," he said with a firmness in his voice. "What did you do to the living pod so the Contros can't see us?"

Ahh, Theo thought. Manny finally figured it out. "RFID blocker."

Manny groaned in disbelief. "Jesus, Theo. That's against the law."

Theo shrugged nonchalantly and smiled devilishly. "That's only the half of it."

Manny felt dread prickling at his skin. "What else did you do?" he asked in fear.

Theo couldn't help but smile at having outsmarted the system. His plan was genius. He explained how he'd designed a self-containment algorithm to make it seem like the four of them were in self-containment mode for two weeks already. That duration passed the requirement imposed by the Contros for entry into the Stanford Pod if it went into lockdown. The algorithms dictated their fate at that point, with the end of the road in sight but unattainable.

Theo continued, "The last time your RFID's went through a gate was in Bridgeport. But by that time, you were already in self-containment for over a week. Well, according to the Contros anyway."

Manny soaked in all the information and considered the dangers they faced. Rosita would be furious if she ever discovered their plans. "What happens if we get caught?"

"Well, judging by the progress your cancer is making, I guess you would die."

Manny remained silent as he searched for the words to respond to this simple fact. After what seemed like an eternity, Manny made his observation, "die in self-containment on the road, or die in a lockdown with the Contros."

"Yup," Theo surmised. He looked away for a long pause and became lost in thought in the viewer. "Might as well die trying."

Manny watched as Theo's eyes moved back and forth as Theo's brilliant mind worked to process all the data that came his way. Finally, looking up at Manny once more, Theo surmised, "Your only chance is to get to the vaccine."

"You're right," Manny agreed, taken aback by how much Theo was able to discern in such a short time. Their paths had become deeply intertwined since they met, as if Theo was an ancient traveler, a "Friend of the Way," sent to show him hope during a difficult time.

Manny and Theo exchanged the last few details of the plan, and Manny was now fully aware of what Theo had accomplished for him. Just when Theo thought the conversation was over, Manny blurted out, "I kissed her."

Theo's face twisted in confusion, his expression barely visible on the holographic visor he wore. He stammered, "Who? Who did you kiss?"

"Rosita."

"Rosita?"

Manny sighed and looked away, feeling a wave of nausea as the events tumbled through his mind like an avalanche. "Yes…what the hell is wrong with me? Why do I keep kissing my friends? Am I insane?"

Theo shifted uncomfortably, the silence stretching out like an elastic band about to snap. "Did you say, friends, as in plural?"

Manny swallowed hard before nodding slowly. "My best friend, Mickey, from childhood…" His voice trailed off as he tried to find the words.

"You're kissing boys too?" Theo asked hesitantly. "I mean not that there's anything wrong with that if that's your thing."

Manny shook his head vehemently. "No, no, no. Mickey is Michelle. She's a woman." Manny explained how the divorce, cancer treatment, kids going off to college, job loss, and failing farm had all taken their toll on him—to the point where he self-medicated heavily. Mickey slapped him across the face after that kiss and he'd regained some clarity. As he shared this story with Theo, Manny found himself feeling oddly relieved. Aside from Mickey, Theo was the only one who knew everything about his current situation. "It feels kind of good to tell someone about all this."

Theo paused; his brow lined with reasoning as he processed what Manny revealed. Suddenly, a few of the missing puzzle pieces snapped into place, and it explained some of Manny's introversion.

Manny let out a heavy sigh as Theo asked about Rosita. Manny explained, "She won't even look at me now. We haven't spoken a word since I kissed her."

Theo considered his friend and ran his hand along his jawline in thought. "I suck at women, so I don't know what to advise you. If it were me, I would give her some space. Give her room to breathe and come to terms with whatever she's feeling."

Manny sighed and shifted his weight from one foot to the other as he considered Theo's suggestion. Just then, the long hauler jerked and Manny felt himself lurch forward.

The door of the living pod opened with a hiss, and Rosita stuck her head out, her face pale, and her eyes wide with fear. She motioned frantically for Manny to come inside. He complied without question, stepping into the bright interior of the pod.

Rosita pointed at the north-facing window that showed a small town about a half-mile away. The gates of the town were closed tight, but not quite tight enough to contain the swarm of Contros vehicles that filled the main road heading straight towards them. The sirens blared and strobe lights flashed, illuminating the darkness around them as external loudspeakers demanded their surrender.

Manny tapped his shield in an effort to contact Coop at the same time Coop was trying to reach him. "What's going on, Coop?" Manny spoke first.

"The bastards threw a tether at us," came Coop's reply.

"What do we do? We can't stop here!" Manny asked urgently.

Coop's face was grim as he replied through gritted teeth, "No choice until the tether is off. We can't move an inch with that on us. Turn off your shields and stay inside, no matter what."

Rosita instinctively picked up Maggie and looked around for a safe spot, her eyes widening with fear as the Contros loudspeaker demanded repeatedly for the driver to step out of the vehicle.

Coop opened his shield and spoke firmly into it, "No, I will not," in response to the loud voice from the loudspeaker demanding identification. He spat back defiantly, "I don't care if you are the king of the world!" His heart sank as he hoped fervently that none of his passengers' shields had opened, revealing their presence.

The voice returned with an authoritative demand from the Controllers of Substances, Time, Authority, and Credit. "Sir, identify yourself."

"I am Amadeus Thaddeus Cooper," Coop stammered. His voice quivered as he repeated his Long Hauler number, LH400798851, followed by a proclamation that he was on self-containment mode for twelve days under Covid 2032-587 policy. "I refuse to break quarantine for you or anyone else."

At that moment, Coop's mind raced with thoughts as he noticed two squad cars slowly driving up right next to Betsy. A man stepped out from one of the cars and spoke emphatically into his megaphone, "Sir, we are in lockdown in the Lake Tahoe region and invoke Lake Tahoe Regional Policy— Covid 2062. We demand you exit your vehicle and accompany us to the South Lake Tahoe Pod until the duration of this lockdown is completed."

"You know as well as I do," Coop began, before reciting the words of the commitment to maintain the food deliveries during lockdowns that all long haulers knew by heart, "that your damn regional policy does not overrule the nations long hauler's food deliveries."

A tense silence fell as the Contros discussed what to do with their superiors on calls in their shields. The discussion broke when a figure dressed in Pod Police uniform suddenly emerged from the vehicle. "Get out of the fucking truck before I have you arrested!"

Remaining composed, Coop said to himself as he addressed them via an exterior microphone, "I invoke the Virus Protection Act of 2054 and claim my self-containment as its own pod. Therefore, your act of hostility can be construed as an act of war."

The Popo standing by the car gesticulated wildly to their partner in the Contros vehicle, their words lost in a flurry of motion.

Meanwhile, Manny took a chance and called Mickey back in the Bronx Pod, and explained the situation rapidly. He heard her quick breathing through the communicator, her voice barely a whisper as she ordered him to try to stall them. "Don't get out of your pod for any reason."

Manny saw Mickey motion frantically for Gary to step into her office. She handed him a piece of paper with encoded instructions for the long hauler pod and the pod at Lake Tahoe. "Just keep stalling them, and let Coop know he shouldn't get out of the cab," she said to Manny.

"But I can't contact Coop or they might see us," Manny explained. Rosita stood by looking at the Popos through the window.

"What do you mean?" Mickey asked, puzzled by the statement. "They can't see you?"

Manny realized his mistake when he mentioned what the RFID blocker could do. He hesitated for a moment before eventually saying, "It's something I can't tell you about."

"Jesus, Manny. You are asking a lot of me. Don't forget this is being recorded."

He sighed, knowing that the surveillance cameras in the walls were everywhere and impossible to avoid. "I know, I know. There's too much data going on here. Even the AI reviewers can't catch everything."

Mickey remained silent; her eyes averted from Manny's face as if to say "That's not an excuse." Manny seemed to get the message; his shoulders slumped in resignation. "Alright, I guess it's a malfunction or something."

Rosita's gaze remained fixed on the activity outside the window until her eyes widened and she spun around. "Manny, they're leaving!"

Manny flew to the window, squinting through the smudged glass on the outside video camera as he saw two Popo vans pulling away in reverse. He spoke into his shield, voice taut with tension, "Mickey, they're leaving!"

Mickey darted a thumbs-up from her office window and flashed it to Gary, who continued talking on his own device at his desk. He returned the gesture before disconnecting with a relieved sigh. Mickey spoke into her shield again, "Looks like everything is set."

Coop watched all of this unfold from the safety of the cockpit, filled with curiosity as to what just happened. Suddenly, a voice crackled through the loudspeaker from one of the police cars. "Sir, we acknowledge your right to declare self-containment and will cease hostilities. We agree to your Food Transportation Priority LH-7822 for the Bronx Pod."

The electronic tether released its hold on Betsy and she began moving once more. Relief swept through every occupant of the long hauler.

CHAPTER 38

A call is sent to find their ways,

After the near miss in Lake Tahoe, Manny waited for Dr. John Strunk to appear on his visor. When he finally did come into focus, Manny could see lines of stress around his eyes. "Sorry, Manny," John said briskly. "Was in a briefing. Where are you?"

"We are passing through the Sacramento pods now and will be there in about two hours."

"Damn good," John added with a relieved smile before turning serious again. "Your vaccines only have two more days of usage. We've got to get them into you or it's all over."

Manny's stomach tightened as he asked how long the process would take if they didn't make it in time.

John made an apologetic gesture with his hands. "About two weeks if we miss this one," he explained slowly. "We would have to draw new blood samples, form the mRNA sequence, and make the new vaccine. But the cost would be incredible."

Manny's worries took over his mind. "We don't have that much time, or money" he exclaimed.

John reassured him, "Rosita already sent the updates to the labs. Surgery might be necessary though, which could be a problem with our schedule."

Manny asked for clarification, "What do you mean?"

"We can't have anesthesia in your systems for eight days prior to the second set of shots, or the vaccine won't work," John explained.

"So, we get the first two shots, then do the surgery, and we'll still have plenty of time for the next set of shots?" Manny summarized.

"Exactly. Just make sure you get here quickly," John said firmly.

"We have to go around these pods to avoid a tether, but it looks like the virus isn't in the San Francisco Bay Region yet." Messages sent via the internet from the World Health Organization kept Manny informed constantly throughout the journey. He knew in advance which highways avoided the lockdowns as they progressed across the regions.

"We'll go straight there then," Manny stated emphatically. He knew that the University of Santa Cruz would have to wait for their delivery.

The stakes couldn't be higher, any delay would mean death.

CHAPTER 39
When the children have no choice,

Alex and Andrea looked at each other, their eyes mirroring the same sadness. "Hi, Dad," Alex said, his voice wavering slightly as he adjusted the holographic visor on his head so their father's face became visible. Seeing him in holographic form only emphasized the fragility of his situation.

"I'm almost to Stanford," Manny announced, with a hint of anxiety in his voice. He explained how his battle with cancer was far from over, the rhizomatous cancer was spreading, and there were no guarantees the mRNA vaccine would be effective.

Andrea's lip trembled. "Oh my God...keep driving, Daddy."

Alex echoed her sentiment while silently hoping the university pod lockdown held off until his father received the vaccine.

The twins pleaded with their dad to let them join him at Stanford, but he was adamant about them staying put at the university pod. He wanted them to stay safe and have access to resources and classes should they need to enter lockdown. But underneath all his words, what Manny really wanted was to spend time with his kids before it may be too late.

Manny looked his children in the eyes, wanting to keep them safe and shield them from danger, but he also feared what might happen if the lockdown lasted too long, or if the cancer consumed him before he ever got to see his kids again.

He ran a hand through his hair and his face softened slightly at the sight of their pleading faces. He thought about all the accessible resources by living in a university pod, and their expertise grew around vaccines and cancer treatments. Finally, he realized the sound of their voices is what he would miss the most. "Don't worry. I'll get there after I get the vaccine," he said softly.

Maggie sat up in her chair, transfixed by the love in Manny's voice as he spoke to his children through his shield. She rose and walked over to him, placing both hands on either side of his face and looking into his eyes with childlike wonder. Gently stroking the bandages covering his injured hand, she asked him why the bandage looked so strange. He rotated it so she could see the air pocket sewn in, created to allow oxygen to reach the wound.

"Open it up!" Maggie demanded, her gaze never leaving his. When he hesitated, she said matter-of-factly, "Show me."

"Why?" Manny replied, a hint of reluctance in his tone.

"I want to see it." Her piercing gaze met his, daring him to deny her request. "I'll show you mine first."

Manny watched as Maggie slowly unwrapped her bandage to reveal the long scar from her wide excision surgery. She pointed at a dark spot on her wrist and said, "I call him Oscar. He reminds me of a angry boy in my class." Manny inhaled at the sight of the uneven and discolored spot, undoubtedly melanoma that had grown larger within the last few days.

Manny quickly peeled off his own bandage and also saw a new growth since yesterday. Although smaller than Maggie's Oscar, denial was useless in recognizing the potential for rapid metastasizing. He remained still, time running out in his mind.

"Hah, that's a little one," Maggie said proudly and compared her Oscar with his little spot.

Manny managed a weak chuckle and shifted uncomfortably as Maggie stated, "We'll call yours Sweet Pea," she said softly. "Because it's so small."

Manny laughed softly at the girl's attempts to cope with the situation. "Don't worry. We'll get some medicine and get rid of these two soon enough."

"Mommy said we have to get surgery as soon as we get to Hawaii," Maggie said.

"We're going to Stanford," Manny said in reply, confusion evident in his voice. "Not Hawaii, we are already in California." He glanced at the dining area door where Rosita sequestered herself once again, and gave Maggie a little push towards the desk.

Manny's heart raced as he walked towards the dining area door to see Rosita. He paused before reaching out for the door handle when suddenly Rosita pulled it open from her side. Both of them stood still and silent until Maggie broke the tension with a joyous exclamation. "Manny has a cancer named Sweet Pea!"

Rosita instinctively looked at Manny's scalp, but Manny shook his head and pointed to his wrist. She stepped closer and noticed the loosened bandage. Rosita locked eyes with Manny for the first time since he kissed her two days ago. She carefully pulled Manny's hand away from his body and led him through the dining area door. "Let me take a look," she said softly.

As she slowly unwrapped the bandage around Manny's wrist, she examined the new growth with a doctor's precision. Then, as if remembering something suddenly, she looked around and said, "I'll be right back. Wait here." With that, she rushed off through the door for a brief moment.

Manny noticed that Rosita wore another one of her nanotechnology doctor's outfits, this one in a fashionable shade of green. He realized she was likely preparing for work at Stanford the moment they arrived.

Rosita re-entered the room carrying an instrument carefully arranged around her neck. The telescoping camera and light attachment reacted to her verbal commands as she tested it with wave-like motions. She guided Manny over to the dining table and helped him sit before taking his bandaged hand into her own and removing the makeshift cast. She studied the cancer spot intently with the special reddish glow of the scanning light, her lips moving silently as though making medical notations into her shield. Then, as if Manny wasn't even there, she focused all of her attention on Sweet Pea.

Rosita announced in a factual tone, "Looks like it has metastasized. You are going into surgery right after I take out Oscar."

Confused, Manny blurted out, "Surgery right after the vaccine, right?" To which the doctor replied, "Yes. If that vaccine works at all, it will take a week or two to know the results. Surgery will take out the cancer before it spreads further."

Manny felt his mouth go dry and he slowly turned to look at Rosita, searching for some signs of reassurance in her expression. She kept her eyes focused on packing away her medical equipment, avoiding eye contact with him. He heard himself say, "Okay, if that's what you think is best."

Rosita finally met his gaze and then quickly looked away again as she zipped up the container filled with medical tools.

"I'm sorry," Manny said quietly as he walked past her toward the main living area. With one last glance back at her, he took a deep breath and stepped into the other room.

CHAPTER 40
We can lend a helping voice,

Dr. Curtis Fauci, the Chief Medical Officer of the World Health Organization, stepped up to a podium in an otherwise empty briefing room. Towering over Dr. Fauci, two men wearing regulation navy-blue suits flanked him. He chose for the occasion a gray pin-striped suit with a coordinating cashmere waistcoat and tie, his style highlighted by a vibrant pocket kerchief. Cameras situated at four points around the room captured his every move and expression.

The little red lights atop the cameras shone like a 1,000-watt bulb in the eyes of the two sweaty blue-suited men as they detailed the statistics showing on the large screen behind them. On the other end of the broadcast sat an estimated 20 billion people across the world.

Dr. Fauci paused before he spoke, taking in his colleagues' words and allowing them to sink in. He represented CATACS, the fourth branch of the government, and guided the lockdown of over 3 billion people throughout Russia and the United States regions. It was the largest virus spread since Miami's COVID outbreak fifteen years ago. "Good evening, everyone," he began. "I'd like to thank you for allowing us to do our job and contain this global pandemic."

Dr. Fauci gave a solemn pause before continuing. "But our efforts must not be taken for granted. We have nearly 1 million deaths already, primarily in Russia, but also here in the United States. Only through continued contact tracing and diligent quarantine measures can we move closer to inoculating all those affected and curing the sick."

He swallowed hard before continuing. "In order to protect our citizens and continue to contain the virus, it is paramount that we maintain stringent lockdown measures across two countries and over seven thousand pods. Any travel at all must provide proof of self-containment for two weeks prior along with a negative test result approved by CATACS."

"In closing, we must all come together during this time of crisis. We call on all hospitals and medical units to work overtime and provide assistance to those in need. Although we believe the lockdowns will not reach the western coast of the United States, we will be ready if it does," concluded Dr. Fauci as he removed his electronic tablet from the podium. He then looked up and gave everyone a reassuring smile before adding, "May the virus miss you."

CHAPTER 41
Guides may lead them western bound,

Mickey studied Gary as he sat at his desk in the squad room, scrolling through his electronic pad to keep track of the special delivery and coordinate its safe passage. She noticed he still wore yesterday's uniform: a tailored suit designed with nanotechnology and marked with an expensive insignia.

Gary rose from his chair and stepped into Mickey's office. "The long hauler is at the Stanford Pod Gate," he reported confidently. "I cleared the way for them to get through."

Mickey recalled Gary as a broken man only a few weeks ago, but now she saw a different man. His calm demeanor was reassuringly familiar, yet foreign at the same time. "Thank you, Gary," Mickey said in sincere appreciation.

Gary ran a finger across the dimly lit screen of his electronic pad, pausing as he scanned over each name before confirming the route for approval from the Pod Police. "They will get through," he announced in a steady voice without any sign of hesitation.

"They?" Mickey asked as she suddenly felt a chill run down her spine. She began to worry about her decision to let Gary guide the long hauler across the country.

With complete composure, Gary looked up from the pad and met Mickey with an unreadable stare. After a brief moment of silence, he continued on with more details about the shipment: four passengers aboard, destined for Stanford Pod and then to the University of Santa Cruz vertical farm where Mr. Cooper would pick up the return load for delivery back to Sunnyside Farm. And now he knew Dr. Manny Rio was aboard the long hauler too.

As Gary finished his update, he asked for permission to help Mr. Cooper complete the delivery so the truck could return home safely. Taking a deep breath, Mickey nodded her head in agreement and stood up from her seat in salute. "Good work, Officer Thurston," she said sincerely.

He mirrored her gesture with a quick salute of his own and smiled softly. "Thank you, Sir. Good to be back."

CHAPTER 42

They soon arrive at hallowed ground.

Theo remained in touch with Coop the entire time they traversed the Dumbarton Bridge, the divided causeway connecting both sides of the San Francisco Bay Area. Coop clutched Betsy's steering wheel tightly and kept his focus on the winding roads ahead of him. After hours spent driving and 3,000 miles behind them, Betsy finally approached the entrance to the Stanford University Pod. "Cut the blocker now," Theo commanded.

"We're only a hundred feet from the gate and it's still open," Coop responded reluctantly. Exhausted, he knew he must finish this job before he could make his way back to Naoko in Sunnyside. He activated his shield and connected it to the living pod's interface, then double-clicked on the RFID blocker switch and deactivated it.

Manny and Rosita's shields beeped in unison and lit up their screens as dozens of notifications flooded through. The Algos data inundated their screens, adjusting credits, allocations, time logs, and forecasting more accurately based on the news that the group traveled thousands of miles and was now at the Stanford gate.

"Mommy! My shield is going nuts!" Maggie screamed, bursting through the bathroom door. She wore a purple tutu and mismatched swimming trunks, her hair now a mess of knots after being freshly brushed moments before. Her mother held out her arms, embracing Maggie as she leaped into them.

"That's alright, darling. Mine too."

Manny grinned knowingly. "It must be because we registered at the Stanford Pod gate; the Algos are probably processing it all right now."

Rosita scrutinized the data streaming across her shield display while Manny and Maggie did the same with theirs. "How can it say we've been in self-containment for fifteen days? I thought we had only been…" Rosita started to ask, unaware of what Theo concocted.

Manny waved his hands frantically, pressing his index finger to his lips to gesture for her to be quiet. He slowly nodded up and down, then motioned toward the cab where Coop sat, trying to indicate that the Contros might be listening. "I know, we've been cooped up for a while," he replied carefully. Now he nodded his head sideways to try and point to the cab where Coop sat.

Rosita stayed confused, but before she spoke, Manny raised his finger to shush her. He explained, "Now we can enter the Stanford Pod without risking further spread of the virus, we've completed our self-containment period."

Maggie and Rosita glanced back and forth between each other; their faces serious. Maggie finally voiced their shared concern, "I want to get out of here Mommy. This camper is too small."

Rosita glared at Manny with a look that could melt glass.

Manny smiled warmly in response and spoke into his shield. "Coop, we will be ready in ten minutes."

"That's great news, Manny!" Coop called back. The self-containment log already became history at Stanford. The gates stayed open.

CHAPTER 43
The powers will watch without fear,

Brock Masterson, the Director of the governing body at CATACS, tapped a few keys on his laptop and two cases immediately appeared on the wall-sized projector screen. Claudia Rosenberg and Andrew Bagsund exchanged worried glances; they both worked hard on these cases in the past weeks, but the algorithms behind them kept producing anomalies, especially when it came to trying to lengthen life spans too quickly. The same two cases were back up on the anomaly list once more.

Claudia asked, "I don't understand why the algorithms can't simply extend a lifespan forecast. What is wrong with that?"

"It goes too fast for safety precautions," Andrew replied in an agitated voice, frustrated over Claudia's optimism. "We'd be better off overriding it."

"Not so fast," Brock chimed in before the debate got out of hand. He scrolled through the data on the screen as he spoke. "Look, they're already together traveling to one of the best hospitals in the country. They avoided all the lockdowns, and they have the right amount of self-containment. That seems like pretty good news to me."

"I agree," Claudia added hesitantly, her brow furrowed as she glanced at Andrew for support. "Seems strange that there are two such anomalies together."

Andrew squinted at another line of data on the screen before adding, "And with the mother of the child, who just happens to be a renowned robotics surgeon."

Brock turned off the video screens. "Let's keep an eye on this. For now, let's approve the new anomaly." He clicked on his tablet twice, and added four years onto each of Manny's and Maggie's lifespan forecasts.

CHAPTER 44
Landing must occur the hour is near,

Coop maneuvered the big rig through the winding roads surrounding Stanford Hospital, passing towering trees and manicured gardens. The morning sun glinted off the arched windows of the university buildings, drawing attention to its importance as one of the highest-ranked research institutions in the nation. The "Farm" as Stanford is called, became famous for its high level of research and numerous Nobel prize winners. Universities across the country tried to emulate their success, but none could match their reputation or fame. Especially known were their think-tanks with luminaries from all over the world. And especially because of the research into cures for cancer.

Betsy hummed along until they arrived at a turnabout between two hospital buildings near the emergency room entrance. The trio of passengers stepped out onto the outdoor deck between Coop's cabin and their living pod, into the warmth of the California sunshine. They each carried packs filled with enough clothing for a week away from home. They'd prepared for any eventuality, unsure of how long their journey to find a cure would take.

Coop stood at the observation window looking out at the three travelers on the deck, and he raised his hand to bid them farewell. Although the four friends stood a few feet apart, the divider between them remained in place to keep Coop in self-containment for his ride home.

Manny walked up to the window and placed his hand against it, leaving his hand on the window to express his gratitude for everything Coop did for them. Coop's much larger hand mirrored Manny's palm, and he asked him to look after Maggie and Rosita during their mission. Manny blinked away a tear as he looked at the hospital, his mind going over Coop's incredible bravery. He thought about how few people would risk their life, career, and future to do what Coop accomplished for them.

Rosita's shoulder brushed against Manny as she rushed to the window and pressed her palm against it, desperately trying to come up with the right words for this moment. Maggie stood beside them, jumping between subject matters like any child would, from asking when they could swim next to being excited about their adventure. Tears streamed down Rosita's face in equal parts happiness, sorrow, and worry of what was yet to come. She blew Coop several kisses and promised to see him back at Sunnyside.

"You take care of that little girl," Coop managed to say as the three travelers climbed down the ladder to step onto Stanford soil.

The trio stepped off the platform and proceeded to the registration desk. Instructions on the video screens demanded they turn on their screens for full protection. The facility rose up in front of them, its red brick facade speckled with white and gray, and its three stories topped with a verdant canopy. Two enormous poles stretched towards the sky, their thick trunks wrapped in ivy as they supported the stylized roof of leaves. It looked like a contemporary jungle-themed artwork. Above the entrance hung an inscription, "The Bass Biology Center."

Manny led the way towards the registration desk where two PoPos, an attendant, and Dr. John Strunk awaited them. Manny felt his heart pounding as he approached the desk, noticing John wore the similar green surgeon's outfit that Rosita also wore. As they walked closer to the desk, John burst out with a booming, "Manny!" He vigorously shook Manny's hand and then looked to the other two and said, "Dr. McKenna I presume, and Margaret?"

Rosita smiled politely and extended her hand in greeting. "It's a pleasure to meet you, Dr. Strunk."

Maggie also offered her hand before correcting him, "My name is Maggie, not Margaret. Howdy do."

Manny watched this exchange with impatience and quickly asked, "How much time do we have?" A hint of amusement crept into John's voice as he replied, "I'm fine, Manny. I see you are right to the point as always."

"He has no patience for formalities," Rosita chimed in with a grin. She stepped closer to the doctor and flashed him a warm smile.

Maggie scolded Manny for his lack of manners in a stern voice. Manny grinned sheepishly before pulling John into a tight embrace, conveying all of his gratitude in one hug. John stood frozen, taken aback by the sudden affection, but slowly patted Manny's back with understanding.

"I know you must be anxious," he said softly, recognizing their situation. "We only have ten hours to get those two doses into you, so let's get going."

Manny and John started walking towards the desk to register, and Rosita followed closely behind. She tapped Dr. Strunk on the shoulder and asked, "And the surgeries?"

John stopped and turned around to face her, his tanned head freshly shaved, and his mustache and goatee neatly trimmed. He smiled warmly at Rosita. "The Mohs surgeries are scheduled for tomorrow morning."

Manny, John, and Rosita stepped towards the registration desk. Maggie trailed along as she looked at beautiful photos on the walls. To their right, a pair of PoPos stood on either side and scanned each traveler's documents and self-containment data to determine eligibility. A bead of sweat rolled down Manny's temple as he held his breath, hoping that Theo's falsified information would remain undetected.

The guards scrutinized the credentials closely. One guard finally came around from behind the desk and spoke quietly to Manny while handing him his nametag, "Dr. Rio, Captain Killian of the Bronx Pod asked me to extend a greeting to you and Dr. McKenna."

Manny's eyes rested on the nametag, adorned with his full name, "Dr. Manuel Rio," and the title of his position while a guest at Stanford University Hospital, "VIP."

CHAPTER 45

One week passes in pastures with haste,

Maggie and Manny endured two weeks of living on the edge, skirting the law, and narrowly dodging lockdowns, all in pursuit of something now within reach. After a tumultuous journey, all it took to complete the next step of their mission was two simple injections for each of them spread over eight hours. The doctors administered the first dose immediately after arrival last night, and now after a nice rest in the hotel attached to the university, Dr. John Strunk prepared to administer the second shot in the confines of his office.

As the second dose entered Maggie's skin, she felt nothing more than a slight pinch. Rosita stood by and reassured her daughter it would be over shortly. John informed them there were rare cases where patients suffered severe side effects after receiving the vaccine. But for now, the only thing left to do was to receive the second dose, with less than one hour remaining on the vaccine's useful life. They were lucky—the third and fourth doses prepared from their own blood samples taken within hours after this shot would be ready in about eight days.

Maggie said while looking up at her mother and rubbing the spot where the vaccine entered, "Mommy, I'm hungry."

"We can go back to the hotel later," Rosita explained patiently and patted her daughter on the head. "Remember it's not good to eat right before the surgery."

Manny interjected and reminded her of the awaiting food back at the hotel. Coop already delivered their belongings, including over two dozen FOUPs filled with nitrogen blanketed fresh food, bags belonging to Manny, and Greenie the odd-looking drone, to the hotel last night before beginning his trek to Santa Cruz and eventually back to Sunnyside. The hotel rooms were spartan but elegant. Each room had a balcony with protective barriers that extended out around them, blocking any possible cross contamination from neighboring rooms. Redwood trees filled their views, tall and thick, with glimpses of other university buildings visible between them. The tranquil atmosphere reminded them of a farm.

Manny and Maggie followed the nurse, their footsteps echoing off the tile floors, until they reached a dimly lit preparation room. A chill ran through Maggie's body as she took in the scene before her: two chairs with white towels draped over them, metal trays with gleaming needles next to each chair, and two nurses wearing protective masks and gloves. Manny sat down first, rolling up the sleeve of his shirt to reveal a jagged scar. He flinched slightly as one of the nurses swabbed the inside of his elbow and inserted a needle into his vein. The nurse slowly filled several vials of Manny's blood, collecting four in total to prepare two vaccine doses for each patient. Maggie watched anxiously as her turn came next for drawing the blood. Her pulse quickened and her heart raced as she felt a cold sting when the needle pierced her skin. The nurse was careful not to take too much, stopping to check if either of the patients had become too dizzy or lightheaded before completing their procedure.

Both Manny and Maggie examined their arms for any sign the vaccine was already working—some sort of miracle healing—but all they saw were the two malignant spots: Oscar and Sweet Pea, which looked like they grew even larger since yesterday.

John stepped back from his monitoring station, pushing up the rim of his glasses with one finger. "That should do it," he said, admiring the precision with which the nursing technician took Manny and Maggie's blood.

Manny smiled at the nurse and patted his fresh bandage in place. Then he turned to Maggie, her polka dot tutu peeking out from her jeans. He knew she'd deliberately chosen a loose-fitting short sleeve shirt; an experienced patient always wore proper attire to support shots or blood collections. "And how about you, young lady?"

Maggie copied Manny's movements, her fingers gently pressing the adhesive of her bandage into place. She let out a low growl and muttered, "I still don't like shots."

John placed a warm hand on Maggie's back and gestured for her to stand up and follow him. "It'll be okay, Mags," he said in a soft voice. "Thanks to this medicine, this may mean a lot less shots in the future."

John guided Manny and Maggie out of the examination room, his voice firm and authoritative. He continued to explain as they walked. "In order for the vaccine to work, nothing can enter the system in the eight days prior to the final two injections. That means no surgery or other treatments during that period. We need to get this surgery done today so the blood will be clean next week."

Manny followed John and Maggie down the hospital hallway, noting the hushed intensity of their conversation. A soothing blue-gray paint covered the walls, but that did not help him relax. Not right before surgery.

The doctors will remove Oscar and Sweet Pea before they cause any more trouble. John will perform the surgery on Maggie in place of the usual Dr. Blanding, and Rosita will perform the surgery on Manny. The emotional baggage of performing surgery on one's own daughter is too heavy for any surgeon.

Rosita bustled into the preparation room, and Manny and Maggie gave each other a gentle hug and nodded to the two doctors signaling their readiness. John arranged them side by side on hospital beds in neighboring curtained areas before administering the local anesthesia block to put their arms asleep. Later, only a light dose of general anesthesia would be necessary to put them both out during the operations. With a gloved hand, John injected the first injection into Maggie's arm while Rosita silently held her daughter's other hand for comfort. The needle pierced through Maggie's skin and she let out an involuntary gasp of pain.

Manny listened to his friends on the other side of the curtain. He chose to stay awake during the block once again as the technicians guided intravenous blockers through his shoulder, staying in constant communication with Manny as they watched the progress on a sonogram video screen. Manny felt every sensation as the blockers wound their way through his veins like a poisonous snake. Initially he could not move the large muscles in his arm, then gradually his wrist stopped working, followed by the larger fingers, leaving only his thumb and index finger active until even they became powerless. In minutes, Manny's arm turned into an unresponsive lump of spaghetti.

The same thing happened to Maggie, but already under in a deep sleep. The technicians wheeled her away shortly afterwards, her left hand already deadened from the medication. Manny remembered she was left-handed; an ironic twist of fate that cancer struck her dominant hand also. The doctors assured him this was merely a coincidence. They made sure he signed the release before his own hand lost all functionality again. If the cancer was too aggressive, once again there was a chance they might have to amputate his hand altogether.

Manny's gurney rolled down the hall toward the operating room, a sentry of fluorescent lights and sanitized air, then entered feet-first into the white room. The robotic surgeon loomed in the middle of the operating room like a four-legged spider, its legs extended with various instruments attached, poised to enter Manny's skin and plumb the depths of his body for rogue cells of melanoma.

As he rolled to the center of the room, Rosita appeared at his side, her warm hand resting on his good shoulder. "You are going to be just fine after this," she said reassuringly.

Manny nodded, though his lips trembled slightly. "I know. I've got the best doctor in the world."

The anesthetic went to work quickly, and in moments, Manny drifted off into another world. When he opened his eyes again in what seemed like seconds, he found himself in another sterile hospital room, unable to move his groggy body. Lifting his head unsteadily, he saw a thick white cast and bandage covering what must still be his hand. Several technicians hovered around him as he slowly woke up.

"Where is Maggie?" he asked weakly, lifting himself as much as he was able.

"I'm right here, sleepy head," came a familiar voice from behind the long white curtain of the bed next to his.

Manny watched as one of the technicians pulled back the long white curtain separating them, then he saw Maggie trying to sit up in bed. Her large bandages wound around her arm and all the way up over her shoulder, so bulky it seemed to swallow her small frame. He stumbled over his words as he stared at her bandages, his heart heavy with sympathy for what she was going through. He smiled weakly at Maggie; his eyes alive with hope. "How are you?" he asked eagerly.

Maggie gave a soft laugh, the sound barely audible against the sterile hum of the hospital room. She adjusted the sling that supported her injured arm, and her blue eyes sparkled with a hint of mischief as she replied, "I'm fine, but Oscar is a goner!"

Manny chuckled and reclined against his pillow, feeling lighter despite all they endured since waking up in this new room. His gaze followed Maggie's as Rosita stepped into the room. She looked years better than when he saw her before the operation, now clothed and scrubbed clean. She enfolded Maggie in a hug before gesturing for her to follow one of the technicians down the hall so Maggie could dress for their departure. Rosita planted a gentle kiss on her forehead and Manny watched as they departed.

Rosita approached then, pulling up a chair until it was close enough for him to see every detail of her face. With careful motions she tucked in the bed sheet below his torso and smoothed out the cover over his chest. "Dr. Rio," she said, finally making eye contact. When their eyes met, Manny noticed a sense of sadness and weariness in her gaze, a stark contrast from the previously relaxed nature of their conversations together.

Her voice remained steady and clinical as she outlined the robotic process and discussed the tests they needed to do, taking extra tissue this time to make sure it would come back clear. "The rhizomatous material is much farther along than we expected," she said. "I expect the results to come back as stage 3 cancer. Possibly stage 4."

The news hung heavy in the air between them, but Manny felt bolstered by the mRNA vaccine coursing through his veins. He met Rosita's eyes and asked, "Any upsides to all of this?"

Rosita's expression softened as she met her patient's gaze and replied quickly, "Yes. It's not in your lymph nodes." She brought a hand up to cover her mouth before tears sprung into her eyes. Rosita stood up abruptly and walked towards the curtain, attempting to hide her emotions from view, but the sounds of muffled sobs betrayed her efforts. Manny felt helpless and confused, unable to move due to his heavy cast and bandages, yet desperate to comfort his friend if only he could.

He suddenly realized why she was crying, and said the name softly in more of a question than anything else, "Maggie."

Rosita's lips shivered as she gave a single nod in reply, her misty eyes never leaving Manny's. Fear crowded his lungs as he tried to take a breath. He wished he could read her expression without having to ask the dreaded questions, but they were already forming on his tongue. He swallowed hard and whispered, "How bad is it?"

Rosita buried her face in her hands and sobbed, the sound of her anguish shaking the walls around them. Manny stepped from the bed, feeling faint as he stood upright. He wanted to comfort her, but when he reached out with his left hand, Rosita flinched away. The bandages around his neck reminded him of the injury that will keep his arm immobile for days.

She edged away and brushed off his attempt at a hug. "We had to remove six lymph nodes in her armpit," she said quietly. "It's spreading fast. She probably won't regain much use of her hand, if any."

Manny sat back down with leaden limbs, his thoughts whirling around what the doctors could do to save little Maggie. Maybe the Algos' were right.

"We can only hope the vaccine works," he muttered.

At his words, Rosita's face flushed red and her dark eyes flashed with anger. She whipped around to face him, her long black hair twirling as she spat out her protest. Her voice rose louder and louder until nearby technicians nervously peered into the room. "What do you mean, 'we?'" Rosita snapped. "There is no 'we' here."

Manny held up one hand in a placating gesture, trying to bring some semblance of order back to the heated discussion. He looked at Rosita warily, softly questioning what she wanted from him.

"Nothing," Rosita seethed. "This is Maggie and me, just like it's always been." With those final parting words, Rosita turned on her heel and strode out of the curtained area, then turned abruptly to Manny once more. "I'll ask Dr. Strunk to take over your case."

Manny sat in stunned silence for a moment, hands trembling as his gaze shifted toward the nightstand. His earbuds softly vibrated, signaling an incoming call. He fumbled with them clumsily until they were securely in place, then clicked the sound shield to block out noise from the outside world. Ahh, it must be his twins calling to check up on him after surgery; at least someone still loves him. After the dressing down he just received, speaking with his children would be comforting.

John came in as Manny spoke lovingly with his children, promising to see them soon at the University of Santa Cruz Pod. He allowed Manny to finish the call before beginning his medical ministrations, asking questions and inspecting the cast and bandages while also reviewing the chart. "Came close to losing the hand there I see."

"Really?"

"You are lucky you had Dr. McKenna on the surgery," John replied and explained the incredible maneuvers Rosita took to catch the rhizomatous material without taking the tendons.

"That good, huh?" Manny asked in awe.

John moved to sit on the bed next to him and looked into Manny's eyes.

"I'm going to ask her to stay here at Stanford," he spoke slowly, almost apologetically. "We need her here, and it would be so much better than the Chelsea Pod One hospital."

Manny's thoughts swept him away. He cocked his head, trying to connect unconnectable dots. "You want her to stay here?"

"Yes, we've discussed it and she didn't say no." John stood back up and switched on a lamp attached to his shield. He carefully examined the scar on Manny's forehead, then moved the light across his neck, scrutinizing the pre-cancerous lesions there. He snapped several photos for comparison with earlier scans in Manny's file. As he stared intently at the results, his expression became increasingly solemn.

Manny couldn't contain his curiosity any longer. "What's up?"

"It's still early days," John replied cautiously, "but the new rhizomatous lines in your scalp appear to be receding. Activate your shield again so I can show you."

Manny fiddled with the interface on his visor and comparison images of two scans featuring a white line appeared side-by-side. He squinted to examine the differences between the two, but it was hard to see any noticeable changes.

"Do you see it?" John asked. "The long white line on the picture on the right from two days ago is now a little shorter in the left photo from right now."

Manny adjusted the focus and zoomed in for a closer look. Sure enough, its narrow white line shortened ever so slightly; he barely made out the thinning of the little white lines trying to erase him from existence. His heart raced as he realized the implications of what he saw. "It's slowing? It's getting better?"

John stood up and slapped Manny on his good arm. "Damn right, my friend. The vaccine is already working." John was absolutely joyous and pumped his fist in the air. "It's goddamn working!"

Manny sat speechless. This news might be the most hope he felt since this whole ordeal began a few years ago. Despite his newfound optimism, he also felt a tinge of sadness—an odd contradiction.

John explained that while ten percent of study patients see results early, most should expect to wait for two weeks or more before seeing any changes. "You are one of the lucky ones. I don't think we've ever seen results so quickly before," John said softly.

Manny remained still and quiet, processing John's words and the sudden shift in his life. He felt overwhelmed with a confusing mix of emotions, almost as if John had just dismissed him from his job as a cancer patient—a job he held for over two years now. Evidence of another of those seven emotions of any life changing event. But why did he feel depressed and why now?

John then leaned against him in silent friendship. The reassuring warmth of the gesture seemed to encourage Manny to keep going despite his doubts. Manny reminded himself there were still two more shots in the oven that would be ready in a week. And he thought of little Maggie.

CHAPTER 46

Received with goods now embraced,

Manny groaned and grappled to find his ear buds in the darkness and activate his shield. The harsh blue light of the display pierced through his dreams. He squinted at the caller ID: Theo was stuck in lockdown in Sunnyside three time zones ahead of them. Theo had found no shortage of projects to keep himself busy, constantly tinkering away: designing a solar power system, optimizing battery life, balancing power on a desalination plant, and fixing random items. His new worker-buddy, Randy, dressed in traditional plaid shirts and jeans, often stood in contrast to Theo's nanotech clothing that self-cleans. But what made Sunnyside so special for Theo were its people, the true magical ingredient Manny recognized and embraced.

Manny's eyes lit up as Theo's face came into view. The last three days were mentally and physically exhausting for Manny, but his newfound exhaustion suddenly dissipated with the presence of his trusted friend. He last spoke to Theo three days ago due to the rigors of the mRNA treatments and the Mohs surgery. Manny quickly summarized all that happened during his absence. As he spoke, Manny paced back and forth, his good hand gesturing wildly as he conveyed every detail. He briefly mentioned the faint optimism the mRNA might already be working its magic. He spoke so quickly that his words almost seemed to run together, and he kept stealing glances at Rosita and Maggie's patio as if he half-expected them to come out any second. Every now and then, temptation nearly drove him to send Greenie II around the barrier to say hello.

"I'm so happy for you," Theo finally said after Manny finished his explanation. Theo stood at the edge of a vast aquarium, seeming almost small in comparison as he peered into the glassy depths of an enormous tank. Countless long-necked fish swam gracefully through the tall stalks of sea grass behind him, their scales shimmering like tiny jewels in the bright light from above. Soft music hummed in the background, just audible enough to give an air of serenity without washing over Theo's thoughts. Fish near and far formed shapes with their swimming bodies; darting in perfect unison from one side to another, almost like diving into a secret underwater world. Theo asked, "Everything okay? You sound a little off."

Manny sighed heavily and slumped back into the chair on the patio outside his cabin. He looked out at the expansive vista of green, lush Stanford fields that spread before him. His eyes were glassy, and he absently sipped from a cold coffee cup. "Yes, but…I can't shake this heavy feeling in my chest, like something is dragging me down and I can't explain why," he mumbled.

Theo let Manny add a few more details to describe his sadness while an uncomfortable silence hung between them. Then Theo spoke with knowing eyes, "Rosita McKenna."

Manny's face contorted with pain as the name left Theo's lips. "Well, she won't even talk to me! She fired me as a patient! I don't understand how someone could do that to another person."

Theo's hearty chuckle caused Manny to pause. He tried to process how someone as intelligent as Manny could be so dense when it came to women. "Don't you think she has a lot on her plate right now? Maggie is going through the same thing as you," Theo said.

Manny nodded slowly in agreement, the words sinking in and making sense. He felt a cold splash of coffee on his pant leg and brushed it away distractedly. "I can't even see her. Rosita won't let me see little Maggie."

Just then, a small voice came from around the corner of the patio wall and drifted onto Manny's patio. "Hi Manny!"

Manny's heart sank and fluttered at the same time. Had she heard their whole conversation? "Maggie? Is that you?" Manny asked.

"Where have you been?" Maggie asked with genuine concern. She explained how she searched for him for days to ask him some questions. Her voice held soft and steady.

"Is your mother there?" Manny asked while noting that Theo remained connected on the call. He quickly whispered for him to talk later, and double-clicked on his end to disconnect the call.

"No, she's taking a bath," Maggie explained while standing out on her patio. The cool morning breeze blew over her, making goosebumps rise on her skin and causing her to shiver slightly. She'd chosen a nanotechnology outfit and added a blue tutu over the top for some extra warmth. Trying to catch a glimpse of Manny, she leaned out over the patio railing but could not see past the dividers extending between them. "Can I see you, Manny?"

Manny stood up and joined her at the railing, only about four feet apart but separated from seeing each other by the large wall. "I can't, Maggie. Your mom is not my doctor anymore. How are you feeling today?"

Maggie sighed softly and gestured to her armpit. "Not so good. My armpit really hurts," she murmured, using her healthy arm to scratch gently at the bandage covering her arm and shoulder. "And it itches!"

"That's a good sign if it itches," Manny said, trying to reason with her. "That means it's healing."

Maggie pouted and scratched absently through the fabric of the sling while answering him, her eyes glassy and tearful. "I don't know why Mommy is crying so much then," she said.

Just then, Rosita's voice came from behind Maggie. "Who are you talking to?"

Maggie turned around guiltily and replied, "Manny."

Rosita placed a fresh towel over her hair and closed her plush, oversized hotel robe. She moved over to the railing without making a sound and leaned over the railing. "What are you talking about?"

Manny's heart thumped against his chest as he felt Rosita's piercing gaze somehow through the dividing wall. He quickly stood to attention, doing his best to ignore the dull throb in his arm, and stammered out a greeting, "Good morning, Rosita."

Rosita nodded politely, though her expression betrayed more than just pleasantries. "Good morning, Dr. Rio," she said awkwardly. Then she asked, "How are you feeling today?"

Manny exhaled slowly before answering her question, "I'm good, thanks," he replied, trying to steel himself for whatever conversation might follow. He leaned farther over the railing, gripping the top railing with his good arm while readjusting his dead arm into its sling. After a pause, he offered, "Are you up for a cup of coffee? I have some good news from Sunnyside."

"Please Mommy, I want Manny to visit me," Maggie pleaded, her big blue eyes full of hope.

"I'm sure Dr. Rio is busy today," her mother responded.

"I actually have some free time, if you'd like," Manny offered. "I would like to see Maggie before I head out for the day."

Maggie's face lit up and she jumped, pleading with her mom to go along with Manny, no matter where that was. Rosita threw out all her best arguments, but eventually saw the sparkle in her daughter's eyes and realized they were speaking around the corner on the patio instead of using their video monitors as any civilized person would do. Wiping away a strand of hair, she said reluctantly, "Give us twenty minutes. We'll meet you at the café downstairs."

Manny clapped his hands together in excitement. He grabbed his grooming kit and set to work tidying himself up—trimming his sideburns and split ends; using a comb-in hair color that dampened the increasing number of gray hairs; brushing his teeth awkwardly using his left hand; wiping away some splashes on his blue nanotechnology shirt that he always thought made his eyes seem brighter than usual.

He then opened one of his FOUPs that contained a batch of croissants expertly stored in a blanket of argon instead of nitrogen, a trick he learned from the Sunnyside Farm. After giving himself one last look in the mirror and running a hand over his neatly tucked shirt, he grabbed the croissants and headed out the door towards the café downstairs where he knew his friends would be waiting.

The late morning sun guided him to the quaint café located at the rear of the main lobby. He stepped through the entrance and greedily inhaled the jasmine-scented air that lingered throughout the courtyard. A trickling brook snaked around glistening cobblestones and lush greenery before settling next to a vibrant bush of jasmine flowers, their yellow petals glowing against the warm sunlight.

Manny chose an empty table near the outside patio and waited for Maggie and Rosita to arrive. An eager smile lit up Manny's face as he spotted Maggie entering the courtyard. She ran towards him in an explosion of laughter and color, her rainbow-colored tutu bouncing with each step. The jasmine-scented air tickled their noses when they embraced, and Manny noticed the arm slings on both of them—matching but opposite—and the bandages on their scalps. Both of their bandages grew smaller as the days went by and the stitches healed. Manny asked Maggie how she was doing and she replied, "Oh Manny, I missed you so much!" before launching into an excited explanation of all that had happened while they were apart. She looked at his arm and pointed. "And I want to see Sweet Pea!"

"Sweet Pea is gone now," Manny replied. He looked at Rosita with a warm smile and tried to move his dead arm in the sling. "Thanks to your Mommy."

Rosita looked away, guilt tugging at her heartstrings. In her desperation to keep Manny and Maggie apart while they underwent surgery, she forgot what a crucial comfort it is to have someone who understands what you're going through. She finally replied, "Nice to see you, Dr. Rio."

Manny watched Rosita as she spoke, while taking in details of her outfit. She tucked her skinny jeans into her long black boots, and a wide leather belt cinched her blue blouse at the waist. Nothing ventured, nothing gained. He decided to test the waters and see how receptive she was feeling today. "Nice to see you too, Rosita," he replied with a sly grin.

Rosita didn't return the grin but merely nodded, her cheeks flushing ever so slightly. Manny knew this could mean anything or nothing, but he was willing to take it as a good sign for now.

Soon enough, a staff person arrived to take their order. She was young, likely a university student. She wore the standard light blue uniform of the university's staff, her young face lit up with a bright smile. An ID lanyard hung around her neck, and she accessorized her outfit with a variety of colorful beads, clips, and pins. "We have some specials today if you would like to hear about them?"

Maggie asked, "Do you have any cake?"

"No, we do not," the staff person replied politely. "We do have a nice ham and eggs special though. Mixed right at your table White Cube style, which means it'll be nutritious."

All three travelers wrinkled their noses in unison at the thought of White Cube food. They preferred the fresh food from the wonderful FOUPs provided by Sunnyside. Although nearly out, Manny devised a plan for refilling their FOUPs for the remainder of their stay.

"Mommy," Maggie whined with her bottom lip jutting out in an exaggerated pout. "Can we please have something fresh?"

Manny interjected before Rosita could respond. He looked at the waitress and said, "That's okay. We brought snacks for now."

"Okay then, I'll be right back with your drinks," she chirped cheerfully as she spun on her heel and moved quickly toward the counter to place their order. Cheapskates, she probably thought as she walked away.

Rosita and Manny exchanged a conspiratorial glance when they were alone again. He reached into his satchel and pulled out three croissants wrapped in paper and set them on the table. Maggie's face lit up immediately. Rosita beamed at Manny and said, "I don't know what we'd do without you!"

Manny's heart skipped a beat, and both he and Rosita laughed as Maggie eagerly devoured two of the treats in quick succession.

Manny slid the last croissant closer to Maggie encouragingly, even though Rosita shook her head in protest. Maggie devoured the croissant, then looked expectantly at her mother for permission to leave the table. Rosita eventually nodded with a smile, allowing her daughter to investigate a bird nearby that caught her eye. Maggie gingerly approached the bird as it bounced along the rocks at the edge of the little stream.

Manny asked right away when Maggie was out of earshot, "Any good signs yet?"

Rosita stared down at her cappuccino, a look of despair on her face. She idly stirred the cup with a spoon, taking small nibbles of one croissant that lay partially eaten on the side plate. "But Dr. Strunk said you already show some good signs, right?"

Manny spoke up again, trying to lighten the mood once more. "He said I'm one of the lucky ones. The second set of doses is in a few days. John said that is when most people start seeing results."

"I can only pray at this point. But I'm so happy for you." Rosita looked at Manny briefly. The only thing that kept her going lately was the idea that some unseen force was listening to her. At night, after getting Maggie to bed, she sat in quiet contemplation, whispering her worries and hopes out loud into the still air.

Manny held his own belief system but he struggled to find the time to talk to God these days with his busy life. His grandfather used to take him to church when he was younger, but that stopped upon his passing. Now it was hard to find the time to carve out a specific time to talk to the force, but like most humans, the time of need causes the time to pray. He glanced at his bandaged hand. "Believe me, I have been doing my share of that lately."

Manny bowed his head and tried to find a connection to the divine, but the pleasant sounds of Maggie's footsteps as she crept toward the bird distracted him. The bird, an elegant sparrow, kept one eye trained on Maggie and hopped away a few paces every time she inched closer. Eventually, Maggie stopped moving and held her breath, watching the bird cautiously. She observed its mistrust of humans, even though it knew it was safe with her.

Rosita glanced from Manny to her daughter and then back again. She took a deep breath before deciding to reveal something. "You know, she has no father."

"Really?" Manny replied, surprised. He noticed the absence of any male figure in Maggie's life and wondered why her father wasn't around.

"Artificial insemination with a scheduled birth," Rosita explained. Tears began to fill her eyes as she thought about all the school required for her medical degrees and how there never seemed to be enough hours in the day for dating or having children in the traditional way; artificial insemination was the only way she could have a baby. She looked up at Manny, feeling ashamed and embarrassed that she chose that route. "My sister helped me the whole way, luckily."

Manny glanced at Rosita compassionately. "I think you've done a marvelous job raising her," he said truthfully as he stirred his coffee with a miniature plastic spoon. "She is an amazing little person."

Rosita shifted her gaze to the wall behind Manny, trying to compose herself. Her fingernails tapped anxiously against each other as she sighed, then said, "What if this doesn't work? What if she keeps getting worse?"

Manny reached out and gently placed his good hand on top of Rosita's trembling one. She flinched slightly but kept still. He gave it a light squeeze. "Don't even think that. Don't say that. Remember *Abraham's Law*."

As Manny spoke, Rosita studied his face intently, and absorbed his explanation of the ancient spiritual law. He said they must stay positive and have faith that all would be well. The energy one gives out to the world is the same energy received back.

Rosita realized their hands were still intertwined and gently edged away from him as she said softly, "You're right. We have to stay strong and trust."

Manny stared down at his empty hand, feeling as though all time stopped for a moment. He finally found his voice again and said softly, "I want you to come to the farm with me."

Rosita's mind reeled at his invitation. "The Santa Cruz farm?" She asked, her voice barely above a whisper.

Maggie walked back from the little creek and must have heard that question. "What farm?"

"My kids are meeting me at the University of Santa Cruz Vertical Farm," Manny explained. "We can take a Beeze and be there in an hour."

"What about the lockdown?"

"Mommy, I want to go, please, please."

"I just read a report from the WHO and it doesn't appear to be spreading this far," Manny explained. He had spoken to John about their trip out to the farm, reporting that CATACS's lockdowns were showing success in containing the virus. But if the farm went into lock down for too long, they might miss their second set of injections. John replied without hesitation that he would break the law if necessary to ensure they got the shots.

Rosita quietly took notes on her tablet, jotting down questions about the farm, its location, its importance, the risks, and numerous other related subjects. Maggie continued her chorus of protests while Manny described the farm's safety protocols.

Finally, Manny finished explaining the plan and waited for Rosita's response. "And we can reload our FOUPs with fresh food," he added.

At this last bit of information, Rosita smiled widely and exclaimed, "Good! I can't go back to eating that White Cube crap again."

CHAPTER 47
All return the very the next day,

The three travelers gathered outside Dr. John Strunk's office, looking for his assurance that it was okay to leave the control group of the clinical trial for the day. He emerged from the small room and welcomed them warmly, reassuring them that their trip was safe. His thin lips curled into an appreciative smile as he mentioned that Manny's children occasionally delivered fresh food to him from the farm over the year since they'd arrived on the west coast, and asked if they could bring him back a few steaks again.

The streets surrounding the Stanford Hospital were fairly empty, with people either walking or cycling along the quaint university grounds. The campus air smelled fresh and resembled the quiet of a farm, yet distant from one—the nearest actual farmland being miles away. This institution had recently introduced vertical farming to its curriculum in collaboration with the University of Santa Cruz's beachfront vertical farm, as access to seawater made it an ideal location for advanced cultivation techniques. The trio waited along the curb for a Beeze to break away from the pack and pick them up for the ride to the coast.

Finally, a four-person Beeze pulled up in front of them and opened its double doors. Manny held out his hand to help Maggie get inside first, but Rosita stepped in without taking his offered hand. Once all three passengers settled into their seats, the Beeze took off towards the coast.

Manny told the others about his twins, describing Amy as loving and intelligent while Alex is abrupt, impulsive, and equally smart as Amy. Both studied agricultural sciences at the local university and now work at the university's vertical farm, called, "Slug Farm," an homage to the school mascot. With nostalgia in his voice, he remembered how the twins rebelled against him during his time at White Cube Research, not understanding why he had to keep his day job to make ends meet.

Maggie listened intently for a while, only asking a few questions about the twins. "Where is their Mommy?"

Manny and Rosita looked at each other, and Manny replied thoughtfully, trying to suppress the sadness in his voice. "She's very busy with her own life, so she's not around much. But the kids can see her every once in a while, when they want to."

Maggie thought about that and changed the subject to point out the redwood trees that towered along Highway 17. The tallest of them stretched into the sky for 300 feet and cast a long shadow over the Beeze. "Mommy, look at how big those trees are!" she exclaimed in awe.

Manny smiled to himself with a shake of his head. He took this same route so many times that the stunning natural scenery was no longer eye-catching; it became like the Japanese phrase, "Kabe ni kieteiku," which meant, literally, "like wall." A piece of art hung on a wall for too long will gradually melt away and become hidden within the rest of the background, becoming invisible to those passing by. In Japan, they switch out artwork in their "Tokonoma," or display area, every week to keep each piece from joining the wall's pattern and disappearing into the wall and "becoming the wall."

The Beeze took the travelers across the top of the mountain range and began its descent down to the ocean, which revealed itself as they turned curves and saw the ocean in openings between the trees. Soon, Maggie and Rosita spotted the Pacific Ocean sprawling out beneath them, a mix of blues and greens and an occasional wisp of fog that drifted in and out with the tides. California contained its own air conditioning system. After several hot days, the fog rolled in from the coast and cooled down the land before disappearing again. This cycle of changing the weather repeated every three or four days.

"Is that really the Specific Ocean?" Maggie asked, leaning closer to the glass with her nose nearly pressed against it.

Rosita smiled patiently, "Pacific Ocean." Then she turned to Manny and added, "we used to come here all the time when I was little."

Manny knew she must be thinking about Dr. John Strunk's offer to come work at Stanford, one of the most prestigious medical establishments in the world. Then she could be back to where she grew up. "I think the Pacific is more picturesque than the Atlantic, but it isn't as warm," he mused with a bold grin on his face.

Maggie gazed up at them with those big imploring eyes. "Can we swim in it? Please?"

Rosita brushed aside Maggie's hair and avoided contact with the sutures on her scalp. She replied with a hint of suggestion in her voice, "Maybe another time, Sweetheart. First, let's go see some chickens!"

Manny beamed with fatherly pride, eager for his twins to finally meet Rosita and Maggie, both of whom heard countless stories about them in the past few weeks. A million questions came at Manny from all directions, with Maggie leading the charge. He smiled, shielding himself from potential mortification knowing that an eight-year-old doesn't exactly have an internal censor.

Checking his shield to make sure their planned noon arrival was still accurate, he confirmed the Beeze's direction towards the farm situated near the University of Santa Cruz Pod. The waves of the ocean crashed against the rocky shoreline to their left as they drove past cove after cove of alternating cliff faces and sandy beaches. Every few miles, the terrain shifted around them while the mountain range to their right stayed constant and stretched its way north across California, like a giant handrail.

The Beeze suddenly slowed and signaled to turn right into a small canyon. The sign at the gate read, "University of Santa Cruz Vertical Farm." The locals called the place "Slug Farm," in honor of the big yellow slimy banana slug chosen as their mascot decades ago.

Manny surveyed the building with pride. He was involved in its inception and development; his knowledge of vertical sustenance growing (VSG) was instrumental in its construction. Though still in its early stages, Slug Farm mirrored the more advanced Sunnyside model—complete with FOUP delivery, solar panels on the roof, and last mile delivery methods—which Manny also helped create.

Just like the Sunnyside Farm, Slug Farm placed the fish aquariums at the top of the glass and structural steel building. Salt water from the nearby ocean filled the tanks to support the saltwater fish, consisting mainly of surf perch, salmon, albacore and rock cod. During winter months, Dungeness crab scurried along the bottom of the tanks. This saltwater then travels through a reverse osmosis system, a high-pressure membrane filter that purifies it, to feed the freshwater tanks. They were very close to getting the fish tanks to a self-sustaining point.

The nutrient-rich runoff that results from this water process feeds the livestock beds below, helping them grow food for the livestock. The cows kept for dairy and cattle for beef produced manure and fertilizer, which is collected in composting systems and sent to the vertical wall farms of the Santa Cruz Pod, just like bigger cities that grow vegetables on the walls of their buildings.

Maggie wanted to go up to the poultry level, between the tanks of fish and the bottom floor of livestock. Her love for chickens and fresh eggs drew her to that floor now that she understood eggs made chocolate cake. This farm raised chickens mostly, but also some pheasants, hens, and ducks. Like Sunnyside, a spiral walkway led fresh supplies upward when the whole ecosystem fell out of balance. Then the farm must ship in fresh crops and poultry from the more rural areas where they grew on old fashioned farms. That happened less often than at Sunnyside due to the lessons Manny shared with other farms. Get things right at Sunnyside first, then spread these teachings around.

The Beeze slowed to a stop in front of the main lobby and Manny clambered out, bracing himself with his left arm. He heaved a huge black bag from the back seat, and Maggie appeared after it. Rosita stepped out much more delicately and glanced up at the tall glass and steel structure. Meanwhile, the twins barreled towards them, shouting Manny's name and waving excitedly.

Amy was first to reach her dad and launched herself into his embrace. "Daddy, I missed you!"

Alex followed suit and joined the hug. "How's your arm feeling?" he asked as he ran his fingers over Manny's sling. Rosita stood a few feet away from the family reunion, her gaze drifting up the tall glass and steel structure of the main lobby.

Maggie arrived next at the scene and stepped tentatively into the group hug. Alex glanced at Manny in surprise but gave Maggie a gentle pat on the head before releasing them all from the hug. Manny introduced Amy and Alex to Rosita and Maggie. Alex regarded Maggie with curiosity, seeing all the bandages wrapped around her arm, all the way up to her shoulder. The large number of bandages covering Maggie's arm was definitely more than those covering his own father.

Manny adjusted the sling that held his dead arm in place, watching as Alex opened the large bag that now rested on the ground. He pulled out a heavy, black and green box with a blinking green light around its edges, which he recognized as Greenie, Manny's trusted drone. Manny quickly activated it to fly above him in follow-me mode. Underneath it in the bag, several empty FOUPs rolled around the bag. Alex slung the bag over his shoulder and watched as his father's Beeze moved back out through the gates to rejoin the swarm outside. "What can Greenie do now?" asked Alex, eager to see just what sort of new gadgetry Manny brought this time.

The group approached the glass doors of the lobby when a technician behind the front desk spotted Dr. Manuel Rio and practically leapt from his chair. He asked Manny if he wanted to see their new freshwater tank improvements, and the twins' eyes widened at seeing how excited their father made this young student, a young man named Matthew Summons.

Amy smiled politely at him, and Manny wondered if that was a factor for why the technician seemed so thrilled. Maggie nudged the twin's arms, insisting they go on the tour of the aquariums and then see the chickens. Alex made sure their bag of FOUPs would be waiting for them in the lab. With that, they all headed off together. Suddenly, Matthew stumbled back to the desk and grabbed a small black plastic rectangle, excitement twinkling in his eyes. He held it out to Manny, voice barely a whisper, "This came in today by drone. It's from NASA!"

Manny accepted the box, his heart racing with anticipation. He shared knowing glances with his children and they all chattered about the item during their ride up the elevator and until they arrived on the top floor. Alex asked his father about the grant he sought - his faint hope that this little box was an update on the grant. A shield-call scheduled for that night may provide more information. This may finally be the much-needed funding for Slug Farm.

The group stepped out of the elevator and onto a terrace area between two large tanks, one saltwater and one freshwater. The light of the sun shone through skylights above, reflecting off the scaly hides of fish swimming in both tanks. Dividers in each tank separated the various species and delicate fronds of kelp swayed back and forth in the saltwater tank, while little schools of bright-colored fish darted from rock formation to rock formation in the freshwater tank. Moss and ferns provided an intricate backdrop to the scene, while at certain angles, one could spot some bottom feeders wriggling among the carefully cultivated natural environment.

Manny's eyes widened as he surveyed this version of the saltwater tank, marveling at the complexity for the west coast species of fish. He knew how difficult it was to maintain the perfect balance of salinity and temperature. Suspended in the water, albacore and salmon swam effortlessly, but Manny was most intrigued by the delicious Dungeness crab; its complicated process of cultivation is why they are so sought-after during winter months. He watched one crab walk sideways while it seemed to be watching Manny suspiciously through the glass.

Matthew waved his hands with enthusiasm, pointing out the details of Slug Farm to Maggie and Rosita, his muscular physique evident beneath his loose shirt, a testament to the hours he spent surfing at the local beach. He'd bleached his naturally light blonde hair even blonder with the endless hours spent in the California sunshine. Manny noticed the blue flecks that shimmered in Matthew's eyes when he spoke about his agricultural studies at Santa Cruz and his admiration for Dr. Rio himself. Manny wanted to have a word with him about the new type of desalination plant they developed, but he knew that would have to wait for another day. Tonight, they must attend a meeting with NASA to talk about how to pay for all of this.

Matthew waved the small group forward, stepping aside so Manny could lead the way. As they walked, Matthew explained a new technique they used to create fresh water. He motioned to the equipment around them as he spoke and explained the electro-active bacteria in an electrochemical system that powers the desalination.

Manny nodded in agreement; his eyes bright with excitement. "You have such a great amount of solar potential here. You could add photovoltaic for electricity and solar energy cells for evaporation."

Alex, tagging along behind Matthew, piped up from the back of the group with an enthusiastic nod of his head. His dark brown curls bounced as he spoke, "Exactly! We can have all three here!"

Manny's eyes lit up in agreement while speaking of the potential for solar energy at this location, his excitement contagious. Alex joined in and vigorously nodded his head in agreement. Alex's dark brown curls bounced as he voiced his enthusiasm for incorporating all three desalination types into their plans.

Manny beamed, his blue eyes lighting up as he related how Sunnyside Farm became independent of the grid thanks to its photovoltaic solar power system. Matthew's lips pursed in admiration, and he implored Manny for advice on an installation at their place. Alex, ever eager, echoed this sentiment with a "Yeah, Dad! Help us get one too."

Amy gently stepped between them, her hand lightly resting on her father's arm. "That's enough for now boys. Daddy has some things that need taking care of first." Her voice was tender but authoritative and Alex, realizing what she meant, trailed along behind them quietly. Matthew wasn't aware of the medical issues and gave Alex a quizzical look as they left him there in the hallway.

"Let's go. I want to see the chickens!" Maggie yelled out and grabbed Rosita's hand, pulling her away from the giant aquarium.

Manny stopped and watched as Maggie and Rosita hurriedly scurried by after admiring a lethargic fish suspended near the glass. With an exaggerated gesture, he pointed towards the exit. "To the chickens! Follow me!"

CHAPTER 48

Some seek reasons why they stay away,

The drop-off at the Slug Farm went by without problems. Isolated in his long hauler for over two weeks now, Coop longed for the fresh air and freedom, only briefly experienced when he took walks in a type of space suit used for repairs on Betsy to keep her functioning properly. The wait was agonizing in his eagerness to get to the Long Island Pod where Naoko waited for him. He must stay inside the truck for another two days to travel the rest of the way. Just as his spirits began to sink further, he heard a voice echoing off the metal walls of the cockpit.

"Cooper-san," Naoko spoke into her shield, her words a lifeline. "Where are you?" She accented her voice precisely, as if she calculated every syllable beforehand, making sure they carried enough weight to reach him even in his darkest hour.

Coop activated his shield and saw her beautiful face on the screen; her hair pulled back in a neat ponytail, her earrings shining in the light—the same ones he sent her before leaving. "Where are you? We need you here," she continued.

Coop swallowed hard before answering. "I'm going around the Chicago pods right now."

Naoko's face softened and a hint of a smile appeared at the corner of her mouth. "Oh, Cooper-san, I can't wait to see you again. But please be careful. The virus spread very quickly to Long Island Pod. We have two cases already in Sunnyside Farm and they are pretty serious."

Coop knew about the news of the severe situation on the east coast -

according to statistics from the United States, there was an overwhelming number of hospitalizations and almost a half-million deaths. Although Russia was rumored to have similar numbers, this information was not believable due to the lies released by the Politburo and its propaganda machine; however, CATACS reported more factual data, indicating one and a half million deaths in Moscow alone. He felt hesitant asking for the names of those infected at their farm.

Coop's face fell as Naoko solemnly replied, "James-san and Sato-san." He felt like James was a brother to him since he'd started hauling for the farm. He also felt sad upon hearing that the virus struck Naoko's best friend from college, Sato, who worked alongside her at Sunnyside. He swallowed hard, trying to extinguish the feeling of dread in his gut. "How are they doing?" he asked anxiously. "Are they okay?"

Naoko nodded her head solemnly. "James was very bad and was hospitalized, but he is back home now thanks to the new Covid vaccine." Coop worried for James' wife, Roberta; often people living together spread the virus rapidly at home. "Did Roberta get it too?"

"No, she was spared somehow," Naoko reassured him. "James is being isolated in their cabin, so Roberta stayed at Sunnyside Farm."

Coop felt a knot in his stomach as worry for all his friends washed over him. He was alone in the world, but he made a family with the people at Sunnyside. More than anything, he wished to be reunited with them and protect them from whatever this virus might bring. "I'll be there in about 20 hours."

"Cooper-san," Naoko said gently, her voice heavy with concern. "I think it would be best if you stayed away until the virus is gone."

"But that could be weeks," Coop replied desperately. "I can't wait that long. I need to come home."

Naoko's heart ached as she heard the desperate love radiating from his words and knew she couldn't deny him his wish, even though she feared for his safety. "But the virus…"

"I understand the risks, but I'm coming home," Coop said firmly. He'd already mapped out a plan to avoid potential tethers reported along the way by fellow long-haulers He approached many of those areas with every mile he shaved off between himself and Naoko. One danger was in his sights. "Naoko, I must sign off for now."

Naoko let out a sigh and stepped into her role of protector one last time. "I understand, my Cooper-san. May the virus miss you."

"And also miss you."

Coop nervously drove Betsy up to a checkpoint and approached a group of PoPos patrolling the jurisdiction. His heart raced as he thought about the precious cargo he carried—electro-chemical bacteria arranged by Theo for an experiment at Sunnyside—and the possible consequences if the PoPos stopped him. But when the PoPos identified themselves as working with the Bronx Pod, they checked with headquarters, nodded in recognition, and stepped aside to let him pass. Coop felt relieved. Evidently, Theo already explained to Mickey at the Bronx Pod the importance of their return shipment, and it seemed they now had preferential treatment.

CHAPTER 49
Before the third charm the plan goes awry,

Dr. John Strunk shook his head, "Maggie is getting worse and I'm not sure we can do much more for her. We can take out the rhizomatous growths in her scalp with a minor procedure, but then we won't be able to do the next dosage of mRNA."

Rosita clenched her fists. "But we could do the surgery right now!" She stared at John, struggling against an internal battle as she considered performing the surgery herself. The hospitals universally discouraged operating on one's own children or loved ones. Even operating on Manny was risky now that he was a source of strength for Rosita over their time together. Did this sense of comfort become romantic? Was she experiencing Nightingale Syndrome, where a person falls in love with those helping them? It seemed almost too familiar in the current situation: patient to doctor was common enough, but doctor to patient?

John leaned forward; his piercing gaze fixed on Rosita as he laid out the difficult situation before her. "A Mohs surgery will take out the malignant cells now, but it won't eliminate the risk of more growing elsewhere. Plus, the anesthetic would contaminate your daughter's bloodstream at an inopportune time just before her second dose of vaccine. That would be fatal to the trial."

Rosita could feel a sudden tension in the air as she took a deep breath and tried to process all that John told her. She ran her fingers through her dark hair, desperately searching for any kind of solution. "How long do we have to wait if we opt for surgery instead?"

John paused for a moment, rubbing his chin thoughtfully as he weighed his options. "At least two weeks," he admitted reluctantly, "but then she'll miss the expiration date of the current dosage being grown in the lab. The next round would take too long. She would miss the clinical trials."

Rosita felt her heart drop into her stomach as she asked, "And when is the next one?"

John let out a deep sigh before replying with a defeated tone, "I don't know. Depends on the success of this one first."

Rosita peppered him with more questions until she was satisfied with the facts. After one long-winded answer, Rosita stood by the window and looked down at the courtyard below. She saw Manny and Maggie standing alongside the creek below near the cafe, both with their arms hanging out of their slings. Manny checked the progress of his paralyzed limb by swinging it back and forth, and appeared to be regaining some feeling in it again. Maggie, however, moved her arm in a careful and slow motion due to the painful stitches in her armpit. Despite all of this, they laughed happily together, a sight that provided some comfort in such a difficult situation.

*   *   *

As Manny looked up at the hotel window, he noticed Rosita looking down at them. She stood in the window wearing simple green nanotechnology pants and a flowing white blouse tucked in at the waist with a cloth belt. The tight bun in her hair indicated Rosita's stress level. She waved an awkward half-wave before stepping away from the window.

Not long after, Rosita emerged in the courtyard wearing a lab coat to fend off the chill as the sun disappeared behind the mountain range. As she filled Manny in on Maggie's predicament, the little girl danced around the bubbling brook wearing her beloved pink tutu. When Rosita finished giving her assessment of the risks in front of them, Manny didn't say anything, mindful not to proffer his opinion unless asked.

"The next dose is tomorrow," he said as Rosita finished.

"And by that time, it could be spread in other places," Rosita quickly answered in a challenging voice.

"What does John think?" Manny replied softly, unsure of how to deal with her growing frustration. He watched silently as she tried to maintain her composure. Her eyes filled with anger and sadness, making him feel powerless. "He told me we should take the vaccine and do the surgery later if it's needed."

Rosita seemed to suddenly remember that Manny was her patient, not just a witness to her emotional distress. She sprang up from the small round table and assumed a resolute stance before him. Her crisp white coat lay open with its arms outstretched as if it actively collected data for a diagnosis. She commanded Manny to remain motionless.

She stepped closer to him and surveyed him with a critical eye. Moving her hands lightly over his head, she carefully removed the ever-shrinking bandage. For a moment, he felt her blouse brush against his cheek as she parted his hair to check the surgery scar. Finally, Rosita peeled back the last of the bandage and illuminated the surgery scar with a special light. Squinting and peering closely at the area, she examined the stitches and searched for signs of melanoma amongst the little white rhizomatous streaks. After what seemed like an eternity, Rosita returned to her seat and met Manny's questioning gaze.

"Well?" Manny asked hopefully.

"I don't see any new growth," Rosita replied slowly, "but I can't be sure unless we go into the office." A slight smile graced her face as she added, "I think you should take the next dose of the vaccine and knock this out of your system."

Manny studied the little white streaks every chance he could, knowing what they meant and how much danger they posed. But hearing it from a doctor, hearing that she believed there was no growth, gave him hope. He broke eye contact with Rosita and looked down at his hands in his lap. His good hand clutched the napkin tightly while his dead arm rested on the edge of the table, its fingers twitching ever so slightly. Tears filled his eyes and rolled down his cheeks unchecked despite his efforts to hold them back.

Rosita understood all too well; she saw countless cancer patients receive both good news and bad over the years. Bad news tended to cause shock, while good news often prompted tears of relief, especially when the patient endured so much agony already. She reached out and placed her hand on top of Manny's motionless one. The gesture didn't go unnoticed by him as he felt a warmth emanating from her touch. They stayed silent for a moment as Manny composed himself by breathing deeply. He looked over at Maggie as she ran around playing with a stick by poking it into water and drawing little diagrams on nearby patio stones.

*   *   *

Later that day, Manny connected to the shield call scheduled for that evening. He apprehensively placed the little black message box to his ear buds, and waited as a viewing screen opened up displaying the familiar NASA emblem. He knew that in order to gain access to the call, he would need to successfully pass several tests, including a retinal scan and DNA probing of his eyelashes. As he waited for the results, the seconds seemed to stretch on forever. Manny breathed a sigh of relief when the results finally cleared him for entry into the conference.

Manny virtually entered the conference room expecting to find colleagues, but instead there were only empty chairs and blank video monitors on the walls. After waiting for a few minutes, an automated message scrolled across one of the screens thanking Dr. Manuel Rio for his patience and informing him they postponed the meeting due to the unavailability of some attendees. Manny then saw a request asking whether he could also attend an in-person meeting at the University of Santa Cruz VSG farm. A checkbox awaited his acknowledgement, and Manny clicked it without even thinking.

CHAPTER 50

Man stopped at the bridge, time he cannot buy,

Coop pulled up to the gate of the Bridgeport Ferry in his long-hauler, Betsy. He glanced out at the windows of his cockpit and saw a long line of other long-haulers, private vehicles, and Beeze vehicles blocking the way. Beyond them he saw the flat skyline of Long Island Pod across the glimmering expanse of water, with his imagination painting beautiful Naoko waiting for him on the Sunnyside Farm. Suddenly Coop's shield activated.

"Coop," said a familiar voice.

"James! How the hell are you doing?"

"This thing nearly killed me!" James exclaimed, referring to the containment unit that held all its "inmates" in lockdown for two weeks now.

Coop speculated that James' athletic build, young age, and health regiment allowed him to recover quickly from the virus. James and Roberta both wore civilian clothes as they sat side by side in Roberta's office. She smiled warmly at her husband and yelled out a hello to Coop.

"I know. I heard. Naoko kept me posted the whole time. I tried to reach you but they wouldn't let me connect!" Coop explained, feeling joyous relief to be speaking with a friend again after such a long drive.

"Yeah, the bastards took my ear pods." James joked tiredly, while rubbing his mouth and nose—a feeling remnant of the days spent connected to a breathing apparatus while fighting off the virus before his own immune system could regain strength. People literally died from exhaustion due to this virus, so James was fortunate to have recovered as quickly as he did.

"Somebody else wants to talk to you too," Roberta said across the space of the room. "Go ahead and accept Theo's call."

"Coop, damn glad to hear your voice," Theo chimed in after seeing the connection fulfilled. His whiskery face showed up on Coop's viewer, his wild mane even thicker since the last time they saw one another. Theo asked, "Where are you?"

Coop seemed ecstatic to hear friend's voices again, knowing they were only a short distance away. Two weeks stuck on the road was too long. "Good to see you, Theo. I'm sitting at the terminal waiting for the ferry."

"I was afraid of that," Theo sighed into his communicator. "I was hoping you were already on it."

"Why? What's going on?" Coop asked as he studied his latest communications from the ferry PoPos, a nervous feeling forming in the pit of his stomach.

"Bridgeport is throwing tethers on all traffic coming through their docks. Too many people trying to get to New York by taking the ferry," Theo explained. "I talked to Mickey and there isn't anything she can do. No way around it now. Just try to sit tight until we figure out what to do."

Coop looked astounded, stalled literally within sight of his destination across the bay after all of this effort and travel. He thought about the shipment in the hold and checked the timer on his dashboard, which was quickly counting down.

"We won't make it in time," Theo warned. "If we don't get it hooked up soon, the bacteria will die."

Theo, Roberta, and James were all too aware of the impact that Santa Cruz's new desalination process could have. If Sunnyside managed to use the electrochemical bacteria successfully, then they would be able to pass on their knowledge to other farms across the globe. Already over thirty vertical farms joined forces with them, which brought them closer to their objective of creating a perpetual food supply, and breaking away from White Cube. This new desalination method was the last piece of the puzzle.

"How much time do we have left?" Coop asked anxiously, hoping his own meter was incorrect.

Roberta answered for Theo, who paced back and forth between them, and said, "Two days max."

Theo suddenly stopped his frenzied pacing, planted his feet firmly on the floor and stared across the room at Roberta and James. His blue eyes were hard and intense as he stood unmoving, brow furrowed in thought and mouth clamped shut. Coop was confused, not knowing what to expect from Theo's seemingly random question. "How heavy is the bag of bacteria?"

Coop visualized the large black container that sat in the living pod of Betsy, and remembered watching the twins delicately maneuvering it with thick canvas straps over their shoulders while they discussed where it would be best stored. "I don't know, maybe seventy pounds? It's in a cooler."

Theo didn't even pause to acknowledge Coop's reply as he continued staring at Roberta and James vacuously, his wheels spinning quickly. After an uncomfortable stretch of silence, Theo finally broke free from his trance with a proclamation, "You know, I bet it floats."

CHAPTER 51
Third path is all in a mess,

Dr. John Strunk trudged down the hallway, his crisp white nanotechnology doctor's smock billowing behind him with each step. He clasped two vials of precious vaccine in one hand and adjusted the bright blue embroidered name tag on the other side with his thumb. The tag showed the label, "Successful Clinical Trial CV78," printed beneath the letters of his name in celebratory gold font. John entered the antechamber of his office expecting to find both Manny and Maggie waiting for him, but only Manny sat there in the seats provided.

Confused by her absence, he asked, "Where is Maggie?"

Manny shrugged helplessly and replied, "I don't know. I've been trying to reach Rosita all morning."

John nodded, then tapped his finger against his electronic shield and spoke in a low voice. He listened to the answers, asked a few more questions, and instantly went to Manny. "She is in OR2 on the third floor." He set the vials down on the counter nearby before turning back to Manny, who quickly jumped to his feet, undoubtedly anxious to get the dosage administered. John motioned for Manny to remain seated but he stood anyway and insisted on following John. In tandem, the two men marched out of the antechamber and up the stairs, eventually emerging in the wing of operating rooms where they continued their swift journey towards one of the operating rooms on the third floor.

Manny and John burst into the operating room, breathing heavily from the sprint. Rosita looked up dismissively and then back to focus on her work, carefully setting up instruments in preparation for surgery. Maggie remained seated upright in the preparation chair at the center of the room, with the block team hovering above her ready to start the anesthesia. Manny spoke first, "Rosita, wait."

Rosita instantly cutoff his request with a thunderous yell, "Get out of here!" Her face hardened with anger, her eyes flashing at this interruption.

"Rosita, it's time for the vaccine dosage. This surgery can wait," John said with a stern and unyielding tone, his piercing blue eyes measuring up his colleague across the operating room.

Rosita met his icy stare head-on, her jaw set firm and her voice determined. "No, it cannot." She squared her shoulders and lifted her chin in an unconscious gesture of defiance.

"You are a visiting surgeon here and nothing more," he countered, maintaining his posture of authority while his gaze held hers. "I will not allow this surgery to be performed without the proper authorizations."

Maggie sat between the two arguing doctors, her head secured by a chin strap that forced her immobility during the block procedure. Frustrated with the adults for raising their voices and forgetting about her, she angrily pushed aside the block needles that hovered too close to her face. "Mommy, I want the vaccine," she said firmly.

Rosita felt her heart flutter as her daughter spoke up. She'd explained previously the surgery would help and she could start the clinical trial over again in a few months. "Honey, we spoke about this."

"I want the vaccine! I'm tired of these surgeries!" Maggie's voice began to rise with determination and without warning, she unstrapped herself, stood up and tore off her sling. She walked over to Dr. Strunk and reached out to him with her barely-alive hand, holding his hand tightly as if to steady herself. Every person in the room stood quietly to the side. The assisting technicians averted their eyes and pretended to be busy.

Rosita looked astonished after Maggie shouted at her. Rosita tried to reason with her, suggesting they have the surgery first and try the vaccine later, but Maggie would not budge, sheltering herself behind Dr. Strunk. Rosita stared daggers at Manny, speechless in her fury, before slowly advancing towards Maggie and the doctor. She attempted to take her daughter's hand but Maggie pulled away. "Maggie, Mommy knows what is best for you."

Maggie shifted her eyes between her mother and the doctor before pausing on Manny. "You're getting the vaccine, right?" she asked flatly.

Manny swallowed hard before answering truthfully, "Yes, I'm going to get it right now."

"Then I'm going with you," Maggie declared coldly.

Rosita glanced between the two of them in confusion. She thought back to Dr. Strunk's offer to work at Stanford and how badly she wanted to accept it, but now it seemed that offer may be gone. Taking a deep breath, she spoke up, her voice steady and calm. "Dr. Strunk, I'm her mother. What do you plan to do about this?"

John eyed her for a moment before responding in a professional tone. "You, as the legal guardian, have the right to choose. However, if you choose to have the surgery, I will assign another doctor to perform that surgery. I cannot allow a visiting surgeon to operate on their own daughter at this hospital."

She stared angrily in frustration. "But I thought I had full approval for surgery here."

The doctor raised an eyebrow at her questioningly. "You must ask yourself, are you a surgeon or a doctor? A surgeon cuts; a doctor treats. Which one are you?"

The words struck hard. Rosita felt a wave of embarrassment and confusion wash over her as she glanced down at the ground. She exhaled slowly before raising her gaze again, preparing herself to answer the inquisition. "I'm a doctor," she said, barely above a whisper. "Can we go to your office and discuss the options?"

Maggie stepped forward with a determined look on her face. "No, Mommy. I want to hear what Dr. Strunk says. This is my life you know." The little girl crossed both arms defiantly, although a slight grimace became evident when she touched her swollen armpit. Manny stared at Maggie in amazement but managed not to show any reaction. Rosita simply stared at her daughter, taken aback by this sudden burst of maturity.

Rosita turned back to John for guidance and asked, "Well then, what do you recommend?"

John answered without hesitation, "I recommend we get the vaccine into this young lady immediately."

Maggie took Manny's arm with her left hand, which had a matching bandage to Manny's right hand with the contrived cast. She pointed dramatically to the door, stretched like she was starting a march, and declared boldly, "To the vaccine!"

CHAPTER 52
But the fourth may be the very best,

Manny observed that Rosita preciously counted each day since Maggie received the third and fourth dosage of the medication—three days counting, and still no improvement. Maggie nervously shuffled her feet, her hands turning to fists, every time Rosita reached out to check for progress. Everywhere Rosita and Maggie went, Manny went too. He had a knack for being present around the hotel, even though Rosita tried hard not to be in his vicinity.

One afternoon while Rosita sat near the hotel room window browsing on her shield, probably searching for other potential treatments for Maggie, Manny looked up from the courtyard and saw Rosita standing at the window, clutching the curtain tightly as she watched them before quickly turning away and returning to her search. Manny wondered if Stanford still wanted her to stay or if she decided on returning back to Chelsea Pod One. Rosita seemed to feel part of something other than hospital life when she was at Sunnyside.

Maggie asked to go back up to the rooms, seeming a little more tired than normal. Manny asked if she had the energy to see Slug Farm today. They held hands as they walked to the rooms, Maggie bouncing in her excitement once more.

"Mommy!" Maggie burst into the room with Manny trailing behind her. "Let's all go to the Slug Farm!"

Manny stood just outside the doorway, and considered something internally. Rosita asked politely "Dr. Rio, how are you today?"

The pattern of two steps forward and two steps back was getting old;

when was he ever going to make any real progress? He responded with an affirmative "I'm fine, thank you" before following her gesture to enter the room. As they reached the table by the window, Maggie excitedly told them Manny planned something special to show them at the farm.

Manny saw the spark of interest in Rosita's eyes as he talked about taking Greenie, the drone, to demonstrate the new FOUPs. The opportunity to show off their accomplishments and Sunnyside's progress towards self-sustainability, with a NASA representative present, seemed too good to be true.

Rosita paused for a moment, and Manny saw her struggling with an internal battle. He recalled his own Three D's strategy for dealing with emotional stress, Delay, Distract, and Deal with it later, and thought maybe that's what Rosita was practicing. Taking a deep breath, Rosita looked back at him and asked, "When do we leave?"

Manny felt relief wash over his body, not only from Rosita's question but also from Maggie's sudden outburst of joy. Maggie jumped into his arms with excitement and hugged him tightly, her two arms functioning perfectly without the previous tugs from her armpit scar. Maggie jumped back down and rushed off to select an outfit for their trip before her mother's voice stopped her in her tracks.

"Maggie," Rosita said calmly, "I need to check your scar again."

"Aw Mom! Not again…" Maggie groaned.

Manny felt a mix of emotions that displayed on his face: sheepishness, worry, hope, and concern. "I'd like to see it as well," he said.

Manny nervously watched as Rosita grabbed a small device from her desk, a little tool that attached to her shield, which she skillfully and quickly assembled. She gently pulled back the little bandage from Maggie's hair, trying hard not to hurt her. With the light on, Rosita studied the scar intently, double-clicking on the previous day's photos for comparison. After a few seconds of motionless examination, she looked at Manny and said, "They're gone." Then she sat down like a dropped sack of potatoes.

Manny moved closer, parting Maggie's hair around the scar to make sure he saw everything. After a few moments his head shot back up in confirmation. The room grew silent, and then suddenly overcome by emotion.

Rosita began to weep uncontrollably. The pain, fear, exhaustion—two years of all that agony culminated into this moment, and now they finally saw the light at the end of the tunnel. Maggie stood perplexed by the display surrounding her as Manny and Rosita looked at each other, stunned by a realization that the cancer was leaving the little girl's body.

Maggie stood still, too astonished by the display around her to speak. Then Rosita lunged forward, wrapping Maggie in an embrace as she kissed her face over and over again while spinning her in circles. Maggie's legs and arms flailed in the wind as she spun through the air.

Manny watched this beautiful scene, which was almost identical to the one he shared with his children the day before when they had heard the same news—the clinical trial for their mRNA vaccine was successful.

Maggie started asking questions, which Rosita answered with cautious optimism. "The vaccine worked...the vaccine worked," Rosita repeated until Maggie believed it. Finally, Maggie pulled away from her mother and jumped into Manny's arms. She planted a kiss on his cheek that startled him, but also made his tears flow freely like a river. Rosita put her hands on both of them and smiled so wide it felt like her cheeks could burst.

Maggie's face lit up with joy, and she threw her arms around her mother in an embrace. Rosita held Maggie close and finally allowed herself to feel the relief that eluded her for days. Maggie stepped back and looked at Manny, tears of happiness streaming down his face. She grabbed his hands in hers and said, "Let's get Mommy to test you too."

Manny replied, "Dr. Strunk already did."

Maggie pleaded to her mother, "But I want you to test him."

Rosita looked perplexed but obliged. Manny lowered himself onto the chair and she leaned in to him, activating the fluorescent light on her device. He adjusted his position slightly so that Rosita could get a better angle, and as he moved his head brushed ever-so-slightly against her

269

breast. She recoiled quickly before continuing with her inspection. When she finished, she stepped back and double-clicked on the previous photos to make sure all were truly gone. With a smile of confirmation at Manny, she nodded that they indeed were.

Manny smiled when Maggie gazed up at him with bright eyes, and then she leaped into his arms. She kissed him on the cheek, jumped away, then grabbed a bundle of clothing and her rainbow-colored tutu and darted to the bathroom, laughing excitedly.

Manny and Rosita stood alone next to the table after Maggie went into the bathroom. Rosita looked at Manny, turned, and lunged at him. Their lips met enthusiastically as Manny actually stepped backwards a bit after the impact. She pulled him against her with a physical strength that shocked his limp body into submission. Still lingering close enough to feel each other's breath, Rosita whispered words of appreciation before showering him with passionate kisses across his face. Manny stood in stunned silence, struggling to comprehend what was happening. A combination of confusion and bliss paralyzed his body. He felt like he'd been struck by lightning or mugged by Cupid himself.

For a moment, he stood lost in the moment; time seemed to stand still as his heart raced and blood thundered through his veins. But then he heard the doorknob twist on the bathroom door, and quickly snapped back to reality. Rosita stepped away hastily, adjusting her blouse which became slightly undone near the neckline. Maggie looked at him with confusion and asked, "What's wrong with you?"

Manny glanced at Maggie before turning his attention to Rosita, who now looked away, a barely perceptible blush coloring her cheeks. After a moment of silence, Manny managed to respond with a quiet, "Oh, nothing's wrong. Nothing at all."

CHAPTER 53
A new mission is about to begin,

The Beeze rumbled down the winding coastal road, with Maggie sitting shotgun with her mother and Manny in the back. The salt air rushed over them as they passed a small herd of cows grazing on a patch of green grass. Vertical farms are the future, but here were cows standing in a field like a nod to times long gone.

Maggie caught a scent so pungent it made her nose wrinkle. "What's that smell?" she asked.

Her mother lowered the Beeze's window. "It's manure," she said. "We're almost there."

"What's manooor?" Maggie asked.

"Cow poop," Rosita said and chuckled, eliciting laughter from Manny. Maggie stared at the two of them, unsure of what was so amusing. As they turned onto a dirt road, Rosita glanced over her shoulder at Manny, who leaned forward to catch a glimpse of something out the opposite window. She caught his eye and smiled, feeling light and giddy.

The Beeze rolled into the grounds of Slug Farm and Manny noticed several private cars parked along the driveway. One car carried an insignia from Stanford, and one displayed the NASA emblem, which made him wonder why they took private cars to this farm? His musings ceased as his children spotted their father and ran over to the Beeze with outstretched arms, embracing him tightly as he stepped out.

As the twins held their father close, Rosita and Maggie stepped out of the Beeze and Amy broke away and walked straight up to Dr. Rosita McKenna.

She wrapped her arms around her in a tight hug that caught the doctor off guard at first, but then Rosita surrendered to it freely. Through tears, Amy mumbled, "You saved my father's life."

Alex approached hesitantly, with more gratitude than affection, and added himself to the group hug. After a pause, the loving embrace pulled Maggie in too.

Eventually, the four separated and the twins thanked Rosita profusely for aiding their father during this difficult time. She accepted their gratitude graciously but then swiftly grabbed each of their hands, looking them in the eye and declaring firmly, "It was your father that saved us all. It was him, not me."

The twins glanced at Manny, their eyes shining with admiration. Rosita released their hands and stepped back as the two of them moved to hug their father again. Manny held them close for a moment before stepping back and taking their hands in his own. "And without your love, I never would have gotten through this thing," he told them gently. "Remember, you're the ones who kept in contact with John. I wouldn't have known about the mRNA study if it weren't for you bringing him food."

Alex and Amy exchanged a quick, knowing glance before Manny noticed the crowd of people gathered in the lobby. Alex waved his arm in the group's direction and said cheerfully, "Dad, you have to meet these people."

Manny was aware of the influx of visitors to the farm, more than he ever witnessed before. His confusion evident on his face, he asked hesitantly, "Are they here to see Greenie?"

Alex and Amy knew the breakthrough with the FOUPs attracted attention all the way from the university, so they'd assembled a small group of dignitaries to review its results. "Greenie, the FOUPs, the farm— everything!" Alex exclaimed.

Manny followed the group into the lobby of the vertical farm and met the members of the team, one by one. Dr. Hiroshi Nakamura from Kyoto nodded in greeting, with Rebecca Banh, from the vertical farm studies at

Stanford, standing close behind him. Next was Ron Johnson from NASA, his friendly smile belying his impressive credentials. Then there were familiar faces Manny had seen many times before at Slug Farm.

The group then made their way to a lab where they watched Greenie's operations up close. The drone hovered in mid-air for a moment before delicately depositing five "straws" of FOUPs onto a mockup door of a pod. Everyone watched in awe as Greenie effortlessly completed the task, and Manny heard the sound of double-clicking from people's shields, and questions flying all around him.

Dr. Nakamura then moved to the sample case and selected an item from inside. He placed it in the FOUP so that no one could see what food he chose. After a few moments, he revealed to everyone the label on the sample he selected. As expected, the AI in the FOUP correctly identified the food, and the room erupted in applause and cheers. Questions filled the air as people conversed amongst themselves about the FOUPs and Greenie's impressive capabilities.

Manny beamed with pride, surrounded by a swirl of motion and discussion as scientists and technicians crowded around the prototypes they developed. He listened to their questions and watched his proteges provide answers with confidence. As he shifted uncomfortably in anticipation, a blue light unexpectedly glowed in his shield, and Theo's face emerged on the screen.

"Manny, how's the demonstration going?" Theo asked, peering out at him intently. His expression was tight, like an anxious student waiting for their exam results.

Manny stepped away from the group to speak privately. "How did you know...oh never mind." He shook his head in amusement, becoming more and more accustomed to Theo's surprises, and continued talking.

"I've been working with your people out there for a few days already," Theo explained. Not waiting for a reaction, he continued talking about the vertical farm project at the University of Santa Cruz. His voice shone with pride, speaking of the hope to create lasting change through this venture.

"That's great, Theo," Manny said with admiration etched into every word. He admired the group's collective knowledge and wisdom more than that of any individual genius. As he stepped away from the lively crowd towards a quiet corner, he felt as if the universe brought them all together at Chelsea Pod One for a purpose.

"Have you met Dr. Nakamura yet?" Theo asked excitedly.

Manny nodded as he stepped further away from the bustling group. "Why is someone from Kyoto here?"

A wide smile lit up Theo's face upon hearing this question. "I contacted him. They use that new electro-chemical bacterium for desalination, just like at Santa Cruz. It could revolutionize our power costs if we use it here too!"

Manny's eyes widened in surprise. "That's incredible news! We should try it at Sunnyside."

"Already on it, boss," Theo replied rapidly. "Coop's bringing a batch from Santa Cruz right now. Should be here soon."

"I feel like something, or maybe everything, is coming together," Manny declared. After all the health issues and problems from the past few years, everything seemed to be in sync now. Coop's heroics saved him, and he thought of Roberta, James, and everyone back at Sunnyside. He felt especially thankful for Micky Killian for clearing the path across the nation for them. And now Theo blazed a trail to success. He told his new friend, "By the way, I think I'm in love."

Theo's eyes widened and he burst into laughter. "No shit! We could all see that every time you looked at her!"

Manny felt his cheeks flush and he managed a sheepish chuckle. "That obvious, huh?"

Theo continued. "Manny, you go for it! Rosita is wonderful and you deserve each other."

"I'm not sure she wants me though," Manny professed.

At this point, the group of people noticed Manny off to the side and began calling him over. With one last nod from Theo, Manny said goodbye and rejoined the group near the FOUPs where a lively discussion took place.

Manny stood off to the side, watching as the group's faces became illuminated by the soft light emanating from the electrochemical bacteria on the table. As they noticed him, their curiosity piqued and they began asking questions.

Dr. Nakamura, the head scientist of the Kyoto project, turned to Manny and asked, "Between the desalination and electrochemical bacteria production, what are your energy costs here?"

Manny's eyes flickered with recognition and he recalled seeing the numbers only last week. "Four megawatts right now," he replied. "But a photovoltaic solar panel system will be installed to cover that delivery by spring time."

"We'll be power-neutral by March," the technician, Matthew Summons, chimed in. He was a former student who now worked tirelessly on the project. He guided most of the demonstrations with quiet authority. Amy stood next to Matthew as they explained the plans to Dr. Nakamura.

Manny interjected, "I want you to meet some of our key players here. May I present Matthew Summons. And this is my daughter, Amy Rio."

Matthew's face lit up with excitement as he shook Dr. Nakamura's hand. "It's an honor to meet you, sir," he said humbly. "I've been studying your work on desalination for years." The enthusiastic chatter resumed as everyone discussed the exciting new developments at the vertical farm.

Dr. Nakamura thanked Matthew for his kind words and then gestured to Manny with a gentle nod of his head. "My daughter is also quite knowledgeable in this field," he said in a low voice.

Manny furrowed his brow, seemingly taken aback by the revelation. "Your daughter? Who is she?" he asked curiously.

A knowing grin lit up Dr. Nakamura's face at Manny's question. "You know Naoko Nakamura at the Sunnyside VSG, correct?"

Ah yes, Manny thought. She'd studied at Kyoto and her knowledge on desalination was priceless. Runs in the family he realized. They were fortunate she joined NYU's Pod and eventually settled down in Sunnyside. Manny grinned and replied, "We feel very lucky that she found us at Sunnyside."

Manny followed the group as they suddenly began drifting off to a conference room, feeling more perplexed by the second. He stepped into a spacious conference room alive with technology, multitouch displays mounted on the walls, and an array of high-definition cameras shifting to each speaker as they entered the room. Dr. John Strunk and Theo watched every person enter the room; their faces illuminated virtually in the glass panels at one end of the table.

Manny tapped his shield and asked Theo, "What's going on here?"

"Just sit back and listen to the proposition," Theo replied, giving Manny a quick nod and smiled tightly before tapping his shield to disconnect.

Manny sat down and watched as everyone around him connected into their shields. Dr. Nakamura's voice filled the room as he began the meeting. "Welcome to the first University Vertical Farm Alliance meeting. UVFA for short."

A giant video screen illuminated at the front of the room and displayed a logo of two hands clasping in a handshake above a group of five-story vertical farms encircling the planet. The simplicity of the design conveyed the purpose perfectly as Manny realized the significance of this new alliance.

The Director from Agricultural Sciences at the University of Santa Cruz took charge and described the intent of this organization. Then she passed the introduction along to the Directors from Stanford, Harvard, NYU, Michigan, Wisconsin, and finally UCLA. Then Ron Johnson spoke last, and identified himself as being the Director of Vertical Sustained Growth for the Mars Exploration Project.

Manny sat with eyes darting from speaker to speaker, nodded in recognition as each director spoke. He knew all their university's work through Sunnyside, but the University of Kyoto was new to him. Naoko would be the connection, he realized.

The UCLA Director then unveiled an ambitious plan: a central governing body to fund vertical farms around the world, managed by the consortium's universities and dedicated to providing fresh food for local communities. Manny already saw the potential in this solution—how Slug Farm was just one example of the achievements accomplished with shared science and resources. He watched as the directors eagerly discussed the proposal, debating its merits and challenges.

Manny marveled at the presentation unfolding before him. Graphs, tables, and videos flashed on the video screens, demonstrating the professionalism of the participating colleges. The presentation featured the Sunnyside Farm, with visuals of Greenie delivering FOUPs to doorsteps. Additional slides showed the tracking of FOUP contents and financial projections for four more farms that adopted Sunnyside's improvements. The final slide displayed a graph of Sunnyside's self-supporting finances, indicating substantial profitability. James must have provided the details, Manny surmised.

An impressive organizational chart filled the screen with Manny surprisingly placed at the top as CEO, Theo listed as CTO, and names including Roberta, James, Naoko, Randy and several technicians spread out over the rest of the organization. As the audience members rose to their feet in thunderous applause for members of the Sunnyside Farm, pride swelled within Manny's chest. He exchanged glances with Amy and Alex, who looked very proud of their father. Rosita stood at the rear of the conference area holding hands with Maggie, who seemed amazed at the graphics on the screens in the room. This was unfolding rapidly and he wondered if he missed something or missed some communication.

The crowd erupted in cheers again at the organization chart, and Dr. John Strunk waited patiently for them to settle down before continuing. He clicked on a button in his shield, and a live video feed came up displaying most of the staff at Sunnyside. Manny felt a twinge of homesickness as he watched his friends smile and wave to the camera. Coop was missing from the picture, and Manny knew he was likely on his way back east by now. He saw Theo standing next to Roberta and James, who both seemed to be in on the secret project.

John explained, "It was only through the exceptional leadership and dedication of Dr. Manuel Rio that these incredible advances were made possible." At this declaration, another great round of applause filled the conference room as well as all the locations attending via shield.

As John continued to praise Manny's work, people in attendance clapped and cheered. He then shifted his attention to introduce Theo, who only recently joined the Sunnyside Farm.

"Theo's scientific achievements in robotic surgery earned him quite a reputation," Dr. Strunk proclaimed, emphasizing the numerous patents Theo filed for medical instruments and accessories. "Now that we have Theo on board for Vertical Sustained Growth at UVFA, we can expect even greater results from this initiative!"

Manny stared in amazement as the audience erupted into thunderous applause. When the room finally quieted down, Theo appeared on the big screen in front of them and addressed the crowd. "I want to thank you for your belief in me, and especially all of you at the universities who will benefit from this technology. I'm delighted to accept the role as Chief Technology Officer for UVFA and look forward to developing new innovations for global distribution."

The conference room came alive with cheers as technicians began showing off the new FOUPs and other Greenie drones in the works. Suddenly Manny's video screen switched to a private channel.

"Manny," Theo said. "I told them I would only go if you were CEO of this whole thing. Have you accepted it yet?"

Manny glanced over at Rosita and Maggie, who looked proud but anxious. Manny knew what was coming and felt overwhelmed. He smiled slightly and said, "They didn't ask me yet, but I sense they are going to in a few moments."

Theo was surprised and said, "That guy from NASA was supposed to meet with you last night."

"The meeting was canceled, but I can't answer right away anyways. I need to talk to some people first."

"Everyone is behind you," Theo assured. "Roberta said she would take over your role at Sunnyside. And James wants to come on board UVFA too. Do you understand what this means?"

Manny remained bewildered by all the data, and all of the changes happening so rapidly, but replied, "I don't know."

Theo smiled widely and explained the obvious to his friend, "This means we are going to Mars!"

Manny looked confused and stammered, "But where am I going to live?"

"I think anywhere you want," Theo replied factually. "Mars is too far, but I do recommend California."

CHAPTER 54
For the hope that we may all win,

Coop stepped out of Betsy, his faithful companion for thousands of miles, and into the cool night air. He stretched and inhaled deeply, there was no need for breathing apparatus anymore. He navigated around the back of the truck and opened the door to the living pod. In the kitchen area, he found the large black cooler bag that held the contents of his mission, the electrochemical bacteria, crucial for the desalination plant addition at Sunnyside Farm. He didn't know much about it, but was determined to carry out his task; after all, he was Amadeus Thaddeus Cooper.

He attempted to hoist the bag up, then found the right handles and began walking eastward toward Long Island Sound, an expanse of icy waters dividing Connecticut from Long Island. The plan relied on him to swim away from the shore, far enough out to avoid security gates and RFID scanners that do not exist in the ocean. His last scanner reading came at the entrance for the ferry at Bridgeport where it picked up his signal. If everything worked out, his next scanner detection would be at the exit of the ferry at Port Jefferson on Long Island.

He loaded the heavy duffle bag onto his shoulders, the weight staggering as he trudged towards Long Island Sound. The inky water at the shore glimmered beneath the night sky, waves slapping against the rocks with a hollow booming sound. His body trembled from the cold as he realized his lack of a wet suit would restrict how long he could remain in the salty waters. Taking a deep breath, he dipped into the icy waters and began swimming. His hands latched onto the handles of the bag, dragging it along behind him as he kicked through the choppy surface. With every passing minute, the shoreline seemed to recede farther and farther away—until finally, after what felt like an eternity, Coop was forced to admit this was perhaps the dumbest thing he'd ever done for love. But with Naoko's name on his lips, he battled against the cold and kept going.

He glanced up and noticed a few large ships slowly passing by a few miles away, their huge bodies cutting through the sea like beasts in search of prey. The cold was intense, but fortunately the high salinity of the water made buoyancy incredibly easy. At times, it felt as if he couldn't sink if he tried.

Theo instructed him to swim at least a mile away from shore before they picked him up. Coop nervously checked to make sure his ear pods remained securely attached, otherwise he would find himself in quite a predicament—stranded until morning, probably near death, and almost certainly arrested by the PoPos if he even survived the ordeal.

Suddenly a strange noise above Coop startled him out of his trance. He remained still, not daring to move until figuring out the source of the noise. The buzzing grew louder and louder as slowly the shape of Greenie II appeared above and hovered just a few feet away from his head. His shield activated and Theo's face filled Coop's video screen.

"How ya doing, Buddy?" Theo yelled loudly to overcome some noise on his end.

"Damn glad to see you, Theo," Coop said, about as relieved as any person could be in the middle of a cold channel. "Where are you?"

"We'll be there in a minute. I've got Greenie's location pegged on my finder."

Coop sighed in relief and remained quiet, waiting for any noise that signaled some type of boat. A faint sound came nearer that reminded him of swishing and then another swishing noise off to the side of that one. As the sounds grew closer, he strained his eyes trying to make out any lights or shadows, but it was pitch black. Suddenly two figures appeared out of the darkness and it looked like they somehow walked on water. They slowly sunk into the water revealing long black surfboards beneath them.

"Coop, hang on," Theo said as he balanced himself on one of the boards. "We've got you."

Suddenly, a quiet yet confident voice cut through the night air. "Cooper-san, don't worry, we will take you home."

Cooper gasped as he recognized Naoko's voice. He could barely see her as she approached him and before he had time to react, she leaped off the surfboard and kissed him passionately. A wave of warmth traveled through his body, melting away any residual fear or coldness that threatened to overwhelm him just moments earlier. Naoko pulled back slightly but kept her lips close enough for Cooper to feel their warmth in stark contrast to the ice-cold channel waters beneath them.

Theo broke up their moment by dragging another board toward them. "Plenty of time for that later, Coop! Get onto this board before you freeze to death, and put this wetsuit on."

"How did you get here? I don't understand," Coop asked as he lifted himself onto the board and felt its slippery glassy surface beneath him.

"These are hydrofoil boards, Cooper-san," Naoko said as she watched him settle into place. "They go really fast."

Naoko helped Coop get on the board and explained how to use the hydrofoil. With every smooch, Coop grew increasingly eager to get on the wetsuit. He then threw his garments into the water and pulled the bib overall type of suit over his legs followed by the wetsuit jacket on top. As soon as he zipped up the jacket, his shivering began to slow as the wetsuit began warming the water inside.

Naoko clasped Coop's hands and sweetly kissed his lips. She then hopped onto her surfboard, the slickness of her wet suit glistening in the moonlight and highlighting her gorgeous figure. "You ready?" she questioned as she handed him a remote-control to the hydrofoil.

Theo went about enclosing the large black box inside another long, tubular board. The digital connection between the boards kept them taut until they formed a line behind Theo. He stood on top of his surfboard and yelled, "Hang on!"

Then, suddenly, the boards shot forward with a momentum that Coop never imagined. He struggled to keep his balance as their speed increased, but soon grew accustomed to the movement.

As soon as Theo gave another command, the digital connection between the boards kicked in. The boards rose from the surface and moved along effortlessly on their hydrofoil wings. At first, the boards simply glided above the surface, but then their speed increased quickly until they zipped across the water like a bullet train.

The wind whipping around Coop pushed him into an awkward leaning position so he could remain aboard his board. He rode many types of vehicles before, but nothing compared to this incredible experience! He glanced over at Naoko and admired her graceful frame as she expertly controlled her board. Her wetsuit hugged her body as she kept her gaze fixed ahead. Coop copied her technique so he didn't lose control.

The boards darted across the channel like dolphins playing in the wave crests. In fifteen minutes, they arrived at their pickup point on Long Island. Coop, unaccustomed to the hydrofoil board, attempted to slow down but instead fell over dramatically. Naoko leapt into the water with a hearty laugh and wrapped herself around him playfully. His laughter mingled with hers as their lips met for a wonderful embrace. They kissed and kissed, laughing heartily as they dragged the boards to the shore.

Lugging their four boards and a black bag, they dragged them from the water and onto dry sand. Two figures quickly approached from the truck nearby and without hesitation ran to Coop's side for an embrace. Roberta and James welcomed him warmly; unbothered by his sodden state, and rejoiced at his safe return. This was genuine friendship, true family.

"We better get out of here," Theo interjected suddenly. "You never know about the PoPos."

CHAPTER 55

Separation of paths when gone astray,

The governing body of UVFA discussed the future while eagerly seeking Theo's input from across the country. Anxiety hung heavy in the air as they needed Manny to accept the position of CEO. Without his acceptance, none of the universities would join them and they wouldn't get NASA funding for the venture. After lengthy deliberation, Manny agreed to take on the responsibility, and a collective sigh of relief filled the room.

While Manny continued talking with the remaining board members at Slug Farm, Maggie and Rosita left in a Beeze to return to their hotel at Stanford. The smaller and nimbler group described plans for expanding into numerous universities and pods, and into NASA. They proposed a five-story portable garden that could travel with a seven-month mission to Mars, where they'd be stationed for at least two years, like Noah's Ark.

When the meeting broke up, Manny spoke with Roberta and James from Sunnyside again. James planned on staying with Roberta while he trained someone else to manage finances at the farm. But it was clear that Roberta's ambitions were expanding, and Manny knew it was time for him to get out of her way.

Alex and Amy saw the potential of their father's sustainable farming project, for it to free millions from the tyranny of White Cube's food production. The twins were a source of support throughout his recovery and now urged him to stay with them on the farm. Manny hugged them both tight, feeling an almost spiritual connection he lacked in years past.

Manny told them good night, mentioning that he may need to go back to Long Island once the Contros lifted the lockdown restrictions. The twins implored him to take up the role at UVFA headquarters in California, reminding him of all the high-profile institutions located nearby, such as Stanford University, University of Santa Cruz, and NASA. They suspected his longing to follow Rosita drove his eagerness to return to Chelsea Pod One.

Trying not to think about Rosita and Maggie for a moment, Manny signaled for a Beeze to head back to the hotel at Stanford. The ride gave him time to think through his new situation. What happened earlier with Rosita when she'd kissed him? Manny wasn't quite sure. She indicated she would travel back to Chelsea Pod One and resume her career there. The offer to work at Stanford must not be on the table any longer.

He realized that they may drift apart over time. Did he love Rosita? Absolutely. Did she love him? Manny didn't know. What happened earlier may have been only emotions rising to the top.

As the vehicle pulled up to the hotel's entrance, Manny took a deep breath and stepped out into the cool night air. He had some thinking to do.

The next two weeks were a blur; he was busy juggling his new CEO role plus trying to tie up loose ends with the clinical trial as well as the new desalination project at Sunnyside. Every so often he'd catch glimpses of Rosita and Maggie, but their meetings were getting further and further apart. Still, Manny waited anxiously for her decision as to whether or not she'd accept the offer to practice medicine at Stanford. John let him know that Rosita planned on returning to Chelsea after the lockdown ended. Manny wondered if could stay here in California without her.

One day, Manny spotted the two in the courtyard speaking with a beautiful woman. He walked hesitantly downstairs to catch up with them. As he approached, Maggie ran towards him with her usual warmth, wrapping her arms around him in a tight hug. Rosita was happy but thoughtful, her romantic gestures becoming more infrequent as each day wore on. It was obvious she was pulling away.

"How are you, Manny?" Rosita asked softly, gently reaching for his hand

and brushing her thumb against his skin in an affectionate gesture that was new. Her jeans looked familiar, paired with tall black boots—one of Manny's favorite looks of hers.

Maggie donned new clothing; instead of her usual tutu, today she wore a shirt with bright colors and patterns. Rosita turned to introduce the striking woman next to her, who stood up quickly and smiled brightly at him. Rosita said, "I would like you to meet my sister, Ashlie."

Manny's hands slowly released Rosita's, but their gaze lingered as questions arose about this sudden sister. He reached to shake her hand, but Ashlie jumped into his arms suddenly.

"You saved Maggie's life," Ashlie said warmly and kissed Manny on the cheek. She lingered a bit as Manny beamed, feeling the love from an older sister.

Maggie stood by beaming at her aunt and Manny hugging. Ashlie then returned to her seat, folding her long and beautiful legs into a casual seating position as the group talked about the events that transpired recently.

They all sat and talked for a while as Ashlie and Rosita shared stories of their childhood in Piedmont, California, where Ashlie still lived and managed the family business, "LoMcKenna Industries," the premier maker of prosthetic devices powered by artificial intelligence.

"My father was a pioneer in artificial intelligence," Ashlie offered as she regaled Manny with story after story of the early days of AI. "He was even part of the Beeze startup."

"He and Uncle Mike drove the first Beeze vehicles," Rosita explained as she talked about the Beeze Project, something their family worked on for years—until the Controllers took hold of the entire industry for the good of the people. Bitterness suddenly filled the air as the two sisters talked about the days when all of their family's work disappeared.

Ashlie stood up with a mischievous look in her eyes suddenly hiked her skirt up a few inches and stood very close to Manny. "Just look at these babies. This is part of the Christi line. Aren't they the most gorgeous legs you've ever seen?"

Ashlie adjusted her legs in various positions as Manny became captivated by their beauty. He was embarrassed to be ogling at a woman's legs while others were there, watching his expressions.

"They're artificial, silly," Ashlie said with a smile. "I designed them myself."

Manny was curious about the technology and began to ask questions, but Rosita remained oddly silent, already knowing the answers. He noticed the likeness between the two women and could tell Ashlie was probably older than the other.

"Go on, touch them," Ashlie coaxed without any hint of self-consciousness. She grabbed Manny's hand and placed it on her thigh. "Feel the skin."

Manny was both shocked and shy as Rosita urged him to explore Ashlie's prosthetic leg more closely. Eventually he let his fingers gently trail over her thigh before quickly pulling away.

"Well?" Ashlie asked expectantly.

Manny looked around nervously before replying in a timid voice, "That feels like real skin. But it is too perfect."

Both women erupted in laughter as Maggie squealed gleefully at his discomfort. Despite feeling humiliated, Manny could not help but crack a smile at the situation.

Ashlie sat back down and crossed her legs again. "My father is the one who perfected the skin. He thinks we need to add blemishes too," she revealed proudly. "My mother used her own legs as a model for the original prototype."

The group then discussed their impressive philanthropic achievements of providing prosthetic limbs for those who could not afford such high-technology— an achievement that everyone was incredibly proud of.

Ashlie began asking her sister about her plans, encouraging her to stay in California again after being in Chelsea Pod One for so many years. "We never get to see Maggie enough."

Manny and Rosita kept exchanging knowing glances as Manny's heart ached when Rosita revealed more and more of the story and plans. He began responding to questions about his job offer at UVFA, but he could feel Rosita's eyes scrutinizing him. He felt the weight of Maggie's gaze on them and knew that if the conversation weren't interrupted, it would only become more complicated.

It was Maggie who broke the silence. "Mommy and I are going back to Chelsea," she said, a note of pleading in her voice. "Please come along, Manny. Please."

The request hung in the air like an invisible thread connecting them all together. Rosita glanced between Maggie and Manny and then to Ashlie, using her hand to brush away a tear as she spoke softly, "Oh, Manny...you should be close to NASA and Slug Farm. And your children...and seeing how we..." Her words trailed off into nothingness as they all seemed to understand what she was unable to say out loud.

"Manny has so much to do here," Rosita tried to explain to Maggie. "But he can come visit us whenever he wants." She knelt down to get closer to Maggie, whose expression turned from sorrow to anger. Rosita seemed to plead for help with her eyes as Maggie crossed her arms in defiance. Then she climbed up onto Ashlie's lap, who remained purposefully quiet while sensing the strain in the discussion.

Manny turned his attention to Rosita in search of guidance. All he wanted was a sign from her, even if it were just a fleeting glance or a simple nod of her head. He would understand any cue that told him to go with them, no matter how painful it might be for him to do so with his new job. But instead, Rosita looked away and let out a deep sigh, silently affirming her own decision.

"Maggie, I'll come as often as I can. I promise," he said as she moved closer to him now and looked up at him imploringly. Manny stared into Maggie's big blue eyes in wonder.

"Please Manny, come with us," she pleaded. "You're like my Daddy now." He felt his throat tighten as he wrapped his arms around her petite frame and lifted her up, noticing the way her tiny hands clung tightly to him.

Rosita looked on in astonishment, a mix of emotions crossing her face. She knew that at eight-years old, children often love fiercely and deeply, their hearts wide open without inhibition.

Manny stood in the courtyard, barely able to contain his emotions as Rosita and Maggie said their goodbyes. Ashlie held his hand and kissed his cheek, an action that spoke of both sadness and determination. The sun began to set in the sky, creating a gentle breeze that seemed to whisper words of warning.

Manny watched them walk away until they were out of sight. He wished something could intervene, anything to make them want to stay. Instead of remaining in the courtyard, he walked into the hotel lobby and passed through the driveway. As he saw all the Beeze vehicles sitting empty and idle awaiting signals for rides, Manny felt a newfound understanding about them that had not been there before. The sleek cars suddenly seemed more alive than they had ever been. He had seen the Beezes so many times, they blended into the background like a long-forgotten painting on the wall.

Suddenly, he heard a voice from behind him. "The shape isn't too dissimilar to the ones we designed thirty years ago," it said. Manny turned around, startled at the man standing behind him, and slowly recognized Rosita's father from the photograph on Rosita's office wall. Walking up next to him was Rosita's mother, smiling brightly and approaching them both with purpose.

She walked straight up to Manny and said, "Dr. Manuel Rio?"

"Yes?" Manny replied confusedly.

She wrapped Manny in her arms and whispered into his ear, "I can never thank you enough for saving my granddaughter's life." As she stepped back, the grandfather and grandmother thanked Manny profusely for all he had done and began sharing stories of their past few weeks together with their daughter Rosita. It was then that Manny noticed a small bandage on Rosita's father's forehead and saw the knowing glance that passed between them.

"Luckily just a carcinoma this time," Rosita's father explained. "I hear you've been going through some of this crap too."

Rosita's mother looked at her husband with a "we hardly know him," look, but he waved her off and said they should get to know him better. "Heard you're quite the genius when it comes to vertical sustenance; heck, you may even be going to Mars someday!"

Manny spent an enjoyable half-hour chatting with Rosita's parents before Ashlie arrived in a strange-looking car with even stranger wheels. The car spoke in a humanlike voice and referred to itself as Dave.

Later, Manny, Rosita, and Maggie in their hotel rooms, attempted to fall asleep in their own methods. Rosita read a story to Maggie, trying to get her to fall asleep even as tears streamed down the little girl's face. Trying to contain her own emotions, Rosita sniffled softly before continuing to read. And Manny in his room simply stared out the window.

CHAPTER 56
Goodbyes are said at end of day.

Dr. John Strunk sat across from Manny in the cramped preparation room, their conversation punctuated by the hum of electronic equipment and the flicker of video monitors. The job offer from UVFA presented Manny with a cruel ultimatum: stay in California and risk losing Rosita forever, or follow her to New York and throw away his career prospects.

Manny weighed his options as he glanced at the obnoxious yellow release form on top of the monitor. One signature could mean a lifetime of regret, but two signatures could mean a lifetime apart. He couldn't bear the thought of losing Rosita, but he also couldn't fathom giving up his dream job to chase unrequited love. He wondered if that was even definable in this relationship.

John cleared his throat, breaking Manny's train of thought. "Are you ready to sign?" John asked, his voice laced with concern.

Manny hesitated before nodding slowly, his heart torn between two equally unpalatable choices. He clenched his jaw and tried to close off the swell of emotions threatening to consume him.

John cleared his throat, breaking Manny's train of thought. "Don't choose just yet. We can do that later," he said, concern written all over his face.

Manny hesitated before nodding slowly, his stomach tied in knots. "Thank you for everything," he said, moving towards John for a hug they rarely shared previously as friends but now was a regular occurrence. At that moment, Manny felt so grateful to have such an understanding friend in this difficult situation—one who not only saved his life, but could help save his future with Rosita.

"I'm so glad it worked, Manny," replied John. The two men stood in each other's arms for a few moments before John composed himself and gestured to the chair in the center of the preparation room. "One final inspection though, for the pilot study." So, it wasn't quite done yet.

Manny felt a chill as John left the room and the door slammed shut behind him. He glanced around at his surroundings—the stark white walls, the surgical instruments laid out neatly on trays near the examination chair, and the harsh overhead light that illuminated the space.

Manny's heart raced as the door opened and Dr. Rosita McKenna stepped in with a warm smile on her face. She wore his favorite green doctor's nanotechnology garment today, which served to further confuse him. Didn't they say their goodbyes just two days ago?

They greeted each other politely. After adding a special light to her shield, she moved closer to Manny and began to part his thick hair, searching for white lines that could signify rhizomatous cancer. He felt like he was drowning in her scent, and it seemed like an eternity before her fingertips finished combing through every strand of hair.

The moment that changed everything happened when Rosita shifted positions again. Manny felt her shirt brush against his cheek, then he felt the heat coming off her body and the softness of her breast glancing against his shoulder as she reached farther back on his scalp. His breath caught in his throat as he reached up almost instinctively, letting his hand reach out and come to rest at the waistband of her pants, right above her pelvic bone. His thumb felt the warmth of her skin beneath her blouse. "Rosita," he breathed out, "I love you. Please don't go back to Chelsea. Please stay with me here."

Rosita stopped moving and stood still for a brief second before she slowly moved away from him. Manny's hand dropped back down to his thigh with gravity's inevitability. Her face displayed a look of worry and resignation written across it as she said, "Well that's that. This is going to have to be my last inspection for you."

Manny wanted to close his eyes, curl up into a ball, and disappear. He thought about jumping out the window.

"I mean…as your doctor that is." Then Rosita leaned in and spoke the unspoken, pressing her body against his, pushing him deep into the examination chair. Her chest grazed against his cheeks as she straddled him in the chair, wrapping her legs around him and sinking her body onto his until their lips nearly touched. A spark of electricity surged between them when their mouths finally connected, and Rosita wrapped her arms around him with a passionate embrace. "How long have you wanted this? All you had to do was ask." She breathed heavily against his lips.

"I wanted this forever," came his husky reply. Manny felt as if time stopped as they continued to explore one another, hardly aware of the ticking clock counting down before someone discovered them in the examination room. Rosita's warm breath tickled his neck as she whispered words of love and devotion, and he knew that wherever this passion was taking them, he wanted her by his side. She stroked his hair and cradled his chin with her hand, and for the first time in what seemed like forever, Manny felt safe. Rosita kissed him with such passionate force that his heart nearly stopped.

"I love you both. I need you and Maggie," he eventually replied, feeling as if his future laid itself out before him.

Suddenly, the door creaked open and Rosita leapt off Manny's lap in an instant. In walked a technician who didn't seem to notice the couple's brief embrace. From behind the technician, Rosita flashed Manny a playful smile before returning to pretending to review something in her shield.

Manny took in the disarray of his life, mulling over his grandfather's philosophy. "Be like the river," he had said. The words that carried Manny through so many storms offered him little solace now, when it seemed every trial and tribulation hurtled his way unceasingly. But maybe sometimes, Grandfather, a water spout is necessary instead of a constant river. Sometimes one must shoot for the stars and create a bit of chaos in order to reach the heights.

Forecast cloudy or sunny

The Algos at CATACS churned feverishly, processing the new data inputted from Stanford's clinical trial. Data from the machine-learning adjusted the algorithms for each person, modified correlations, and moved parameters with each successive cycle. The clinical trial results made a significant impact to their AI models, taking previously disregarded anomalies and discovering new pathways for treatments for melanoma cancer. The algorithms then extend the patients' lifespans, creating opportunities for increased wealth while consequently resulting in more contentment—amplifying the positive outcomes even further. An extraordinary breakthrough for algorithms.

The Contros could not ignore the pronounced variations in the results of Dr. Manuel Rio and Margaret Ann McKenna. They had to rewrite their algorithmic code accordingly. With each iteration, the Algos became more intricate, allowing for longer lifespans and greater contentment with life.

Algos Updated:

Dr. Manual Rio's lifespan increased to 92 years.

Margaret Ann McKenna's lifespan rose to 94 years.

Dr. Rosita McKenna's lifespan remained at 94 years.

Incidentally, a Mr. Theodore Wiggins found his algorithm adjusted to 108 years without anyone raising an eyebrow.

A poem about the Last Mile from the chapter headings

Act One:

Meet the neighbor in his cell,

Neighbor's fate and time must tell,

Discovers the neighbor's true plight,

Battle is on for the first fight,

The doctor is in,

We wanted a win,

Travelers go to the coast,

Only one is diagnosed,

Some have secrets that they've kept,

Take the property with respect,

Young and old on the quest,

Special gifts arrive when best,

Man and woman oft collide,

One sets out on a wild ride,

Controllers present, one bad, one good,

Father and children in the brood.

Act Two:

Medicine needed for young and old,

Friend's distractions often bold,

Medicine is a father's guide,

We all go for another ride,
Man, and friend on a quest,
To the farm they'll invest,
Remedy might the answer be,
Devices fight with constant glee,
Children know what occurred so far,
Engage a flight to reach afar,
Power steps in with all their might,
Friends get back to their delight,
Code for escape but 'tis too late,
Change of plans with family's fate,
All destined to pastures away,
All have plans it seems today,
Escape is the mission that they seek,
Next stop over by travel unique,
The winding road brings doubts ahead,
Mistakes are made that must be shed,
Trouble looms in offshore bays,
A call is sent to find their ways,
When the children have no choice,
We can lend a helping voice,
Guides may lead them western bound.
They soon arrive at hallowed ground.

Act Three:
The powers will watch without fear,
Landing must occur an hour near,
One week passes in pastures with haste,
Received with goods now embraced,
All return the very the next day,
Some seek reasons why they stay away,

Before the third charm the plan goes awry,
Man stopped at the bridge, time he cannot buy,
Third path is all in a mess,
But the fourth may be the very best,
A new mission is about to begin,
For the hope that we may all win,
Separation of paths when gone astray,
Goodbyes are said at end of day.

The Beeze Series

Book 1: Last Mile

Forty years in the future, Dr. Manny Rio, little Maggie McKenna, and her mother Dr. Rosita McKenna must find hope in a world run by Controllers. With only a brave team of scientists, long-haulers, and Beeze AI vehicles to help them, they fight against algorithmic control as they venture across the country looking for a cure to their disease. Every step of their journey is fraught with danger as they pass through pod after pod, escaping each one prior to their closure and before electronic leashes place tethers on them to prevent escape.

Book 2: Tales at the Top

Young engineer Brian Lomax arrived in San Francisco, hoping to capitalize on the rapid growth of Silicon Valley. Computers boomed in the 80's, dot-coms crashed in 2001, a financial crisis hit in 2009, yet people still dreamed of a future with growing computer power. The 2019 pandemic increased the need for control in order to save lives, but soon people realized that algorithms were attempting to dominate their lives. This led to the origins of artificial intelligence and the rise of the Controllers.

Book 3: Critical Paths

Ten years after the great pandemic of 2019, Brad Baumers and Dexter Lomax, Brian's son, worked at MAST Technologies in San Francisco, a developer of artificial intelligence computer chips. Dexter invented DAVE, an AI-driven car designed to prevent fatal crashes, but he was too late to save his own wife from a fatal crash years before. DAVE was the first Beeze vehicle and the prototype used to create a fleet of swarming Beeze vehicles. Megan Sumners and her cameraman teamed up with Dexter's group to make a five-night TV series on the dangers of AI overuse. When authorities covered up a disaster, the team set out to reveal what really happened.

Book 4: Rise of the Contros

Dexter Lomax's dream of leading a team to create a fleet of autonomous Beeze vehicles faced the pandemic of 2050. With his trusty vehicle, DAVE, by his side, he used AI technology not only to battle the Controllers at their own game, but also to provide sensory feedback for his daughter's prosthetic limbs and control the growing fleet of Beeze vehicles. He, Ashlie, and her mother Christi faced a clash between their own ethical values and those dictated by the increasingly powerful AI-fueled Controllers.

Book 5: Roots of Mars

Later in the year 2075, despite the restrictions of post-pandemic life, algorithmic manipulation, and artificial intelligence, the reins of the Controllers seemed to stretch ever tighter around society, leading it into a state of carefully controlled stasis. Yet, Dr. Manny Rio, Maggie McKenna, Dr. Rosita McKenna, and techno-wizard Theo Wiggins formed a plan to build an innovative form of vertical farming that could sustain its inhabitants independently from the Controllers. This story portrays the strength of the human spirit as these individuals strive to create a self-sustaining food production system which may benefit us all—here on Earth and beyond.

About the Author

Residing in the San Francisco Bay Area with his wife and children, David Lee Luedtke is an author, inventor, engineer, and traveler. In addition to writing for various magazines, he wrote a weekly column in a regional paper for many years. His career took him from engineering to executive roles in the semiconductor world before diving into robotic surgery, which incorporates artificial intelligence to provide sensory feedback to surgeon's hands. He holds several patents for his inventions and has a huge interest in advancing autonomous driving—all of which helps to generate ideas for his novels.

www.ingramcontent.com/pod-product-compliance
Lightning Source LLC
Chambersburg PA
CBHW060403260626
47160CB00006B/2420